R U N N I N G

W R E C K E D

**FORTHCOMING BY MARK COMBES**

*Clowns and Chameleons*

a PHIL RILEY NOVEL

# R U N N I N G

# W R E C K E D

# MARK COMBES

MIDNIGHT INK
WOODBURY, MINNESOTA

FIRST EDITION
First Printing, 2007

Book design by Donna Burch
Cover design and illustration by Kevin R. Brown

Midnight Ink, an imprint of Llewellyn Publications

**Library of Congress Cataloging-in-Publication Data**
Combes, Mark, 1964–
   Running Wrecked : a Phil Riley novel / Mark Combes.—1st ed.
     p. cm.
   ISBN 978-0-7387-0982-6
   1. Divers—Fiction. 2. Americans—Caribbean Area—Fiction. I. Title.

PS3603.O4725R86 2007
813'.6—dc22

                                  2007002238

Midnight Ink
Llewellyn Publications
2143 Wooddale Drive, Dept. 0-7387-0982-4
Woodbury, MN 55125-2989, U.S.A.
www.midnightinkbooks.com

Printed in the United States of America

Even in civilized communities, the embryo
man passes through the hunter stage of
development.

HENRY DAVID THOREAU
*The Writings of Henry David Thoreau, vol. 2*

The violence of beast on beast is read
As natural law, but upright man
Seeks his divinity by inflicting pain.

DEREK WALCOTT
"A Far Cry from Africa"

# ONE

I wonder what the shrinks back in the States would say if I told them I was dreaming about a marlin swimming the Serengeti? Ah, fuck 'em—I'm not crazy. I've seen crazier things in my life than some fish where it ain't supposed to be. Hell, I've seen a *little girl* where she wasn't supposed to be and the damn shrinks didn't believe that either. Besides, what can dreams tell you anyway?

Lost in that phantom conversation with myself, I almost miss it. But Chubby sees her—a beautiful Beneteau sailboat, maybe forty feet stem to stern, off to starboard. I pull back on the throttles and ease the boat over on her starboard chine, making a tight circle back to the sailboat. I'm drawn to the boom as it slams back and forth, the main sheet too slack to keep the heavy hunk of aluminum from pitching to and fro with the waves. Watching the boom from my boat, I'm reminded of a crazy, out-of-control metronome. It strikes me that the sailboat looks sick, or lonely, if a sailboat can look like either. Something is wrong.

When we pull up behind her, the *Miss Princess*, that strange feeling wells up—the one you get when you walk into an abandoned building. You sense the life that was once there but now only lingers in erratic, weak energy. You become aware of it when those pinpricks on the back of your neck start. Combining that feeling with the sound of the sails flapping in the wind and the boom out of control, I know, before I even hail her, that she is abandoned.

Nevertheless, I shout through cupped hands, "Hello, the boat! Hello, the *Miss Princess*!" No response.

Chubby and I look at each other simultaneously and shrug. I pick up the marine radio and hail, "*Miss Princess, Miss Princess*. This is *Tortuga One*." Nothing. I repeat my call and still no response. Maybe this is a charter out of Grenada and they don't know their boat name. "Sailboat at South Gap off Isla Tortuga, please respond." The sailboat is picking its way into the wind, tacking back and forth in the same manner that a novice might set his boat to heave to. It's like a wounded animal fleeing.

"Now what?" Chubby asks.

"I have to go aboard and see what's going on. We may have to take her in. I need to let Callie know what's going on." I turn my back to the wheel of my boat to shield me from the wind and shout into the radio, "Callie, Callie, this is *Tortuga One*. Callie, Callie, this is *Tortuga One*. You there, kid?" I wait what seems like thirty minutes, and I feel Chubby moving the wheel under my butt. He nudges the throttles a bit, to keep us in line with the sailboat. I wonder, *where the hell is that kid?* He should still be at the shop working on the air compressor and he should be able to hear the radio. I look in the direction of my shop, Dive Tortuga, some seven miles around the southern end of the island. I envision Callie sleeping out on the dock

2

while my voice bellows over the radio. I chuckle to myself, knowing it isn't true, but I am still curious about why he isn't answering.

The wind has shifted and is blowing through the South Gap from the southwest. The South Gap is a quarter-mile-wide passage between the main island of Isla Tortuga and the small pinnacle known as South Point Island. The passage acts as a funnel for the wind between the high cliff of the mainland and the smaller, sheer pinnacle. It is like standing in a wind tunnel with the fan on high, and we would have to head into that wind tunnel to get home.

Chubby's impatience escapes its always-tenuous bounds. Acting his role as the impatient fifteen-year-old, it's clear he can't understand why we have to go to such effort for this abandoned boat.

"Isn't this government business?" he asks.

"We just can't let an expensive sailboat wallow out here."

"Anchor it," he demands.

"Dammit, Chub, you know how deep it is here. I doubt that they have seven hundred feet of rode."

He rolls his shoulders. "Where is Callie?"

To move the project along for Chubby, I'm about to give up on raising Callie when the radio squawks, "*Tortuga One, Tortuga One,* this is Dive Tortuga. Come bauk, ya read. Over."

"Dive Tortuga, this is *Tortuga One.* Have Bill meet me at the pier. I'm bringing in a sailboat we found out here by South Gap. Seems to be abandoned. Over."

"Abandoned? Overboard?" Callie questions.

"Yeah, just tell Bill to meet me. We'll be back in about a half hour or so. *Tortuga One,* out."

In deference to Chubby, I shut the radio off before Callie can come back. I'm annoyed with him for not answering fast enough

3

and don't want to get into it right then as to why he was so slow in responding to my hail. Actually, I'm annoyed at the whole situation—Chubby's impatience, Callie's inattentiveness, and this damn sailboat owner's recklessness.

Isla Tortuga sees its share of bareboat charters out of Grenada, so I've seen a lot of dumb stuff in my short tenure on the island. Bill refers to these bareboaters as "credit card captains" because anyone can be a captain if their card is platinum. It's amazing that more of these guys don't get themselves killed, considering their skill levels. The sea can be an unforgiving place and Isla Tortuga is an especially unforgiving, strange little island surrounded by jagged pinnacles that, at times, rise feet from the surface like teeth on a saw. I've learned great respect for the waters around this island. They have taken many ships and many lives and I don't want to be another stat on a form, another soul lost at sea. So to see a boat this close to shore, its mainsail cracking like gunshots, and no one responding to my calls makes me more than a little concerned. Clearly, something is not right. I need to do something, as inconvenient as it might be to both Chubby and me. "Look Chub, I just want to get back to the shop and have a beer." A gust of wind reminds me that we need to get moving. "Let's just do this."

I quickly go over the plan with Chub, telling him to take the wheel of the *Tortuga One* as I prepare to jump aboard and investigate.

When on board, my plan is to take a cursory look belowdecks and see what, if anything, I can find. I really don't expect to find anyone—we've been behind the boat for some five minutes now, shouting and calling on the radio with no response. The boat is abandoned.

After that, I figure I'll motor the sailboat around the point and back to Pelican Bay. Sort it out there in the calm of the bay, with a cold beer in hand. And that will allow Chubby to drive *Tortuga One* back to the shop and let him get on with his oh-so-important life.

Really, I shouldn't be so hard on the kid. He's worked his ass off this past week in some pretty rough sea conditions with some fairly unpleasant French divers. Yesterday was their last day of diving so Chubby was looking forward to having today off, but I pressed him into service, making him help me with a dive site marker buoy that had a frayed line. I was concerned that the line would snap and we would lose the buoy.

Plus, I haven't been sleeping very well lately. Weird dreams.

The short version is last night I dreamed of Africa. I was alone on safari, wandering the bush, hunting big game. I came across a pride of lions in the open savannah. There were at least six lionesses with cubs. As I drew closer, I saw they were feeding on a fish, a very large fish, maybe twenty feet long. It looked like a shark, but the curve of the tail was beautifully formed, a sickle. It was a marlin. The lions looked at me with little concern, as if they were expecting me. Then I woke up.

And it's been variations on that theme for a couple of weeks now.

The *Miss Princess* is wallowing badly, as boats do that are at the mercy of the wind and currents. My plan is to board her from the swim platform. It will be tricky; Chubby will have to inch up slow and close so that I can jump from the bow of the *Tortuga One* to the swim platform, and all of this when the two boats are in a hollow of a wave so that the platform will be relatively level.

The odds are good that I'll get wet. I do.

Chubby does his part, gets me up close, but just as I pounce, a shore-reflected wave tilts the platform, effectively swatting me into the sea. I bob to the surface to see Chubby looking over the side of *Tortuga One* with an obnoxiously broad smile on his face.

*You try and do a good deed*, I think to myself as I sidestroke to the sailboat. I pull myself up onto the platform, slog my way up to the companionway, and poke my head down the opening. "Hello. Anyone home?"

No answer, just the sound of sails and hardware rattling and banging as the boat pitches in the confused seas. So with both hands I push my too-long bangs back over my head and make my way toward the mast. Holding onto the portside stay, I discover the mainsail halyard winch is jammed. Smashed, actually, with the wire halyard miserably wrapped and kinked in the broken winch. It looks like someone has been at it with a sledgehammer. I know I'm not going to get the sails down with it looking like that. Not easily anyhow. From where I stand on the coach roof, I can tell that the jib is badly furled on its roller-furling headstay, bumpy and offline. The jib sheets, the ropes that control the sail, are chopped off, unraveling in the wind, flying like crucified snakes at the clew of the sail. What is going on here?

*Hell*, I muse, *just run the damn thing in and be done with your Good Samaritan deed for the day.*

I retrace my way back to the stern of the boat when an unexpected gust of wind rolls the boat and makes me reach for the wheel for support. I then notice—I'd walked right past it before—that the wheel is bound with rope, very distinctive rope. It is polyethylene, with red and blue threads wound around a white core. I've never seen this kind of line on a boat before. It looks like thick clothesline. Strangely, the rope binds the wheel to the compass binnacle, a very rudimentary autopilot, especially for such a nice boat. My eyes drop to the throttle, fully forward—wide open. The transmission lever is down, forward for a sailboat. My eyes scan the gunwale for the fuel gauge and I sink when I see it reads empty. Someone set this boat off motoring full steam ahead and it ended up here, at South Gap, when it ran out of fuel. My great plan of motoring the boat in is shot now, and I can't sail it in with the all the hardware out of commission. The only other option is to tow it.

I turn my attention back to the rope securing the wheel. *Man, this is strange*, I think to myself. I look back at the gunwale. The boat is equipped with an electronic autopilot, so why the rope? Didn't the owners or charters know how to use the autopilot? Unlikely, but possible.

I pull my Leatherman tool out of its sheath, open the serrated knife, and begin cutting the rope. As I saw away, I yell to Chubby, "Hey, buddy. Bad news."

His head drops to one side, registering his frustration. "What?" he says, plaintive as a small child.

"I'm sorry, but we've got to tow it in. It's out of gas and it's unsailable."

"Can't we call someone? Can't the police tow it in?"

A good idea, but the weather isn't cooperating. I'm not too thrilled with the prospect of waiting for relief on an uncontrollable boat. It could easily end up smashed on the rocks, and I'd be swimming before help would arrive.

"I'm sorry. I don't think we can chance it. We should tow it in. I'll make it up to you. I promise. Hey, dinner on me at the Beachcomber, huh? How does that sound?" *Pretty damn generous to me,* I think. It seems to soothe him. He doesn't respond. With Chubby, I've learned that no response is a tacit agreement. "Start setting up a bridle for towing. Use the dock lines in the back bench." I finish cutting through the rope on the wheel, and as Chubby searches out lines, I decide to check belowdecks.

I skip down the four steps of the companionway into the salon area, and realize suddenly that this is the first time I've been below. I'm surprised at myself, slightly, for not checking there first. Someone could have been hurt below, but I presumed no one was aboard when I shouted down earlier. I didn't see the need.

"Hello!" I shout. I'm right, no one home.

It smells musty below, like a damp cellar. The sliding companionway roof is pushed forward and the protective boards at the steps are not in place—the boat is open to the weather. I notice salt stains on the sole, irregular white blotches, evidence of intruding saltwater. A good storm with high enough seas could have downflooded the boat and possibly sunk her.

The companionway stairs put me almost directly in the middle of the boat. From this vantage point, I quickly scan the area. Nothing unusual. Everything seems in place. The navigation table is directly to starboard; I think that a good place to start. I can at least get an idea where the boat is from by reading their charts.

I find nothing. I lift the lid to the navigation table, not a single chart or note. In fact, not even a set of parallel rulers or dividers. Odd. Whoever was sailing the boat, no matter their skill level, would need to have these basic navigational tools. And they would want the charts of the area out and ready. Hell, I know these waters pretty well after six months but anyone new to the waters would use—no, need—a chart to avoid the ever-present pinnacle or sandbar. I open the cabinet above the table and find three charts rolled neatly in tubes. I pull out the one on the left, unroll it, and find that it is a sectional chart of the area, but with no course plotted. In fact, the chart looks brand new, never used.

"Hey boss? I'm ready up here!" Chubby yells from the *Tortuga One.*

"OK!" I yell back. I can hear the wind whistling through the rigging topside and I quickly calculate that with towing we are about an hour from the bay and a safe harbor. I decide that a thorough search of the boat will have to wait until we got back into calmer waters. I roll the chart back into its tube and latch the door of the cabinet.

When I pop back up on deck, Chubby is staring at me.

"The weather, boss," Chubby says.

I look at the water and the tops are starting to blow off the chop. We need to beat it around the point. There, we will be protected from the wind, in the lee of the island.

"OK, toss me the line." He tosses me a two-inch line that is about twenty feet long—just long enough to allow the *Miss Princess* to settle behind the wake of my boat. Good choice. The sailboat won't get tossed considerably in the wake so we can chance running at a faster speed. Chubby is thinking. But then, despite his age, Chubby is an experienced seaman.

I find what look like brand new dock lines in the starboard lazarette and then walk the towline up to the bow of the sailboat as Chubby putters alongside. I tie off the *Miss Princess*'s dock lines to the base of the mast and lead one starboard, one port. I lead them around their respective bow cleats and then make them fast to the towline. Chubby keeps some slack, being careful not to foul our props with the dangling line. I need to get back to my boat and it is clear I'm going swimming. I strip my T-shirt off and catch Chubby's sidelong glance at the scars on my chest and shoulder, and I reflexively cover myself, hands crossed at the wrists, wet shirt swinging slowly. He turns away, ashamed, and I stuff the shirt into the back of my cargo shorts. As I brace myself to dive in, I hear a crash belowdecks directly beneath me.

I decide I better go back below deck to secure as many things as I can to limit the amount of stuff that will get tossed as the boat pitches and wallows during towing. "Just a minute, Chub." I move quickly back down the side deck to the companionway.

As I half jump down and half slide down the stairs, the door to the main cabin at the stern of the boat swings open and slams against the wall. The noise startles me so much I nearly fall into the salon as I spin around. The Beneteau has a double stateroom layout: one cabin in the bow, the other cabin astern. From topside, I heard the noise in the forward stateroom, but the door to the rear compartment just swings there, open and close, open and close, periodically slamming violently into the wall, as if it were waving me to come in. I step to the door and grab it on one of its closing cycles and hold it half open. Curiously, I lean against the door and the jamb of the door, my modest six-foot frame just fitting into the opening, and peer into the cabin. The bed is made, and everything, like the rest of the belowdecks area of the boat, seems in order. Something catches my eye.

As if someone flicked it out with a finger, I see a pacifier roll out from the far side of the queen-size berth. The pacifier is opaque blue and with every passing wave, it lolls back and forth on its hilt, like it is waving to me. It is a halting sight, and an even more halting realization. There had been a baby aboard this boat.

# TWO

THE SETTING SUN MAKES Tony White's eyes look molten. Tony cups Martha's face. "Don't cry. Please try to compose yourself. Let's show them that British stiff upper lip."

The little girl hugs Martha, legs thrown around the woman's waist, her arms locked around her mother's neck. Tony runs his hand through his daughter's flaxen hair, "It's OK Sophie, everything is fine."

But Martha knows better. The situation is not fine. How could it possibly be fine? She hasn't a clue where she is, save that her small family is belowdecks on a barely seaworthy boat steaming who knows where.

"What will they do with us, Tony?" Martha asks.

"I'm not sure, Mart. I have to believe they would have killed us by now if that was their intent." She cringes at his choice of words as she feels her daughter wriggle tighter around her, as if the little girl were trying to meld back into her.

Tony turns and moves onto the first step of the companionway. From her vantage point, Martha can see the larger of the two men. The man has the revolver slack at his side; the rolling of the boat makes his arm swing like a lethal plumb bob. The man's broad back is to them and only a few yards away. The man is clearly watching something or someone. Tony ventures another step, but with a groan, the step gives him away. The broad-backed man half turns, raises the gun, and points it at Tony's head. He thumbs back the hammer. "Bam," he says quietly.

──────────

The pacifier rattles me.

A child on board—certainly not what I was expecting. Yet, it makes sense, I guess. Many families take cruising holidays and even though Isla Tortuga is not a hot spot for sailors, we seemed to get our share. Nonetheless, the reality of a child being on board strikes me hard, harder than it should, perhaps. Now back on my boat, towel draped over my soaked head, that one primal human object makes me wonder what happened to the people on the *Miss Princess*. I finger the soft plastic now in my pocket.

All those weird, mismatched details. Smashed hardware, roped up wheel, yet tidy belowdecks. The violence topside doesn't match the calm below.

I reach out and touch the towrope, feeling the tension. The *Miss Princess* bobs and weaves in the hollow of our wake.

I swing around the bench and stand next to Chubby behind the console. "Sorry about the speed. It's just that I don't want to tear out the cleats or snap the line."

"Not a problem," Chubby says quietly. He appears solemn, concentrating on the water ahead. And with that response, I realize I've underestimated this young man—again.

Chubby is a good kid, a strong kid with more maturity than his years. After I showed him the pacifier, Chubby thought to scan the area with the pair of binoculars we have on board, just in case the owners were swimming and forgot to anchor the boat. A ridiculous thought on his part, but his earlier impatience disappeared immediately the minute that pacifier showed up. He was clearly concerned.

I look sideways at him, attempting to read him. I watch his eyes constrict and flex as he works out hidden thoughts. One minute he's as petulant as any fifteen-year-old on the planet, the next he is an adult, concerned about a missing child. I guess that polarity resides in us all. I nod my head, signaling my departure, and move back to check on the *Miss Princess*.

I watch the sailboat for several minutes as she nods and canters behind us quite nicely. The sailboat's motion in the water is hypnotic—like swinging in a hammock—and I find myself fading away from the present. *I need to get some sleep*, I think to myself. I try to focus on the boat and the pacifier and the clearly missing family, but my mind won't stay fixed. Like a child or kitten or puppy, I'm easily distracted and I find myself thinking of a conversation I had with Bill Tomey, my friend and previous owner of Dive Tortuga. And then, seemingly out of body, I find I'm no longer on my boat but back with him on the porch of my shop and it's last night, dusk.

———

It takes on the color of a blanket I had as a child. My mom washed that red cotton blanket so many times that the original crimson became every hue of red—tangerine, fuchsia, and plum spread throughout the fabric with all the care of a toddler's watercolor painting. Sitting here, I feel like I have that old blanket thrown over my head and I'm looking up through it. I can almost taste the unraveling polyester border, laundry soap, fabric softener—comforting tastes to a four-year-old boy.

*Just another one of those bruised Caribbean sunsets*, I think to myself.

"Jimmy Buffett is a genius," Bill says flatly.

The statement shakes me out of my reverie. I don't respond immediately, but glancing over at him, I notice he is contemplating his bottle of beer and for a minute I think he is talking to it instead of me. I'm hoping he is talking to the beer and not me.

It's something Bill Tomey and I do most afternoons, sit on those heavy Adirondack chairs in the shade of the deck of my SCUBA-dive shop—which used to be his dive shop—discussing the day's events or other topics of minor importance. This is Isla Tortuga and not much happens down here in the deep southern Caribbean, so there are often long lapses in conversation, but that's just fine with me. We are just two guys looking out over the green apple sea enjoying the jumbled breeze and a couple sweaty beers. Words are often superfluous. It's the mood that counts. It's those mind-warping sunsets that count.

"Jimmy Buffett is a *genius*," he states again, a smidge louder.

Oh no, he is talking to me.

This has been the issue *du jour*—or perhaps I should say "du month"—between Bill and me. Don't get me wrong, I like Jimmy Buffett as much as the next guy, but I don't share Bill's conviction that the troubadour from Key West is the second coming of Mozart or Aristotle. "I don't feel up to this today, Bill."

"There is more to the man than 'Margaritaville' and 'Cheeseburger in Paradise.' The man has a preternatural understanding of the wandering soul, ya know that, don't you, Philly?" He takes a minute sip from his beer.

"Yes. You've told me that before—many times before." I take a large pull on my beer.

"'Remittance Man,' 'La Vie Dansante'—he understands what it means to be alive, he really understands."

"Yes, Bill, he really understands," I sigh.

Bill swivels his head and says, "You are not looking at this with the kind of open mind needed to grow your soul. Like a tree, you must branch out to grow. Take in that sunlight—convert that chlorophyll, my friend."

"This tree is a bit baked today, if you don't mind."

In my peripheral vision I can see him staring at me, eyes bouncing around my face, searching.

"All right, Philly. If the teachings of Jimmy Buffett do not interest you—and they should because the man is an aesthetician of the highest order—then what would you like to talk about?"

Silence, save for Bill's long fingers impatiently drumming on the arm of his chair and the staccato scream of some unseen gull. It goes that way for a few minutes. The gull finally quits; Bill's fingers do not.

"Can't we just enjoy the sunset in peace?"

"Sunsets are just fine with me, but I'm sensing a tone in your deportment that suggests agitation. You must cleanse yourself of that agitation to truly appreciate the beauty around you." He finishes his pronouncement with a couple raps on the arm of the chair.

Turning to him, I counter, "What the *hell* are you talking about?"

"See? That's what I mean. Look how quickly you jumped at that. It's in your careworn face. It's in the way you sit rigidly in that chair that is designed to be sat in languorously."

"Isn't that 'languidly'?"

"They mean the same thing, Philly. Don't argue semantics with me, sonny boy."

*Boy ain't that the truth*, I concede. And it hits me. He has succeeded again, getting me to talk when I don't want to talk. I can feel it in the quiver in my hands, the excited trembling in the legs. I know we will spend hours talking now. Talking about what, I don't know. Perhaps everything, perhaps nothing really. Just idling time until we both grow hungry enough to break off the discussion to find a bite to eat. The sun is wrapped in clouds now, revealing its restful light on the smooth water like a road of light leading to the horizon, or a road of light leading to me from that far horizon. It's unclear.

"So what's up, Mr. Phil Riley?" He hops his chair around so he is now facing me.

And I spill it all.

"I don't know. Well, it's kind of weird."

"What? What?"

"Ah, what the hell, it's you, right? You're just a fifty-some-year-old hippie with a penchant for Australian wine and nude metaphysical retreats. How weird can it be? Hell, it must be pretty tame in your book. I followed a guy around today. There."

"That's ex-hippie, remember? You followed a guy around today?"

"I still don't get how you can be an 'ex-hippie.' I don't see how that works, but yeah, I followed a guy around today. Pretty darn interesting, huh?"

"On the face of it, no, but for you, it's a slight deviation from the norm, so I'm intrigued. Proceed. But wait until I get another beer." He pushes himself up from the chair and ambles into the shop.

"Ah, man. I don't know. It's really nothing. Really. I mean, I was looking for an excuse not to work and I found one. That's all it is," I yell at the ceiling of the porch, head tilted back so he can hear me in the shop.

"*I* think not," his voice is muffled, head stuck in the small refrigerator behind the counter.

"Oh Jesus. Here we go. Damn, Bill, not everything someone does is some clue to some deep-seated inner conflict or something. My following a guy doesn't say one thing about me. It means I was bored, that's all."

"There is a reason you followed the guy. You could have found some other way to kill time, but you decided to follow this guy. Why?" He is back out on the deck, fishing in his pocket for a bottle opener.

"I thought ... hell, I don't know what I thought. I never learned the answer. And where is my beer?"

"The answer? What answer? Aha! Here it is, damn opener likes to hide from me! What answer?" I hear the pop of the cap releasing from the bottle and the clink as the cap hits the deck. He heads back into the shop to fetch me a beer.

"I followed the guy 'cause I wanted to know what his story was. He fascinated me. I'd never seen him before, and his mannerisms, the way he carried himself, impressed me. You know, when you're just sitting around letting your mind wander, you tend to fill the voids with... stuff. Your imagination fills in where the facts leave off. I did that with this guy. I made up this whole story about him and I never found out if I was right or not."

"Interesting, for several different reasons. So you gonna to tell me this story or not?"

"All right, 'Doctor' Bill ..."

"And from the beginning—and with details. Give the details." He was at my side, extending the opened beer.

I took the beer and sucked the foam out of the neck. "Details, huh?"

———————

I pinch the pacifier between my fingers. The rubbery resistance brings me back to the present. Refocusing, I find that we are through the gap and making our way up the western side in the sheltered lee of the island. I hear and feel the engines respond as Chubby gooses the throttles a bit, urging the *Tortuga One* on home. I half look over my shoulder at my young captain.

Chubby rolls his shoulders and head, like a boxer before a fight. Chubby is built like a tree trunk, so the name "Chubby" doesn't really fit him. I would have called him chunky. It's a tradition on Isla Tortuga that everyone has a nickname. Mine is slowly spreading around the island. I hope it doesn't stick. But Chubby is what his friends call him, and he doesn't seem to mind it. So I call him Chubby as well. Standing at the wheel, legs shoulder-width apart, feet slightly splayed, calves doing most of the work of stabilizing him as the boat bounces about on the water, he leans into the wheel, chest almost touching it, right hand on the twin throttles. His stance makes it look like he is willing the boat to go faster.

"Keep the speed right there, Chub," I say, reflexively. I take a quick look at the towrope. It's fine. The cleat feels solid under my hand. I look back up at Chubby and watch him drive the boat.

Chubby reaches up, scratches his head, and combs his Afro with his fingers. He fishes out a piece of sea grass stuck in his hair and holds it gently in his open palm. He gazes at it with his fingers curved to shelter it from the wind. He sighs, lowers his fingers into the wind, and lets the grass fly off his hand. It cartwheels through the air past me. I lose it immediately in the wake of the boat.

"Boss!"

I turn back to see Chubby pointing directly ahead just off of Sandy Beach, the landmark that introduces the entrance to Pelican Bay. He is pointing at a small launch, silver, a little Avon inflatable. Sitting in it is Bill Tomey, long silver ponytail flapping against his back as he charges out of the shelter of the bay into open water. His little rubber boat, no more than ten feet long with a little nine-horse outboard, is a bronco bull. He must have the outboard throttle opened all the way.

He is sitting sideways on the rear plank, left hand on the tiller of the outboard, right hand wrapped in the painter of the dinghy. He is a man on a mission. Salt spray slaps up so badly that at times you can't see him. I throw my head back and laugh. Chubby turns around with a huge smile on his face. It is quite a sight, a six-foot-seven, 250-pound, fifty-nine-year-old ex-hippie in what looks like a toy boat tearing at us like he is running for his life.

"Should I idle down?"

"Yeah, Chub, pull back a bit so he can poke alongside."

"He doesn't look happy," Chubby observes.

Chubby is right. Bill is close enough now, maybe seventy-five yards, that we can see him snarling like a feral cat. It isn't a look of concentration; it's a look of anger. I wonder what has gotten him so pissed. I don't have to wait long for my answer—Bill is upon us, whirling out to pull along port side.

Bill screams, "Is your radio dead, or just your brain!"

"What?" I answer, puzzled. Not the welcome I was expecting.

"Why did you turn off your radio? We have been trying to raise you for a half hour! We thought something had happened to you."

"I told Callie what was up. Didn't he tell you?" I respond, defensively.

"He told me you guys were abandoning ship, for Christ's sake! I thought you guys had a fire or something!" Bill, both mad and relieved, begins to calm down, his face relaxing.

I begin to understand where the communication broke down, recalling the conversation with Callie. *Abandon? Overboard?* He clearly thought that *we* were abandoning ship and going overboard, not that we found an abandoned sailboat.

Callie is notorious for that sort of thing. Callie is slightly "hindered" and frequently doesn't get the story straight. Combine that with a rather active imagination, and a fairly simple story can get out of hand in a hurry.

"Callie heard me say 'abandoned' and thought it was Chub and I that were abandoning ship," I inform Bill.

"The poor kid was in tears. He came running up to my house, all out of breath, saying you two were drowning, that the boat had gone down. Jesus, I couldn't get him to calm down enough to get him to tell me your location. Didn't you tell him where you were going?"

"I'm sorry, Bill. I didn't. Chubby and I were going out for a couple hours to fix the buoy at Catherine's Rock. Didn't see a reason to," I apologize.

"What the hell! Would it fucking kill you to tell someone what the hell you're doing? Sorry, Chub. Not mad at you." Bill's anger boiled up again—at me.

I catch the slightest smile spread on Chubby's mouth just before he turns away.

"Just leave your damn radio on next time! You know how Callie is. The damn kid's a mess! By the way, what the hell is that?" He throws a thumb at the *Miss Princess*.

"Good question," I nod.

During Bill's scolding, Chubby has taken us around Sandy Beach and into the bay. Dead ahead lies the gray, sun-bleached dock that juts out directly in front of Dive Tortuga. Scattered in front of it are three sailboats—one more than yesterday—each tied up to one of the half dozen or so mooring buoys in the bay. They stand at attention, tight on their painters, facing into the southwest wind.

There are people on the dock. I can make out three forms, one of which is shielding his eyes, hands forming an awning against the oblique sun. I know the other one, the one with the police cap pulled low.

Chief of Police Bourgois is a physically impressive man. Six foot three or four, 250 lean, athletic pounds. Skin the color of coal or slate with a slight sheen to it. I don't know the man well. Only met him in passing a few times, but his reputation is excellent. A thorough, accurate man, everyone says. It is, however, interesting that he is

21

here, on my dock. I clearly remember that I told Callie to ask Bill to meet me at the dock. I hadn't asked for anyone else. Or did he know of the *Miss Princess*? Isla Tortuga is a small island, but not that small. No way he would know about the sailboat yet. What did he want?

My attention turns to the other man on the dock standing at Bourgois's shoulder. I clearly don't know this one.

My quick assessment: White guy. Not quite fat, not quite in shape. Slightly balding, wearing knee-length shorts, a loose batik-printed shirt, and dark brown huarache sandals. Pallid skin. Fresh to the islands. A tourist. But why with Bourgois?

The owner of the *Miss Princess*? My heart jumps.

"Bill. Who is that with Bourgois?"

Bill idles his skiff allowing it to drift back to parallel with me. "I don't know. Callie was the only one on the dock when I set off a few minutes ago. He's talking to Bourgois. They must know one another."

I nod in agreement. My eyes turn to the third person on the dock. Callie, my seventeen-year-old shopkeeper and general repair-man. He stands bare chested, sweat making his cocoa skin glisten in the low angle of the sun. Callie is standing slightly ahead of the two other men, hands clenched together and shaking, like he is about to roll some large dice—his sign of agitation. I smile and say to myself, affectionately, *Callie, what am I going to do with you?*

Chubby pulls the engines back to neutral, allowing us to slip up to the mooring buoy, momentum bringing the *Miss Princess* slowly up to us. As we secure the sailboat, Bill motors in to report to Bourgois our intentions and to take Callie home. The poor kid is bawling with relief. Bill is still in the dinghy, holding onto the dock, when

Bourgois yells out to me through cupped hands to turn my radio to channel six. I do.

"Riley?"

"Yes," I say, with a playful lilt to my voice. We look at each other across the water.

"Don't search the boat until I get there."

"It's too late. I've sort of searched the boat already. No one at home."

"No one?" he says, looking quickly at the pale man next to him.

"Yeah. No one. Is that guy next to you the owner?"

Bourgois furtively looks at the man. The man stares out at me without acknowledging Bourgois's glance. Bourgois comes back after a beat, "No. No he isn't. He is a customer of yours—potential customer."

"Hey, great. Have him stay there. We shouldn't be long. You can come out if you want, but there isn't much to see. I can fill you in when I get to shore. Like I said, I'm just gonna take a quick look, try and find the boat's papers, then come right in."

"Don't go on that boat. Just come in."

We gape at each other for longer than is comfortable. I shrug and shut the radio off, thinking, *odd*—odd that he took my word for it that the boat was abandoned. If I were the police chief and someone brought in an abandoned sailboat, I would be asking a hell of a lot more questions *and* I'd be out here searching the boat. Looking for clues. He wasn't doing either. Didn't look like he was that interested in the thing. It seemed like he already knew, or suspected, that the boat was unoccupied. With eroding equanimity, I watch Bourgois walk up the dock toward the shop, pale man in tow. Their conversation is intense. A customer, huh?

It is clear to me that on some level, Bourgois and the man know one another. I can sense it. Strangers don't talk with that kind of animation.

Furthermore, the man doesn't look like a diver. Granted, SCUBA divers come in all shapes and sizes, but this guy didn't fit into the typical mold, especially for Isla Tortuga. I, as a rule, get the hardcore American diver who is tired of diving off of cattle boats and seeing the same old things over and over again. They usually look like Navy Seals, thick and tattooed, on a little R and R in the islands. This guy looks like an insurance salesman from Cleveland, right down to the obvious island shirt.

When I turn around, I see Chubby trying to pull the sailboat in, but he is actually pulling us to it. The *Tortuga One* is significantly lighter, apparently, than the *Miss Princess*.

"Just tie off the line where it is. It's short enough. I'm not worried about the swing. We're out here far enough and if another boat comes in I can deal with it then."

Chubby quickly complies, securing the line with a flourish, like a rodeo cowboy. He spins on his heels, eyes expectant.

I nod, pivot on the bench, and nudge the throttles.

"You can tie up, can't you?" Chubby asks.

"Sure. And thanks for your help today."

His head bounces on his shoulders.

We are several feet from the dock when he jumps from the boat, landing with a few short balancing steps. He turns, waves to me, and sprints up to the shop. He grabs his bicycle that is leaning against the wall and throws it on his shoulder. I lose sight of him as he makes his way up the embankment to The Road.

I sidle the boat up to the dock and cut the engines. With stern line in one hand, I flip the round orange fender over the side, then jump off and make the stern fast. I work quickly, tying off the stern before the boat bounces off its fenders and the bow swings out of reach. I catch the bow easily. I secure the bow and throw on a spring line then shape up all three lines. *Tortuga One* is ready for the night. I turn toward the shop.

I'm very hungry for some reason, the saliva in my mouth like glue. As I make my way up the swayback dock, I glance up the embankment in a vain hope that Michael's roti stand is open. Rotis are burrito-like things made from beef, chicken, or conch mixed with fried potatoes. They are very tasty and a staple of my diet. But I know before I look that Michael will not be there. Yes, the flip-up shutters are down. The tin-roofed shack just squats there in the scrub.

I twirl, walking backwards, looking back at the mouth of the bay. The sun is balanced between the twin cliffs of the bay entrance, like a spicy, orange ball wedged atop a crack. I look at my Omega Seamaster. 6:17. I'm surprised by the time. It's getting late.

I spin around and continue up the wooden dock that connects with a poured concrete ramp that runs directly into the front door of the dive shop. The ramp makes it exceedingly convenient for loading equipment in and out of the boat. Bill was really thinking when he put the ramp in.

"I understand it is your responsibility, but . . ." Whoever was talking stops short.

I am about twenty feet from the open front door of the shop. I freeze, searching the shadows in the shop. I have a hard time making anything out because of the sharp contrast from the slanting outside light and the darkness inside. When my eyes finally adjust enough for me to see any detail, I see the two men standing deep in the shop, looking out at me, silently. I flinch. It spooks me a bit. Like walking into a dark room to find someone silently sitting on a couch.

"Come on in, Riley." It's Bourgois's voice, but I can't see his mouth move. His companion turns and moves away from the door, off to where my desk is, in the back corner.

I proceed timidly, feeling a little like a teenager being called into the den for a scolding from his father. I try to shake it off, but I'm only partially successful. Standing in the doorway, I alternately turn my eyes from the pale man to Bourgois. Bourgois stands next to the doorway that leads into the back room where I keep my equipment and repair station and the other inner workings of the shop. The pale man leans, rear against the desk, ankles crossed, left hand holding right elbow. He is smiling a very broad smile, too broad.

"Donald Bennett, meet Philip Riley. Philip, Don," Bourgois offers, a pinch too enthusiastically.

I nod to the pale man who now has a name. "Pleased to meet you, Don. May I call you Don?"

"Likewise, and but of course." A distinct British accent.

I grin, and bounce a bit with internal laughter. I hate diving with Europeans—they are the worst-trained SCUBA divers on the planet. They have no regard for safety and even less regard for underwater etiquette. They, to a type, act as if diving is nothing more than taking a very complete bath. I was hoping that my supposition that Don really wasn't a diver was correct.

"I prefer Phil." I look over at Bourgois, who now is smiling that damn smile, too. There are some odd vibes going on in this room.

Three men standing around grinning at each other masking something that I instinctively know won't be said. I try anyhow, in a roundabout way. "So you're looking to do some diving?"

"Why yes. I've heard from Charles that the diving is outstanding. I'm looking forward to it."

"Charles is most correct. The diving here is outstanding in its own way," I say, with contrived formality.

"Perhaps you gentlemen can talk about diving later. I would like to know what you saw on the sailboat," Bourgois exhales, steering the conversation.

"Yes of course, you men talk about your business. Just quickly, when do you go out in the morning, Phil?" Don is unexpectedly heading for the door.

I turn sideways in the doorway to allow him to pass. "Actually, I usually buy my clients a beer, to welcome them to our fair island. Are you and your wife free tonight?"

He stops just before reaching the door. He is about five feet from me and for the first time I get a good look at him. My first impression of his fitness was fairly inaccurate. Popeye forearms and tree trunk legs sticking out of a whiskey barrel torso—a thick and sturdy fellow. Not the typical diver type for sure, but a man who looks like he takes reasonable care of himself. I quickly measure that I would not want to tangle with this guy unless I had a very large club and an ample supply of surprise.

"I'm solo, actually, so I would love to dine with someone. Are you free for dinner as well as that beer?"

"Yeah, sure," I agree. "How about the Beachcomber?"

"The little café up the beach?"

"Yup. Best seafood on the island."

"That sounds nice. I'm down at the Tortuga Beach Resort, so shall we say seven thirty? At the Beachcomber?"

I mechanically look at my watch. "That would be great. Gives me some time to change and clean up."

He smiles again, and moves past me out the door. There is barely enough room and I suck my stomach in to give him room to pass. Outside, he turns, gives an abridged wave, and disappears around the corner of the shop.

I stand in the doorway a moment, looking down the beach through the empty space where he turned the corner, thinking, *that was a fast escape.*

I try to formulate some questions for Bourgois. The only one that I come up with is the obvious, "What the hell is going on here, Chief?"

He doesn't answer immediately. He leans in the rear of the store in the shadows. The tender sunlight angles into the shop past me, onto his shoes. They shine a silky black. They are the only part of him that I can make out clearly, so I focus on them as I talk. "There's something going on here. I can feel it. Hell, it doesn't take some Sherlock Holmes to figure that out."

"There is nothing going on, Riley."

I turn my eyes up to his featureless face, an articulate silhouette. "Come on. This is all a little too conspiratorial for me, Chief. You guys don't do this very well. I know there's something going on. Between you and Don. And the boat . . . " I let my words trail off.

Again silence. I jump in with both feet, thinking that surprise might wedge open an unrehearsed answer.

"Who *really* is Don? Why aren't you out searching the boat? Why aren't you pounding me with a thousand questions about the boat and what I saw?"

"You saw nothing on the boat," he interrupts.

I step into my shop, closing the distance between us. "Is that a question or a statement, Chief?"

No answer. He moves slowly out of the shadows and into the slanting light. I read on his face that he wants to say something, I think.

"What is it, Chief?"

He pauses, mouth slightly open, as if he does indeed want to speak. He shakes his head, and moves toward the door, closing on me. I move deeper into the shop to give him room.

"Show Donald a good time. He is an old friend," he says, moving past me, brushing my chest.

"Hey. Wait."

He is in the doorway, ready to turn the corner.

"There was a baby on that sailboat."

He hesitates momentarily in the doorway, back to me. I watch him roll his shoulders, subtly, then move on. Outside the shop he turns and moves along the front of the shop. He stops in front of the large open window that looks west out over the bay. He is framed in the opening, silhouetted again by the sun. His head hangs down, sad dog. After a moment, he lifts his dark head and turns toward me.

"Stay off that boat, Riley." His disembodied voice rings deep and sober.

He steps away from the window, leaving me squinting into the setting sun.

# THREE

HONOR. HONOR AND DIGNITY. That's what I thought the minute I saw him. He looked majestic, though he was only about five foot seven, at best. He certainly had a bearing about him. Like I said—majestic. But majestic isn't the right word. Majestic is a mountain, or a lion. This guy exuded a sense of right and a sense of wrong. I can't explain it. I'm sure you've seen people where you think they are righteous people. They are good people. You could tell—I could tell—this guy lived the right life. He was good people.

Anyway, I couldn't take my eyes off him. He was standing on the beach out in front of the dive shop. Straw hat over heart, chin on chest. His feet were bare, half buried in the wet surf sand. His faded powder-blue pants were threadbare. They were so thin and pale that they looked like the color of the sky when it's really hot or humid. When the moisture acts like gauze softening the blue. But they were clean—the pants, that is. His white shirt was spotless, too, except for the hint of yellow perspiration stains under his arms.

As I watched him, I tried to place him. I finally decided that I'd never seen him before. He looked Latin. Perhaps Venezuelan, perhaps not. I'm not very good with accents or nationalities. But about an hour earlier I heard the flight from Caracas go overhead when I was in the back room working on the damn compressor, so I figured Venezuelan was a good guess.

I watched him for about five minutes, I figure. He didn't move. Just stood there. Chin on chest, hat over his heart. I watched the lapping surf softening his footing and several times, when the water had eroded his base, he would take a correcting step back to keep his balance. It looked like someone was pushing gently on the front of his shoulder. It was subtle, gentle, and yet distinct. He would wiggle his feet deeper in the sand after each retreat, but the water would eventually win out and he would be forced back a few more inches.

I eventually went back to the green beast that for some damn reason won't run Monday through Saturday, it seems, and I've got that group coming in and I need to be able to pump tanks or I'm in it deep.

But I couldn't keep my mind off of him. So after a few minutes of staring at the laid-open compressor, shaking my head, thinking that I'm going to have to get Callie out of school to fix this damn thing, I decided to see if the mystery man was still on the beach. He was.

Poncy—you know, that stray mutt that runs the beach? Well he was sitting next to the old man, tail sweeping an arch in the sand, long tongue dripping with anticipation. The old man smiled down at the mutt and laid open his hands to show that he had nothing to offer. Poncy licked both palms, one stroke each, then sat back down and continued staring up at the man. The man laughed. I could hear him. Deep. Full. Honest. He reached down, cupped Poncy's head, and tousled him good. The dog's ears flapped wildly. When he released the mutt's head, the dog just stared up at him like nothing had happened. The man smiled down at the dog, rolled his head to the side, raised his chin to the sky, and gave Poncy the one-eyed look. The kind of look a mother gives her son just before she is about to say, "What did I tell you, young man?" I got that look from my mother more than once, as you can imagine. But Poncy didn't understand the nonverbal communication because he just sat there, tongue lolling, skinny chest bouncing with every pant.

The man realized that he wasn't getting through to the dog, so he returned to studying the bay.

Then he quickly crossed himself, adjusted his hat on his head, spun, and made for the path leading off the beach, Poncy in tow. The quickness of his actions snapped me out of my trance. I watched him plod through the soft sand with purpose. No hunched back, no teetering steps. I went out onto the deck here to watch him make his way up the rim of the beach to The Road. You know where it banks there, heading back into town? I could see his head slowly disappear as he angled across the sloping pavement to catch the northbound bus.

The minivan spluttered around the corner and slowed. He must have got on. I heard the sliding door both open and shut and the minivan struggle to pick up speed.

I stood there a moment and as I was about to turn back to the compressor, Poncy came running down the little ridge and onto the beach, right to where the man was standing. He snuffled the sand for a moment, then turned and ran full out up the beach.

I drove my truck into St. Christopher, ostensibly to buy a part for the green beast of a compressor, but really, to see if I could catch up with the man.

After the old man left, I began my mind-wanderings, wondering what the guy was all about and what he was up to. If he did get off the plane, then why did he come to the beach almost immediately, then within minutes head back into town? Why not stay in town, do your business there, then come to the beach? It . . . intrigued me.

When I first got to town, I of course had no idea where to find him. Then it hit me—he would have to clear immigrations once off the plane. Just talk to my old buddy Sam Cartier down at the immigration office and see who it might be. The flight from Caracas is rarely full, so old Sam would surely remember my man. That may have been wishful thinking, but I figured it was as good a place to start as any. Proud of myself for being so industrious, I headed for the Customs and Immigration Office to see if Sam was in.

Of course, he was out. You know, that guy never works. He is *never* there when I want to see him. He always tells me "make an appointment." Christ, this is Isla Tortuga. Little, sleepy, backwater, nobody-knows-we-exist Isla Tortuga. Maybe, and I mean maybe, ten thousand people live on this island and we get, on a good day, two flights into the airport, right? So how busy can the guy be? There can't be *that* much customs and immigration going on. Anyway, Cartier wasn't at his office—so much for my grand plan.

I headed toward the square and the market. Plan B. Figured I had as good a chance there as anywhere. Maybe get lucky, and besides, I was hungry.

So I got a roti at Benny's cart because he puts the most chicken and vegetables in the thing. And his wrap is tasty, too. I think he puts rosemary in the bread. You know, I'm not sure why rotis haven't caught on around the world. Hell, they sell enchiladas by the millions, why not rotis? But I digress.

I sat on the low seawall overlooking the market. The market was busy today. A nice assortment of fish, it looked like. I was glad to see that. Saw Alan there, in fact. Red snapper will be on the menu at the Beachcomber tonight. I guarantee you.

I sat there for a while and saw several other people I knew, but no old man. I was beginning to think that maybe he didn't come into town at all. Or was I jumping to conclusions and assuming that he was coming into town when he got on the bus? There wasn't any indication of any sort that he might ride the bus all the way into St. Christopher. Hell, I don't even *know* if he got on the bus. I didn't *see* him get on. I heard what I *thought* was the man climbing aboard, but I didn't see him. I wondered what I was thinking to assume that I would just drive into town and find the guy. Pick up the trail just like that. Like he would be waiting for me. How the hell did I figure I was going to find him?

I began to really hate myself for going on this boondoggle when I should have been back at the shop fixing the compressor. *This was a waste of time*, I told myself. No matter what I thought of the guy, or thought he was, I should have been tending to business. He *could* have been someone important or interesting, but I wasn't going to find anything out about him sitting on the port wall people watching.

But, of course, he appeared just as I was about to head home. But how I saw him is interesting.

He was standing, his hands clasped behind his back, behind Peter's fruit cart up under the awning of Jana's Boutique. He was in the shadows, but his white shirt stood out. That's how I saw him. I was scanning the crowd and he stood out against the gray stone. I leaned forward from my perch, instinctively trying to close the gap between us so that I could get a better look at him. It did little good, until he stepped out of the shade into the full light of day. He still had his hands behind him, like a professor addressing his class. He was looking right at me.

There was no doubt he was looking at me because I self-consciously looked up and down the low wall—I was the only one sitting on it. I flushed. He caught me.

Like the young boy caught staring at the pretty girl in class.

Then reason kicked in. He didn't know me, because I didn't know him. And there was no way he saw me back at Pelican Bay. I was in the shadows then, inside the dive shop. There was no reason for him to be staring at me. But no doubt, there he was, looking right at me.

We must have stared at each other for five minutes. People passed back and forth in front of him on the sidewalk, but he simply stood there undistracted, tunneling a hole in me. For my part, I sat there feeling the hole spinning deeper in my chest until I was certain that it would bore through the other side, letting the sun behind me shine through and form this little spotlight on my lap.

Oddly, though, I wasn't uncomfortable with the situation. Typically I would be, right? I would usually be very self-conscious in a situation like that. And that uncomfortable feeling would grow to anger—from a simmer, to a low boil, to confronting the guy that was making me uncomfortable—but not this time.

Why, I don't know. Maybe I didn't perceive the man as a threat. I don't know how much of a threat an old man like him could be, but nevertheless, I wasn't offended by his staring. Hell, how could I be? I was gaping at him in return.

The stalemate finally ended when he dropped his hands to his side, revealing his hat in his right hand. He plopped the straw thing on his head and made for Upper Bay Street. Again, like on the beach, his quickness surprised me. Almost otherworldly. Ghostlike.

I had to beat it through the throngs in the square if I was going to catch up with him. I had this great urge to rush right up to him and ask him his name. Find out why he was staring at me. And what he was doing out on the beach.

I lost sight of him almost immediately. He was to the corner of Upper Bay before I could make my way around the outside of the stalls. Upper Bay runs at an angle away from the market, so I knew I wouldn't be able to see him until I reached the corner. I began to jog, and because I was wearing my Tevas, I had to cobblestone hop from one rounded stone to the next. Like hopping across a shallow river on the exposed rocks. I can't believe how deep the gaps are between the stones. Anyway, that slowed me.

I finally worked my way to the corner of Upper Bay, and swung around the corner, left hand gripping the smooth, cold stone.

Upper Bay is about wide enough for four skinny goats, and I felt like I was standing in the barrel of a gun because there he was, standing about halfway down the block, maybe twenty yards away, hands behind his back again, hat forward on his head, staring right back at me. He was waiting for me. I thought I was going to crap my pants. I *did not* expect him to be there, or at least that close.

This was the closest that I'd been to him since I first saw him on the beach. I knew his pants and shirt, but now I saw his shoes. Simple flip-flops. Dime store flip-flops worn thin from many miles of petrified coral and hand-laid pavement. His toes curled like thick talons, gripping the front of the sandals. And something lay next to his left foot. I couldn't make it out from where I was standing, in spite of a tight squint. The object's gray color blended too well with the cobblestone walk.

When I looked up from his feet, he nodded slightly, spun, and strode quickly up the street. It was like he was leading me to something. I felt like a dog—like Lassie taking Billy to the fawn with the broken leg. Or maybe he was playing me like a fish on a line or something.

I let him turn onto Center Street, heading into the heart of St. Christopher, before I ventured after him. I moved quickly, knowing that I *could* lose him—though that didn't seem to be his intention—at the roundabout that is about fifty yards up Center Street. From that spoke, he could go any of five ways, and I would be left wondering again. Although, again, I didn't think that was his intention. Especially when I picked up the small wooden fish lying on the sidewalk in the spot where he was standing.

It was a marlin—wooden, painted gunmetal gray, and about two inches long. I turned it over and on the tiny base was one of Jana's oval stickers. Clearly he had bought it at the boutique. I wondered if he had placed it there on purpose or had dropped it by mistake. I slipped it in my pocket and hustled to the corner.

He was in the middle of Center Street, crossing to the other side, moving quickly. Gliding. I loped along after him. He never looked back. He hit the roundabout and turned west heading down Grandby and I picked up the pace.

I got to the corner and kind of skidded around it. I stood looking down the deserted street. Scanned back and forth. No old man.

37

Poof. Biff. Whammo. Whatever you want to call it, he vanished, right into thin air. Like he was never there.

I slowly, cautiously, walked toward the cathedral. I looked into the shops, some open, most closed, to see if he had ducked into one of them. Nothing. I hadn't a clue where he had gone. He had utterly vanished on me.

I was growing a bit weary of this little chase by now. Actually, to be quite honest, I was feeling rather foolish for having let an old man lose me like that. Besides, I felt silly for having even begun this little game in the first place.

I had parked my truck down by St. Matthews, so I walked all the way down Grandby, continuing my halfhearted search. When I got to my truck, I couldn't believe it, but there it was sitting on the roof right above the driver's door. Another wooden marlin.

I drove back to the dive shop, thinking about this crazy old man the whole time. I turned the two small wooden fish over and over in my hand, trying to determine what they could mean. Symbols of something, I figured. Was it significant that the fish were marlins? Was he trying to signal me or give me a sign? Or maybe he was just playing with me. And how the hell did he know my truck? That one really threw me. But it wasn't the final straw, so to speak.

When I got back to the dive shop, I tromped through the sand up to the front door, and what did I find? Yes, of course. Wooden fish. There were a dozen at least, and all marlins. He must've bought Jana's stock. They were all sitting on their bases like soldiers or guards or something. And that, I'm afraid, is how the story ends, me wasting an entire day chasing some crazy old man with a fish fetish.

———

"Manolin," Bill says, smiling.

"What?"

"Not what, who."

"Who, then?"

"Sounds like Manolin. Manolin is an old fisherman on the island. He did something similar to me when I first came to Isla Tortuga. Didn't lead me all over the island like he did you, but he left little wooden marlins here at the dive shop just like he did with you."

"Manolin? That's kind of an odd name."

"Yeah, perhaps. Came from Cuba long ago so I presume it's Spanish. Somebody once told me that Manolin was a great fisherman. The guy has got to be eighty if I'm a day."

"So what's with the wooden fish?"

"Don't know. He never told me. I never asked."

"You weren't curious?"

"A little at first, then I saw it as a welcoming gift or something. And I like the mystery of it."

"You said he lives on the island? Where?"

"Yeah, Windwardside. Not sure where in Windwardside. He doesn't come over here to this side much. Occasionally to the shop here in Pelican Bay and just when there is a new guy to see—to break in, so to speak."

"Well, I want to go meet the guy. Find out what the deal is."

"Yeah, sure. I can see how you might feel that way. But do you really need to know? He gave you a poesy of sorts. A hint of what he is. He allowed you a glimpse of himself and he gave you a token. A few tokens, really. Symbols of what he is. You don't need to know that he lives in a shack on the beach, or that he uses old newspapers for blankets. Or, perhaps, he is a long descendant of an Inca chief. Embrace the mystery, Philly boy. Let your mind wander. Let it go. You said yourself that you let your mind meander and fill in the voids. Your imagination fills in where the facts leave off. So fill in the voids, like you said."

"Now you really sound like a hippie."

"Don't give me that crap. You said you like to fill in the blanks. So fill in the blanks. OK, then. Let's hear it. What is it? What are all those blanks filled with?"

I can smell the tangy smoke from the wood-fired oven from the Beachcomber restaurant down the beach. They don't burn oak in the southern Caribbean so the smell is something completely different from those log fires back in the States. The smoke smells like the lushness of the land, like the verdant island itself. It's a pure incense of life.

"That Jimmy Buffett is a genius." I push myself up from my chair, thinking of red snapper and rice.

---

But that was *yesterday*; this is *today*.

Standing there under that lavender moon, looking down at my bare feet, I realize I'm standing where Manolin stood yesterday. Oddly, I feel the connection is still there. Like he left a bit of his energy in this spot and I'm soaking it up through the calloused soles of my feet. That if I stand here long enough, I will understand this mysterious man's message.

But looking back over my shoulder at my dive shop that now sits muted and restful in this special light, I feel the contrast of yesterday and this evening. I remember that hard angled light and the tense exchange between Bourgois and myself. There was no mysterious message from Bourgois, but his energy is also present in the heat radiating from the sand.

A puff of cool breeze off the bay brings in the smell of the night ocean and I raise my chin to it. During the day, the sun draws out the scent of the water, scattering it like dust motes in a shaft of light, making the nose work harder for the sensation. At night, the scent condenses in the cooling air, mixes with the warm land air, and creates a knowable cologne, like the scent of a woman's nape. It revives me as I continue along the shore toward the Beachcomber for my dinner date with the mysterious British gentleman. But it's not enough to hold down the dread that wells up in pulsing waves. It's an old feeling that I thought I'd conquered but clearly there are too many voids to fill in. I know without really knowing why that this beach, this island, has changed for me.

# FOUR

I CONTINUE ALONG THE beach toward the Beachcomber, moving at an island pace.

The Beachcomber is owned and operated by a transplanted Canadian, Alan Greenbauer. Some twenty years ago, Alan came to Isla Tortuga on a merchant ship and fell in love with the place. Alan is not a large man, maybe five foot seven, 140 pounds, and is the hairiest man I've ever met. He is the only man I know with thick hair on his back from the tops of his shoulders to the small of his back. Black hair, too, making him a very distinctive figure when he goes for a swim. I tease him that he looks like a dog coming out of the water, water streaming in small rivulets off his pelt. He's very good-natured about the ribbing, and is one of the most peaceful and even-tempered men I know. I'm proud to call him friend.

From where I stand, I can see the swaying drilled-out conch shells that house lights that line the narrow path from the beach up to the patio bar of Alan's small restaurant. The conch shell lights cast odd undulating shadows making it look, from a distance, like the path is slithering up the slope.

I stand there, at the base of the stairs, lingering, letting the cool breeze off the water blow through the hair on my arms—a soft tingling sensation, the touch of a lover. Standing there, sandals in hand, the coolness of the sand caresses my feet after a day in the sun.

The tranquility of this beach stirred me from the first night I arrived on the island. Coming from Minnesota, living in the city with all its noises, you never fully hear the sounds of nature. But here, at the water's edge at night, all you hear is nature. The wind through the manchineel trees, the surf hissing as it recedes back through the sand to its source—impossible back in Minnesota. The beach at night is, in a word, magical.

I look at the glow of my watch, seven thirty-five. I'm on time by Caribbean standards but late, I suspect, by European standards. Grudgingly, I start up the stairs, reviewing my plan for interrogating Don. It's a hastily put-together plan that I came up with earlier in the shower.

The only method that I could come up with was to get him talking about his relationship with Bourgois. Maybe through talking about their relationship, I can get him to reveal something that I might use.

I catch myself. *That I might use?* What am I, a P.I.? The thought came to me earlier in the shower and my answer is still no. Just curious, truly curious, I try to convince myself. Idle minds need occupying. Summer in the Caribbean can get pretty slow, especially on an out-of-the-way island like Isla Tortuga. I don't believe myself. *Remember Manolin?* I remind myself.

I try to focus on the facts at hand. It's a fact that the *Miss Princess* is an abandoned sailboat, that Bourgois and Don know one another, and that something odd surrounds all three. These facts are the framework and I hope my new British friend can enlighten me on the details. Unlike that crazy Manolin character, I have a straight line to the answers I need. Pump a couple beers into this Brit and find out what the hell is going on.

Halfway up the path to the Beachcomber, a muffled burst of laughter seeps out of the jungle from the direction of the patio bar. Alan—always the perfect host—entertaining his guests. I take the remaining steps two at a time.

At the top of the hill, I stop short of the patio to roll my chinos down and put on my sandals. I see Don sitting at the bar with two French tourists that I recognize. They sailed into the bay a couple of days ago. I recognize them from the shop. They stopped in to get their SCUBA tanks filled, but didn't need or want a divemaster; they were going out on their own. That was fine with me. But the detail I remember most about the men is that two women accompanied them. The women stayed outside, talking in French, as the men got their tanks filled. One of the women, in particular, caught my eye. I determined that she was the tall one's companion as he called out to her in French, "Annick, bring me some money, please."

Annick wore a black string bikini and a short red wrap that came to the top of her thighs. Her dark auburn hair was rolled into a small loose ball on the back of her head, held there by a plastic clip shaped like a scallop shell. She was maybe late twenties, tall with broad hips—hips that gave the appearance that they are broader than her shoulders. I remember that she removed her cat-eye sunglasses to reveal large onyx eyes, the same color as the pearl earrings she wore.

Copper skin, long V-shaped face, a lean, long-muscled throat—stunningly exotic looking. I recall her casually scratching under her crescent breast, the sun backlighting her, softening her features with a bronze glow. My heart gently flipped with the thought of all that softness.

I scan the small restaurant. No Annick. Just the three European men sitting at the bar facing a hairy Canadian. I think it's odd—all of these foreigners gathering in the southern Caribbean. You can go halfway around the world and still finds spots where fellow countrymen—or at least people from the same continent—gather. Birds of a feather...

Because he is facing me, Alan is the first to see me lurking in the shadows. "Hey! Hey! Get in here!"

All heads swivel toward me, smiling, eyes searching the darkness for the recipient of Alan's greeting.

I step over the curb that frames the tile patio. Heads bob up in recognition as I weave my way through the small square tables toward the bar.

"Gentlemen. Good evening. *Bonsoir*," I offer.

"*Bonsoir*," say the two Frenchmen in unison.

"Good evening, Phil," Don says quietly.

I select a stool next to Don, putting me on the end with Don to my left, the Frenchmen to his left. I notice Don is drinking a Hairoun, poured into a mug, and before I can ask for one of the same, Alan slides me one, no mug. The beer is very cold, just the way I like it. Frosty, with the melting ice sliding down the bottle.

"Give one to my friend over here," I say, nodding toward Don.

Don raises his mug as a thank-you.

"Two more for the brave sailors, too. Put it on my tab."

Alan cocks his head incredulously, but the tall Frenchman saves me.

"We must be going. Thank you. Perhaps another night."

His friend adds, "Our companions are interested in a restaurant downtown." He quickly realizes his faux pas, and adds, "But we will be back another night before we go." Embarrassed, he searches everyone's faces for a sign of compassion. We all smile, letting him off.

Alan says, "You've seen my wine list. I think you will be back."

The "foot eater" says, "Of course." He does a double take, looking over my shoulder. His face brightens considerably. "Annick, Yvette. *Puis-je vous présenter* Alan, Don, and Phil."

I didn't hear the women come in. At the mention of her name, I whirl a little too obviously on my stool. They are standing right behind me. My eyes immediately meet Annick's. Those glistening eyes, pools of liquid ebony. I feel foolish, like a teenager smiling at the high school beauty queen.

"Hello," I croak.

The ladies respond, "Hello."

Annick wears a yellow flowered sundress that hangs loosely from spaghetti straps to just above her knees. She has on white strap sandals with a modest heel that accentuates her bronzed calves, round, firm, small.

The men move next to their ladies, arms falling easily upon the women's waists.

The four talk quickly, too quick for me to understand with my limited French.

The tall man explains, "We must be going. Good night."

"*Bonne nuit*," I say. I notice that the shorter man is pinning me with his eyes. Suspicion. I flush with recognition. Caught ogling his friend's lady, my discretion blurred by too many months of celibacy.

The four leave quickly and I imagine the conversation in the cab to town. I would not fare well at the hands of the "foot eater."

I swallow the last of my beer and push the empty bottle with the tips of my fingers across the bar. Alan grabs it by the neck and slides it into a plastic case that contains about a dozen empties. He reaches into the bunker and fishes out another Hairoun, pops the top, deals a fresh napkin, and places the beer on it all in one smooth motion. *The man is a pro*, I think, smiling.

Alan reaches behind him and grabs a bottle of red wine that is sitting on the windowsill, a bottle of Australian Shiraz. He pours the dregs of the bottle into a glass, filling it half full.

"Can't let good wine go to waste." He raises his glass in salute, and takes a modest sip. "You fellows staying for dinner?"

"Why yes, we are, but I'm afraid we do not have a reservation," I joke.

"I think we can accommodate you. Let's see, how about any table in the place."

"That is the table I was hoping for."

I slide off my stool and gesture toward the second table from the rear. It is my favorite table as the light above it is only a forty-watt bulb softened further by an aqua blue paper shade. Soothing, but not so dark that you feel like you're in a cave. Don nods his approval and I let him lead the way back.

"Good choice," Alan says over his shoulder as he moves down the hall toward the front entrance to the restaurant.

The Beachcomber faces St. Christopher Road, which is the road that runs out of St. Christopher, the capital, south toward Pelican Bay and out around the southern end of the island. When it reaches the opposite side of the island, directly perpendicular to the city, it intersects Qualie Beach Road at, of course, Qualie Beach. Qualie Road, which in reality is St. Christopher Road after a ninety-degree turn, cuts back across the island into St. Christopher on the east side of the city. Everyone calls St. Christopher Road, as well as its sibling, Qualie Road, "The Road" as it is *the* main road on the island. In fact, it is the only paved road on the island, with the exception of the streets of the capital.

Alan's host stand sits out front on the porch facing The Road. He keeps the menus there. He is running the operation solo tonight, as it is a Tuesday in the middle of July. There isn't much business for the Beachcomber mid-week off-season. In fact, the three of us are the only people in the restaurant.

Don and I arrive at the table. He chooses the seat that faces out into the night. I take the one opposite him and we settle into our chairs. As I slide my chair up to the table and lift my head, my eyes meet Don's. He is looking at me like he is looking through me. Like he's trying to read something that I have written just under my skin. I smile limply, an uncomfortable and inadequate response.

"What brought you here to this island?" Don asks pointedly.

I'm taken aback. No one has ever asked me that question since my arrival six months ago. Not Alan, not my friend Allie, not even Bill. I certainly didn't expect it from a man I had just met a few hours ago. I stumble for a response. "Everyone has their reasons for being here. Mine is no different than theirs." *A rather deft response for off the cuff*, I think to myself.

Don smiles. "I'll have a go at it, if you are so reticent. Hum. You are running from something and it is still chasing you. Even here, it chases you. What do you think?"

*Fuck you*, but I say, "Sufficiently ambiguous to cover every possible scenario. Do you give horoscopes as well?"

Again that smile—the smile from earlier in the day at the shop. Intuitively, based on God knows what, I know I am not going to like this guy.

He continues. "Everyone I meet in these locales that is not native seems to be running from something or looking for something. Actually, they are rather the same, running and looking. Wouldn't you agree?"

I see an opening and take it. "You are not from around here. What are you looking for? Or is it running from?" Not totally on point, but I am trying to move the subject off of me. The response is a laugh this time, a deep, substantial laugh. Head tossed back, pink mouth wide. When he calms down, his eyes settled back onto mine, the searching again.

"It strikes me that you would like to tell me something, Don," I venture.

He pauses a moment, adjusts his fork on the table, and says, "Strike one, I believe the saying goes."

Alan arrives with two menus, handing one of each to Don and me. "Another round of drinks?"

"It's my shout, I believe," Don offers. "Another pint for you, Phil?"

I nod.

"As would I, thank you."

"Very good. Two Hairouns." Alan turns and heads toward the bar to gather our drinks.

I open the menu, then quickly snap it shut and set it on the table. I know the menu by heart. The Beachcomber has a limited offering, but Alan serves the very best seafood on the island. It is even better than the Brigadoon, the fancy restaurant downtown, where I am sure the French couples are going. No one can compete with Alan's expert touch with a fillet of grouper or red snapper. I know I will order the grouper, if grouper is available, with grilled vegetables.

Don is less certain. He studies the menu like it is a manual for diffusing a bomb. "What's good tonight?" he asks.

"Everything," is Alan's reply, with a smile, as he walks up with our drinks.

"I recommend any of the fish fillets. Alan can pick the freshest fish on the island," I boast for my friend.

"We have both grouper and snapper tonight. Prepared any way you would like," Alan states. He sets the drinks down and begins to pour Don's beer into a fresh mug.

"Very well. I'm in the Caribbean. I'll take the snapper," Don snaps, handing his menu back to Alan. "Grilled with garlic."

"Grouper for me," I say, and also hand my menu back.

Alan bows formally, spins, and retreats to the kitchen.

I opt for the offensive this round. "So you and Chief Bourgois are friends."

"Yes, we are. Friends from school." He is comfortable answering my questions, too comfortable sitting there pondering his beer.

"What is your relationship to the *Miss Princess*?"

It shakes him only slightly, registered only in the short, short pause of the lift of the mug.

"The *Miss Princess*? Of what are you speaking?" he says too formally.

"The boat I towed in. Today. At the shop. Remember?"

"My. Your questions do jump about. I know nothing of the—what did you call it, the *Miss Princess*? I've come to visit an old friend, two fellow Cantabrians catching up on old times. The boat is Charles's concern. *I* would like to concern myself with some diving and relaxation."

I have no idea what "Cantabrians" means, but I presume it refers to some school in England. My pause to digest his explanation gives him the opportunity to probe me.

"Why so aggressive in your line of questioning?" he asks.

I can't answer. My grand plan for unraveling this mystery man is dissolving before my eyes.

The thought of all those stupid little wooden fish flashes in my mind.

"Don't be alarmed. I'm not offended. You clearly must think something is amiss with the sailboat. Your concern is admirable."

"Something is wrong about that boat, and I think your dear old friend knows it. What I don't understand is why he isn't doing anything about it."

"Perhaps he is, but he simply isn't telling you. After all, you are not an official of the government, are you?" he asks. I answer with a stare.

"Then, perhaps, he wants you to stay clear of it. So that he and his department can take care of it. I would venture to guess that is the reason for his actions."

I can't argue with his reasoning; it's too sound. But something just doesn't fit. Everything seems too secretive on Bourgois's part.

If what Don suggests is true, then why doesn't Bourgois just come out and say that? Just tell me to stay off the boat while he conducts his investigation? But instead, I get a not-so-veiled threat.

Moreover, Bourgois didn't search the sailboat immediately. Bourgois is keeping something from me, and perhaps this analytical man in front of me is also trying to pull the wool over my eyes. It is an instinctual feeling, born of juices and electricity deep down in the dark corners of my guts, that tells me Don Bennett is full of shit.

# FIVE

THE MAN EATS LIKE a wolverine.

Alan just brought us two steaming fish dinners, and Don and I settle into a silent, tense dinner. Perhaps it's more accurate to say I eat; he inhales. I thought the Brits were supposed to be a mannered breed, but this guy must have misplaced that gene. I can't help but stare in disgust as I pick at my fish.

To occupy my thoughts, I rebuild my plan for solving this personal mystery of the wayward sailboat. I decide to approach the task from the side and bypass Bourgois and his department.

Despite the warning, I know that I need to get back on the sailboat. I will start there and that might be all I need, I reason. The boat is probably chartered and the registration will be on the boat somewhere. The names of the family on board will also be on that document. All I need to do then is call the charter company, ask them a few questions, and the case is closed—at least for my part. My curiosity satisfied.

As Plan B, if searching the sailboat proves fruitless, I'll go into town and talk to Sam Cartier. He should know something. At least he can tell me if the *Miss Princess* ever put in on Isla Tortuga.

What I don't want to consider is the end result of all this investigating. It seems pretty clear to me that something tragic has happened to the family aboard the *Miss Princess.* They either went overboard or ... They must have gone overboard. There really is no other explanation that I can think of. Chalk it up as just another case of careless, novice sailors misjudging the unforgiving sea.

Unfortunately, when the inevitable conclusion is reached, then notification of the next of kin will be necessary. I know, all too well, how difficult that kind of information is to take. I'd leave the ugly, uncomfortable stuff for Bourgois to handle. After all, that is his job. I just need to get the information to satisfy my own curiosity.

My curiosity. Why so curious? Again that question.

I look up and find Don smiling his smile again.

"Penny for your thoughts."

"Just thinking of all the things I need to do tomorrow."

"Like where you're taking me tomorrow. Diving, that is."

I completely forgot that dear Don, friend of Charles, was looking forward to seeing some of the underwater wonders of Isla Tortuga.

"I must confess that I haven't dove in quite some time. You may need to refresh me on some of the finer points," he confesses.

Great. Not only must I postpone my research, but I've got to dive with a beginner. I'm not real patient with beginners. I never earned my SCUBA instructor certification because of my impatience. I fully realize that everyone, including me, was a beginner at one time, but that only reinforces my admiration for instructors. It doesn't make me want to deal with beginners any more than I have to. I think to myself, *I need to find a way out of taking this guy out.*

"I've got some things I need to do tomorrow. I think I'll send you out with my divemaster. He's a very capable diver."

"Oh," he says. "What sort of things do you need to do tomorrow?"

I tell him, "I need to run some errands for the shop. Things in town. Nothing too major."

"Then perhaps you might postpone them for a day. I would prefer that I dive with you the first day. I would like to review my skills with you before I have a go at it with your divemaster. Charles says you are a very good diver, and I would feel more comfortable with you. If that is satisfactory with you."

"Sure, no problem," I lie. "Then perhaps we should turn in, so that we are well rested for tomorrow." I was looking to end my night with this troublesome man. And, considering this change in plans, get out to the *Miss Princess* tonight and do a little "research."

"I am quite tired. I think that is a good idea," he states with sincere cheer.

I look over at the bar and Alan is doing paperwork. He looks up over his half-lens reading glasses and catches my eye.

"Put the dinner on my tab, monsieur."

"Oh no. I insist on paying. If nothing else, at least my share." Don reaches into his trousers for his billfold.

"You can buy another night. You are staying for a while, I presume," I counter.

"Yes, indefinitely. I'd like to spend some time getting to know the island."

Indefinitely. Great. "Then I insist. We will have dinner again," hoping my tone is sufficiently sincere, while my mind is already lining up the excuses.

We make our way toward the front of the restaurant and Alan, looking at his watch, says, "Hey, no hurry, the bus won't be here for another ten minutes. It's due by here at ten."

Don says, "Yes. I rode one down here. They are quite the adventure."

"Yes they are, but very reasonably priced," Alan says, turning his attention to me. "Hey Phil, where is Bill tonight? You know?"

"On one of his soul-searching missions."

"Ah, yes. The fifteenth of the month. That's right."

"Yeah. He didn't say which cay he was going to. I'd sure like to know," I say.

"Probably Pardo."

"Yeah. He does seem to prefer Cayo Pardo lately. I'm not sure why, but ..."

Don interrupts, "Is Bill the man at the dock today?"

A bit peeved, I answer, "Yes. The tall, older man."

"Looks a little like a gray Chewbacca," Alan suggests.

I chuckle. "If you know who Chewbacca is."

"Oh yes, the *Star Wars* character. Yes, he does resemble the beast. Not to say he is a beast, but he is a very striking fellow."

"Nice recovery," Alan replies goodheartedly.

"Yes, Bill does make an impression," I offer, smiling.

"What is this soul-searching trip you say he takes?" Don asks, quickly moving off his faux pas and onto other terrain.

I scratch my throat and try to quickly compile a cogent explanation for Bill's monthly excursion to the cays to work on his karma, or whatever he does out there. I don't feel any obligation to divulge too much information to this man. I realize I'm uncomfortable giving him information. It feels like I'm talking to a cop that just pulled me over for speeding. It feels like he is pulling information out of me. He asks too many questions, far too many questions.

"Well, as he describes it, he is looking for the 'preterhuman experience.' Something beyond him. A kind of a vision quest. I'm not really sure how he does it, or what he gets out of it, but he has been going on these things for years now."

Smiling, Alan adds, "And he does it in the nude. Wanders around those cays for days naked as a jaybird."

That puckers Don's mouth. I can see that he is building the mental image of big Bill Tomey strolling around in the altogether.

I cringe. I knew that detail and purposefully left it out. I try to repair Bill's slightly tarnished reputation. "Bill's a terrific guy. The best. He just has a few odd habits, but he would do anything for you," I say, defending my friend. Hoping to head off any more unfortunate disclosures, I purposefully look at my watch. "We should get outside. They only stop if you are there to flag them down."

"Ah, yes. The bus." Don seems relieved as well.

"Hope to see you again, Don." Al says, extending his hand.

Don receives it, giving it a hearty shake. "Oh, you will. You've got a great place here."

"Thank you. I appreciate that." And to me Alan adds, "And I know I'll see you again."

"But of course."

Don and Alan release their handshake and I give Alan a quick wave. I make my way down the narrow hall to the front of the building, passively guiding Don toward the front of the restaurant.

The Beachcomber is a simple enough building. A wooden structure, kind of a modified Cape Cod style, with a nice open front porch with rattan chairs placed just so, for effect. The sign for the restaurant is a large hunk of driftwood with the name routered into it, the concave letters painted light blue. The building is bright white, freshly painted this month by one red, sweaty Canadian.

We step off the deck the one step down onto the crushed rock and shell parking pad and march, leaning slightly forward, up the gentle incline to The Road. I'm afraid to begin any conversation for fear of igniting something that we can't finish before the bus comes. Luckily, I timed my escape well. The bus is buzzing up over the rise as we reach The Road.

The bus is a Nissan van, burgundy, with orange, yellow, and red geometric designs painted on the side. A loud zouk beat leaps out of the vehicle as the sliding door glides open. The van is empty, except for the driver and his assistant, who collects the fare from the passengers as they disembark the bus. Neither of the men says a word as Don studies them. I recognize the two men, but don't know their names. They look like they are at the end of their shift, haggard road-weary eyes staring at nothing in particular. Their mouths hang loose. The driver scratches his armpit and it suggests the tart stink of a day's worth of sweaty passengers.

"Have fun," I say to Don. I notice his concern, like he is unsure of whether he wants to get in the bus or not. Not quite scared, but less than comfortable. I feel a certain sense of sadistic pleasure in the unnerved look on his face.

"It's OK. They'll take you to the resort." Then, to the assistant, "Tortuga Beach Resort."

The assistant quickly wiggles his head a couple of times and stares at Don, waiting.

Don says to me, "Don't you need a ride?"

"No, I don't. In fact, I live right up the hill there. You can't really see the place from here, but it is about seventy-five yards up the slope from the shop on the other side of the road. I can walk from here."

Silence again, except for the pulsing idle of the van as it struggles to stay running, clearly out of tune. It is the only sound in the calm warm night, a spattering, uneasy noise. Then Don says "OK, then. I guess I'll see you in the morning?"

"Not too early. Remember, this is the Caribbean."

"Be safe." And with that, Don pours himself into the van and before the assistant can get the door closed, the van is tearing down The Road, taillights blinking a nonsensical Morse code.

---

I head for the beach because I know I won't be able to sleep.

It's become a common occurrence for me since arriving on Isla Tortuga, this restless wakefulness. It's not that I'm not tired; it's just that I can't turn it off. I feel like one of those runaway cars that just wheels in circles round and round while bystanders look on, waiting for the possessed auto to run out of gas. And the odd dinner I just had coupled with its equally odd ending at the van keeps those wheels spinning.

I hike down a well-worn path that leads from The Road past the roti stand and find myself back on the beach. For the second time tonight I find myself in Manolin's spot at the water's edge. The man sure seems to have a way of making me think about him. Allie would not approve. She certainly didn't when I told her about it last night...

―――――――

"I don't know. I kinda lost track of time. Bill and I talked maybe two or three hours or so," I tell Allie Tennison, the mango-shaped Australian expatriate that now owns the Isla Tortuga Beach Resort.

Allie came to Isla Tortuga from Western Australia, Perth perhaps—my memory on those kinds of details has always been sketchy—after a failed marriage of nine years. Or was it ten? When I first met her some six months ago, I noticed a reserve in her bearing and I attributed that to her uneasiness about her status on the island—an Anglo divorcée on an island full of dark-skinned Caribs, out on her own for the first time perhaps, running a business in a land far, far from home. Of course, that was a rash judgment based, probably, on nothing but some chauvinistic seed in my psyche— or perhaps a bit of projection. Maybe I was the one uneasy about moving two thousand miles from home to a place I'd never seen before and taking on a business I only knew peripherally.

But I was wrong then about Allie. I quickly learned that Allie is no wallflower. She is a woman of intense pride, intense honesty, intense privacy. She will tell you what she thinks and expects the same of you, but she will not tell you what to think or divulge her inner secrets. She insists on honestly arrived-at answers, but no pouring of emotion. No cheap theatrics for this girl. You will be honest with her, but she will not press you to be honest. If you fail this basic test, you will be viewed as less. You'll be set aside gently. I like to think I carry some of those same characteristics.

60

And because of that vinculum, that wayward soul connection, that understanding of personal lives lived personally, I've counted her as one of my good friends on the island, a confidant.

That's why after dinner and the subsequent conversation with Bill about this mysterious Manolin character, I hopped in my beat-up Nissan pickup and drove down to her resort. I knew I would find Allie awake, sitting on the low ocean wall. She liked the night, she once told me. I asked why, and her response was typical Allie, a shrug of the shoulders.

Sitting there, digging equal signs in the cool sand with our bare feet, I decide to ask her opinion on this mysterious Manolin character.

"The island will do that to ya. Damn mossies!" she squeals, slapping at the diminutive but baleful pests. From the minute I sat down, the mosquitoes honed in on us as if I had brought them with me.

"As I was saying, the island can do that to you—lose track of time, I mean—and make you think crazy thoughts. Bill Tomey likes to think there is some connection between everything, but this Manolin guy is probably just playing a joke. It sure sounds like you talked about this character a fair amount of time. Why are you asking me about it if you've already gotten your answer from Bill?"

I run my hands up and down my arms, then my legs, brushing off the hectoring pests. I sense I've irritated her and I fall silent, head down.

"I don't know this Manolin fellow—he never gave me any wooden fish and Bill never mentioned him to me," she continues. "I just want you to make up your mind for yourself, mate. Bill can be very convincing, and you came down here to get some balance, from a woman that is ultimately practical and not prone to making wild connections for the sake of . . . conversation." She stops digging, pulls her heels up under her butt, withdrawing into herself like a turtle into her shell.

"*Sorry* to bother you, Allie," I say with a bit too much venom. "I'm just looking for answers, you know? I'm just trying to . . . fill in some voids."

"Fill in some voids, huh? That sounds like something that *Bill* would say. Look Phil, I've known you a couple months now and I've noticed that you rush to judgment frequently. Perhaps you need to take a step back, think about what is going on and what your re-action will be. You seem childlike in that way. I don't mean to be critical or run you down, but childlike is the best way to describe it. Like you don't have the breadth of experience to make an informed decision." She is looking at me now, eyebrows straight, intense but not incensed.

Allie never raises her voice. It is never louder than it needs to be. It strikes me that if she did raise her voice it would be out of tune, a bray, a cruel note like a French horn played poorly and loudly. She talks to me like that now. Measured in her words, measured in her tone.

Her statement pushes me off balance. I've never thought of my-self as rash in my judgments. Certainly not the opposite either—a guy that never moves on his ideas—but surely a guy that makes reasonable decisions based on the facts at hand.

"Not sure how to respond to that, Allie," I say honestly, but too defensively.

She snorts loudly. Then quickly she says, "Make of it what you want, Philly. I'm beat. Time for bed."

And that is the clear "period" to the conversation. I've hit a wall with her. I'm not sure I know how I got to that wall, but this conversation is over. She brushes off her feet, straps on her sandals.

We walk in vespertine silence through the lawn of St. Augustine grass. The dew of the cooling night wets my toes through my Tevas. We make for her bungalow (an oversized utility shed, really, room enough for a bed, bathroom, and a small sitting area). Allie spends most of her time with her guests, seeing to their needs, ensuring their comfort. Her living quarters are a formality, really, utilitarian. It is a place to rest and store stuff.

We arrive at her door and she gives me a quick squeeze on the back of the arm, then takes a fistful of my hair in her hand. "You could use a haircut."

I smile and nod my agreement.

"Good night, my little fisherman," she says. And with that, she slides inside her bungalow and lets the door latch slowly under its own weight.

———

Now back on the beach, I think of swinging into the shop for another beer, but decide against it. I am already getting that granular taste in my mouth from too many beers, the malt tasting slim at the back of the throat. That's my sign to stop. I wish I heeded that sign more often.

I make my way down to the sound of the burbling surf. The tide is waning now and I walk the scalloped line between wet packed sand and fluffy dry sand. It strikes me like night and day—dark cold sand versus bright airy sand. I stay just this side of the dry sand and turn south, toward the dark half of Pelican Bay.

Pelican Bay is a strange little cove. From a plane, the bay looks like someone has taken a hole punch and snipped a perfectly clean hole into the side of the island. Rather high cliffs frame the opening to the mouth of the bay, guarding both sides. You steer through the deep channel between the cliffs and then out of the shadows into soft green-blue water. It's a sandy bottom that is consistently twenty feet deep throughout the half-mile-diameter bay. The relatively shallow depth has traditionally kept it from being a more important bay on the island. Only small crafts can navigate these close waters, so St. Christopher, the capital of Isla Tortuga, was built two miles north up the coast where there is a natural fjordlike channel that is quite deep, offering better harborage for larger vessels.

Long ago the Spaniards gave the bay its name, *La Bahia del Pelicano*, the Bay of Pelicans, because of the huge number of pelicans that gathered there. That was more than a hundred years ago. Now the birds go elsewhere. Only a few come back, the lame and the very old. The majority of Tortugans now see the bay as a place of death because the mass of birds no longer return. The bay used to be a nice fishery. The fish, too, are gone, fished out long ago. Which, of course, explains the reason for the absence of the pelicans. The Tortugans see it differently. A higher power has spoken and condemned the bay. It is a place of infertility to them. Very few of them, especially the old, will come to the beautiful sugar-white beaches that ring the tiny bay. Quite a waste, but it does keep the place quiet. The only visitors the bay gets are a handful of sailboats that anchor or moor out in the bay and the smattering of families that live in the area. No one is on the beach at this hour and the two sailboats other than the *Miss Princess*—a nice ketch and smallish sloop—are bundled up for the night. Neither has its anchor light illuminated. The three-quarter moon low on the horizon makes their shadowy silhouette split—one in the air, one waving on the calm water. The *Miss Princess* looks left out. Forgotten by her schoolyard playmates, all dark and disheveled.

My dive shop sits squarely at the six o'clock position of the bay, if the opening of the bay is at twelve o'clock. Go south and you wander deserted beach; go north and you pass by the Beachcomber restaurant, now dark. I like the south end of the bay. The beach of the bay is a crescent, starting in the north at a line of casuarinas and the Beachcomber and curves south past my shop to the south cliff that borders the opening to the bay. A stand of coconut palms towering seventy-five feet, gliding trunks curving out over the water, marks the halfway point between the shop and the terminus of the beach. I make that my stopping point.

The warning is to never sit under a coconut palm, for obvious reasons. I'm not a guy that takes warnings too seriously. Besides, it worked for Newton. Well, apples are slightly different than coconuts and I am all too aware of gravity—or at least the laws of momentum. Regardless, I love sitting under those broad trees, the filtered light through their fronds makes the whole world soft to my eyes. I scoot up under a particularly bent tree, hugging my knees. I look up to check on the coconut situation and I'm relieved to find all of them green, or so it seems in the dark. The wind rustles the fronds and my eyes drift toward the moon, striped by the leaves. The moon looks like a winking eye, the fronds like eyelashes. I unconsciously wink back.

The desire for a beer surfaces but quickly flees. I release my hug and lean back a bit too hard and my head hits the trunk with a hollow thud. I wince and shake my head to clear the brief burst of electric impulses in my eyes.

I sneeze loudly, not bothering to muffle the noise with my hands. I feel chilled. I hug my knees again against the nonexistent chill in the air. It's eighty degrees and no wind to speak of—no reason to be chilled. But I am. Now I feel restless. I get up, brush off my butt, and continue south along the beach. Agouti tracks run in chaotic patterns in the sand in front of me.

My mind wanders back to Allie's parting words, "Good night, my little fisherman." Then Don's "Be safe." What did they mean? Allie's words struck me as a bit condescending, but more odd than derogatory. Something to do with that Manolin character, I presume.

I replay the Manolin escapade. Maybe it is the time of night, maybe it is the beer, but I am more confused than ever about this mysterious man Manolin. I want answers—maybe that's what Allie meant about fisherman. That she knew I would go "fishing" for answers to my questions. She's right. I'm not a guy that likes to let things go. Bill told me that I had the answer already, it's just that I'm not seeing it. He told me that I needed to look elsewhere—not necessarily deeper—but elsewhere for the answer. Answers are not always where you want them to be.

Well, that's bunk in my opinion. Answers to questions are either knowable or not knowable and looking around under rocks or behind trees is not going to make the answer any more clear. I need to go to Windwardside and ask this Manolin guy what the deal is. I'd then have my answer.

And I chalk Don's words up to some arcane British farewell. But the way he said it struck me as a blessing rather than a wish. Like he was casting a good luck spell over me—a priest with holy water. And Lord, he did not want to get into that van. Whatever.

The curve of the bay is constant, like the curve of a watch face. I'm at nine o'clock on that watch face and the beach narrows here as it approaches the rock facade that forms the southern cliff to the opening of the bay. It's quiet now, scree flowing up in a perfect inverted cone of tumbled rock and parasitic vines. A wayward rock the size of a lion stands sentinel to the cone. I sit down on it and look out over the bay. Unseen animals rustle in the underbrush behind me. The sea wrack is piled in rolling mounds, oozing tidal water. I think I smell high-octane fuel.

"Why am I so cold?" I ask weakly.

# SIX

IT FEELS THE SUBTLE vibrations and reacts without hesitation, backing into its hole, eyes on stalks scanning the dark night for movement. The family walks well above the waterline, in the soft sand, too far from the hole to be a threat. So it moves out slowly, alien eyes trained on the intruders. It is cautious.

They have their heads down and move slowly through the soft sand. In his arms, the man holds a small girl, her hair the color of the moon. The woman follows a few steps behind. Her face is wet.

"Tony, why can't we stop here? We need to rest. Sophie needs to rest."

"Only a bit more, Mart. I have a feeling there is a nice stretch of beach just around the point."

"We need to eat. We need to stop and eat. We haven't eaten since they took our boat."

"We'll eat when we stop. Let's just press on."

The surf hisses back through the sand but the fiddler crab ignores it. The danger now is in front, not the waning tide. With its disproportionately massive claw, it thumps the sand lightly as the family disappears into the shadows of the coconut palms. No more vibrations. It is safe to come out and feed and it does, shoveling sand into its mouth, excreting pellets onto the sand. A coconut falls and the vibration sends the crab bolting for its hole, but it is intercepted by a whimbrel. The bird snatches it up and begins to break off its legs. The fiddler uses its massive claw, but in vain. With a toss of the head, the bird swallows it whole.

---

I can't help but think about Don as I make my way along the path up the hill to my little concrete block house.

It was as if we were talking in some code that proved new to both of us, rattling on, even though we weren't really sure if communication was happening. We spoke in short bursts of accurate dialogue, then long periods of silence—a regrouping. But, as in some clicking code, the silences became periods of communication as well. In those periods of calm, our ideas and thoughts seemed to seep out of our skulls and make the short journey across the table to each other's brain. It all seems so fuzzy to me now, yet I feel I know more about him than I did before dinner. But is this new information of any use? I'm unsure. The only thing I know with confidence is that he is definitely feeling me out. I can feel the probing. It is palpable.

But probing me about what? I know my intentions for the evening, but what were his? What was Don Bennett all about and why is he so cryptic? I am positive that he isn't just an idle tourist visiting a friend; however, after that, it's anybody's guess. It appears I will have more time to figure it out—indefinitely is what he said. Dread tempers my curiosity.

Then there is the van. He seemed awfully nervous to get into it, even though he rode in one, perhaps even the same one, earlier tonight. It was a strange, unexpected reaction from a man that both physically and verbally is quite able to defend himself. Odd. This Englishman has me stumped, I confess.

I'm at the top of the hill and the path turns to follow the rim of the hill up to the clearing in front of my house.

It's a simple structure, my house, a large box, really. It's thirty feet by thirty feet of hollow concrete blocks with a skim of cement over them to give a finished look. The big box is sectioned off into four large rooms: a kitchen, a bedroom, a living area, and a bathroom, although the bathroom only contains the toilet and a sink. The shower, an afterthought for the previous owner, is on the back patio. It is a simple faucet head that runs out of the back wall that is common with the bathroom. The shower is open to the world and requires that the shower-taker not be modest; you are literally there for the entire world to see. It took a couple weeks for me to become comfortable with the arrangement. I'd even thought of building a privacy wall when I first moved in, but after those first few weeks the situation became normal to me and I now think nothing of it. Besides, being basically lazy, building a wall is too much work. Also, a couple incestuous banyan trees flank the patio and the underbrush around the house is rather thick. A person would need to go to a great deal of trouble to see something.

The house sits facing the bay, maybe twenty yards from the edge of the hill. When I first got the house, I cleared out the underbrush and chopped down some small trees to get a better view of the bay. I'm standing there now, on the edge, looking down over The Road beneath me, and out over the bay. I scan the water, quickly finding the *Miss Princess*. From this angle, she looks even farther removed from the other two boats. She floats there, looking small and dark on the clay-gray bay.

I can see the rooftops of the Beachcomber and my dive shop and a few odd buildings scattered just off The Road in either direction. I meander to the very southern edge of the clearing and from there I can see the glow from the grounds of the Tortuga Beach Resort.

I again reflect on Don, bumping along in the van, all by himself, sitting nervously next to a teenage Carib, listening to some whacked-out Caribbean rhythm. He is no doubt at the resort by now, thankful to be in his mosquito-netted bed, the ceiling fan turning quickly, helping the faltering sea breezes through the bungalow.

I shift slightly and look out over the resort and toward the southern tip of the island and consider Bill. He is out there, on one of the little cays, doing his thing. He is probably sitting in front of a small fire, drinking his wine, and musing about the wonders of the planet.

I have a hard time understanding aesthetics. I love the beauty of the world just as much as the next guy, but I've never understood why a person needs to strip down and go off into the wilderness to fully perceive or appreciate it. Bill and I have these discussions often—most recently the other night at dinner. He loves to talk about ideas, especially with a person like me that doesn't particularly like to talk about ideas. I think of myself as more of a doer. Experience it, don't talk about it—that's my motto.

That always brings a smile to Bill's face. He says I have promise. He says he knew it the first time he saw me. He tells the story that he knew I would be the one to buy his little dive shop and that we would be friends. Actually, he said soul mates. A yin and yang sort of thing, or something like that. He was right. We quickly became friends, right from our first meeting.

---

I'd just flown to Isla Tortuga to take a look at the dive shop I'd read about and was waiting to meet Bill, after calling him about the place earlier that week. I was standing on the dock in front of the shop watching a pelican struggle to its feet and stretch its wings in the new morning sun. The bird was battered—really beat up. Its wings were warped; its flight feathers thin, mangy. I noticed that its bill was discolored. I stood only feet from it, and yet it seemed not to notice me. I shifted my weight and the wooden dock groaned. The bird snapped its head toward me, and I looked into its eyes. They were glassy and gray. The pelican swung its head frantically, looking for the source of the sound.

"It's blind, or nearly so," a voice called from behind.

The lame bird waddled to the edge of the dock and flopped into the water with a crash louder than you would think an eight-pound bird could make. I swung my attention from the bird to the voice behind me. It was Bill, I would soon learn. I remember being surprised by his stature—at least six foot five and solidly built. As today, he wore what remained of his balding head in a gray ponytail that reached down to the middle of his back. He stroked his equally gray beard as he surveyed me.

"They come here to die, the pelicans, that is. It seems they eventually go blind diving into the water all their life. The impact really takes a toll on their eyes. Tough way to go, seems to me. You're alive yet unable to fend for yourself until someday you fly into a building or starve to death. They seem to come here by the, well, dozens, the blind and crippled ones, that is. Been that way for some time now. Legend—or better, history—has it that this little bay was once full of birds of all feathers. Flamingo, ibis, pelicans—you name it, they came here by the thousands. A virtual avian paradise. The old ones on the island say it was that way until the Spaniards shot all the birds for food. Those crazy cats must have been pretty damn hungry, 'cause I can't think of a more unappealing bird to eat."

I looked over my shoulder at the decrepit pelican as it struggled to swim away. "Sure doesn't look like he is managing very well," I said, not really knowing what to say. There I was, talking about the island's ancient history with this huge man I didn't really know. At the time, I suspected it was Bill Tomey, but he still hadn't introduced himself.

"Aw, just a natural thing. Gotta be a reason, I guess. The pelicans, that is. Must come back here out of some deep-seated instinctual drive. It dictates all life, you know. Instinct. Even humans. We don't like to admit it, but we rely on our instincts more than we would like to admit. Too animalistic, I guess, for most people. People want to think of themselves as above the animals, when in reality, we are just at the top of the food chain." His tone was matter of fact, as if I already agreed with him. He spoke as if what he said was an irrefutable truth, as irrefutable as the air I breathed, or the water that surrounded me, or the poor mottled bird that swam in circles around the dock.

"You have pelican eyes."

"Excuse me? I don't think I follow you."

"Oh, not like that bird there." He pointed to the sick pelican that now nestled against a piling. "Your eyes are sharp and clear like a young pelican. You've seen 'em, I'm sure. Cruising over the water until they see a fish and then *wham*! They fold up and dive. Sometimes they catch the fish, sometimes they don't. But every dive takes its toll. That's you."

He reached into his shorts and pulled out a jangle of keys tied together with a yellow nylon cord. "Want to see your new business?" It was then that I knew for certain that it was Bill Tomey. He tossed his head toward a bright pink building with a sky-blue door. Written in lavender paint above the door were the words *Dive Tortuga*. Painted next to the name was a very realistic-looking, albeit yellow, marlin. Occasionally, I think of painting the shop in a less offensive color scheme, but the colors have grown on me. The shop looks the same today as it did that day.

"Come on, I'll give you a tour." Bill moved up the beach toward the shop, clanging the keys against his thigh. I remember standing a moment on the dock and surveying the area. To me, the shop sat on an idyllic stretch of beach with coconut palms lining the fringe of the beach. Mature macadamia trees grew along the side wall of the shop. The dock was perfectly situated. One could walk out of the dive shop, down a gradual concrete ramp and out onto the weathered dock. Beautiful, simply beautiful. With a skip, I jogged up the dock and ramp. As I hit the doorway of the shop, the smell of wet neoprene hit me.

I had found my new home.

———————

That was six months ago; I'm a good deal less sure of myself these days.

I stride up the slight incline of the clearing, then up the steps into the house. The house sits pretty much wide open and I like it that way, not ever having to worry about theft or vandalism or having to remember my keys. Crime is nonexistent on the island. Maybe you hear about a petty theft here and there, but never anything to really worry about. In fact, I don't have a heavy door, just a screen door to keep the insects out.

I hit the light switch that is just inside the doorway and the living room glows warm from the table lamp next to the rattan sofa, cushions covered in a washed-out floral print almost invisible in the faint light. I habitually make my way into the kitchen and look inside my small refrigerator. A collection of limes, in various stages of ripeness, a plastic bag containing a half-eaten roti, two bottles of beer—remember to pick some up tomorrow—and a fresh gallon jug of purified water. A bachelor's refrigerator. I pull out the water and pop the snap-on lid. I gulp it, perhaps as much as a pint, before replacing the lid and placing the water back in the refrigerator. I slip out of my sandals and pad across the cool tile out through the living room and around the corner and into the bedroom.

The bedroom is a good-sized room, maybe twenty feet by twenty feet, with a queen bed and a nightstand. That's about it. On the nightstand I find the current book I am working on, the latest Doc Ford mystery. I scoop it up and saunter back out into the living room and plop down on the sofa next to the lamp.

I just open the book to the dog-eared page when a flash of orange-white light snaps my head in the direction of the bay. A second later, a tremendous explosion rumbles up the hill like rolling thunder.

"Shit!"

I toss the book on the sofa and sprint out to the edge of the clearing. I look down at the bay and I'm frozen by what I see. A sailboat, or what I presume to be a boat, is burning—a roaring inferno. It looks like a bonfire in the middle of the bay. The neighboring boat owners are already out on their boats, some of them tossing hunks of burning debris off their decks into the water.

The little bay is as bright as morning, the fire is so ferocious. I take a quick inventory of the boats and shake my head with recognition even though I don't really need to confirm it. I know exactly what boat it is. It's the *Miss Princess*.

# SEVEN

I HALF RUN, HALF stumble, falling back on my palms when my feet slide out from under me, all the way down the path to The Road. Out of breath with adrenaline, I quickly, habitually, look both ways up and down The Road before sprinting across. People are coming out from all corners to see what is going on in the bay. It surprises me, momentarily, to see so many people on a beach that is normally deserted.

They all talk at once, excited, pointing at the roaring boat. The blaze shows no signs of subsiding and the people seem drawn to it like insects to a flame. I stand at the water's edge, water cold on my bare feet when, looking down, I suddenly realize that I didn't put my shoes on before running down the hill. I scraped them up pretty good coming down the hill. The bottoms of my feet are burning and the water feels good washing over them, soothing.

I look out at the *Miss Princess*. I can't believe my eyes. I don't want to trust that what is projected on them is really there. What the hell is going on here? I recall asking myself that question not so long ago.

Out of the corner of my eye, I see Alan break through the crowd, loping like a Saint Bernard. "Jesus. Is that the boat you towed in today?"

"Yup. There is something very wrong with this, Alan. Who the hell would want to blow up that boat?"

"What? What are talking about? Blow up? You don't think it was an accident? Fumes in the bilge or something?"

"Shit no! Christ, the thing is—was—totally out of gas. Not a fucking drop! And look at the thing. Clearly someone had to dump a ton of fuel, or something, on it for it to go up like that. I'm telling you, Al, someone blew up that fucking boat!"

I look over at Al and catch him staring at me like I just shot lightning bolts out of my eyes. He quickly drops his wide eyes in an attempt to avoid the eye contact that will tell me he thinks I'm full-blown bananas.

In a moderately more controlled tone I say, "Al. Buddy. I'm telling you. I think someone blew up that sailboat. I really do." My voice trembles with adrenaline. He still won't look at me full on.

It's clear I've startled him. I try to envision what this mild mannered Canadian man is thinking as he looks at me in snatches. My bulging eyes, lower jaw working back and forth, hand pushing the sweat on my forehead up into my hair.

I am typically a quiet and reserved guy. But now, with the glow of the fire lighting up my face, he must think he is looking at a man possessed. That he is talking to my Mr. Hyde.

"I called the fire department before I came down. They should be here any minute," Alan says, too meekly.

"Oh come on, Alan. You're acting like I'm nuts or something. I'm sorry I yelled, but man, this is just too damn weird." I reach out for him. I feel like I'm a father that has yelled at his young son out of frustration and now regrets it. I don't like that feeling—Alan is not a little boy. I pull my arm back after a quick slap on his shoulder, feeling a little foolish for both of our overreactions.

I turn my attention back to the *Miss Princess*. Trying to keep myself under control, I say, "I'd love to know what started the fire—shit, the explosion. But you know as well as I that we won't get a thing out of Bourgois. He'll shut us out like that." I snap my fingers for effect.

"Hey, you know, maybe we should leave it up to him. I mean, it's his business now. You just towed in a boat, you did your part, and now there's been some foul play, you think, so you should be getting out of the way. Leave it to him and his officers. *You* are done with it."

Alan sounds tired, as if he anticipates the direction of the conversation. I sense that he'd prefer not to get into a heated discussion about the detached way that all the expatriates on the island are treated. It's a common topic of discussion for Alan, Bill, and I.

In my mind, we are treated like second-class citizens. He's heard Bill and me talk about my concerns on this topic on numerous occasions, and when I begin my bitching, he always shies away. Bill, a longtime expat, has come to terms with the situation. Says he sees the islanders' point of view. A point of view I know Alan shares, although he won't admit to it openly.

Isla Tortuga is a quiet, quiet island, with little going on politically or otherwise. So it is quite easy to remain apart from the internal workings of the island's government. However, as in this situation, I still want to be able to get some answers out of the local law enforcement officials. Especially when I'm involved, tangential as it may be. I'm not an old hippie or merchant mariner with a foggy past. I've got nothing to protect and I'm not running from anything.

Without fail, that always brings a smile to Bill's face. "Some day you will tell us your demons." Does he mean a little girl on a red bike? Not a demon as much as an eraser, an excuse for a fresh start. The rationalization feels comfortable most of the time.

I pull myself back into the situation and decide not to push—to even bring up the issue here. It would be worthless. I force down the desire and spew out pap. "Yeah, you might be right. Just get back to the business of running a thriving dive shop," I joke.

Alan smiles firmly, getting the joke, but also sensing my insincerity. The little snort of air out of my nostrils was just a little too loud.

I hear the fire trucks roll up, and think, *where is the fireboat?* Then I remember that Isla Tortuga doesn't have a fireboat, nor a navy or coast guard for that matter. The fire will have to be put out from here on shore or a boat will have to shuttle some firefighters out to the *Miss Princess*. That is, if they have a hose long enough. I looked over at my boat, the *Tortuga One*, and half cringe at the thought of hauling hoses and men out to the *Miss Princess*.

The lone fire truck of Isla Tortuga rolls up. It's a beaten-up old pumper right out of a small-town parade. Out of that antique emerge half a dozen men dressed in blue work shirts and blue canvas pants. None of the men have any safety equipment. No helmets or protective jackets, just their shirts and pants. Five of the men scramble down the hill hauling a well-used hose while the sixth stays by the truck and works the ancient valves and levers.

The five men manning the hose immediately understand their dilemma when they see the burning sailboat some seventy-five yards offshore. They look at one another while the crowd watches them. I begin to walk toward them, reluctantly, to offer my services when one man, presumably the chief, shouts out some orders that I can't quite make out. I see the man point down the beach to a wooden skiff that crouches on the beach, pulled up just out of the surge. The waves lap up to the stern of the vessel, rocking it gently in the wet sand. They didn't see my boat tied off to the dock, opting instead to the first vessel they could find.

A bit relieved, I wonder aloud to Alan who might own the boat as two of the firemen run down the beach toward it. No local ever leaves his boat on the beach at Pelican Bay and it isn't a skiff from one of the sailboats moored out in the bay. A quick accounting of those dinghies puts all of them tied on short painters behind their respective boats. The little rubber dinghies look like baby animals hiding behind their much larger parents. The skiff looks more like a fisherman's boat, even though I don't recognize it, and I know a good many of the fishermen on the island. We tend to ply the same waters.

All the fishing on the island is done off the south end of the island, out by the series of underwater pinnacles that run around the southern underwater wall. Large schools of fish congregate there and the fishermen and I make our respective livings going there. I go there to show the fish to my clients; the fishermen to catch them. Besides, no captain or boat owner worth his salt would leave his boat so close to the water. Any capable seaman pulls his vessel way up onto the beach, out of the rising tide.

The two firemen sent to retrieve the boat push it into the water enough to float it, then they run it, both men on the land side of it, toward the waiting three.

I'm unsure why the men are going to so much effort. The *Miss Princess* has been burning for about seven or eight minutes or more, and it looks from shore that the boat is a total loss. The mast has fallen over into the water and it appears that the cabin is gone, the hull the only intact piece of the boat. I wonder if they know that the boat is abandoned. That they needn't hurry on the account of some poor trapped souls, as there are none.

Four of the five firefighters crawl into the skiff, the fifth stays behind to feed the hose out to them. One of the men, the largest, finds the oars and slides them into their locks and begins to row. The coordination with which the men go about their work is impressive. Just before the men reach the *Miss Princess*, the water in the hose is turned on prematurely and catches the men in the boat unawares. The water gushes, sending the little boat spinning. With a lot of shouting, they quickly get the hose turned off on the boat and then continue on to the *Miss Princess*.

While watching the firemen work, I survey the scene out on the bay, my eyes moving from sailboat to sailboat. Shortly into my pan, my eyes lock on a boat about fifty yards to the starboard side of the *Miss Princess* and about thirty yards in front of me. There, standing on the foredeck, hip against the jib stay for support, is Annick. She is still wearing the sundress of earlier that night, but is now barefoot. The light from the fire casts her lean body in silhouette in her dress, her long legs spread wide for balance. She is facing away from me with hands intertwined on the top of her head, the pose hiking her dress enough to show the lower curve of her hamstrings. I can see in the dancing shadows where the muscles meet the tendons that produce the twin dimples on the back of her knees. That electric feeling shoots through me again, a mild tingling in the arms and fingers. She turns at her waist and looks down the open front hatch just behind her. She speaks unheard words to the hidden recipient and shakes her head, her face awash with sympathy.

I look away quickly, hoping that Alan hasn't caught my furtive stare. Too late. I looked over at him and he is smiling up at me, head slightly cocked. His face reads, *you naughty boy*. I wonder what secret thoughts my face expressed when he caught me staring at the girl.

"What? A guy can't look at a pretty girl?"

"Look, sure. But you were more than looking."

I look for an opportunity to end this tangent before it goes any further. "Have you seen that red skiff before?" I ask, pointing to the firemen.

"No. No, I haven't. Looks like a fishing skiff."

"Yeah, but for as long as I've been here, I've never seen a skiff here in the bay. Nobody fishes around here that I know of."

"Yeah, you're right. Who knows?"

And just like that, Alan is satisfied. *Who knows?* He lets it go, just like that. I'm incredulous. "You don't find that a bit suspicious?"

Alan shrugs. With pursed lips he says, "Not really."

The appearance of yet another mystery boat, the skiff, confirms my suspicion that there is something seriously wrong with this fire. This is no bilge-fumes fire, as Alan suggests. It's without a doubt a case of arson, I'm certain. Only a fool would conclude anything else.

Smiling thinly, I wonder what Bourgois will conclude, then realize that I haven't seen any police officers on scene. I turn to see if any arrived unnoticed—surprisingly, no. I look up and down the beach, up on The Road—nothing. Then, as I turn back to the boat, I see Bourgois pull up in his car. He rolls up quietly, no lights flashing, no siren blaring. It's as if he is responding to a cat in a tree rather than a burning inferno. I watch him unfold out of his car and lean onto the open door. Bourgois looks out at the *Miss Princess*, shaking his head. He considers the beach, his head stopping periodically to focus on something or somebody that catches his attention. When his scan finds me, he gives a slow nod and makes his way down the embankment in my direction.

As I await Bourgois, I resume my investigation of the skiff, looking for any distinguishing markings that I can attribute to someone I know. Unfortunately, the little boat is too far away and the intensity of the fire backlights it so badly that I can only make out forms. I will have to wait until the firemen row back in to check out the boat.

I turn to check Bourgois's progress and find him standing directly behind me, all six-foot-three, two-hundred-some lean, muscular pounds of him. His head aims down, chin almost on his broad chest, white eyes against black face looking back at me. "Phil Riley," he says in his thick southern Caribbean accent.

"Where have you been?" I look at my Seamaster. "The firemen have been here ten minutes."

Bourgois raises his head off his chest. His eyebrows arch tellingly. His face reads: *Don't question me. I'm the official here.* He asks, "Did you see what happened?"

"No, but I certainly heard it. Like an A-bomb went off."

He looks at Alan. I forgot that Alan was standing next to me, he was so quiet. "How about you, Alan? See anything?"

"No. Like Phil, I heard it. Ran down to the beach at the end of my path, over at the restaurant, and saw the fire. Ran right back up and phoned the fire department in St. Christopher."

I can see that Bourgois is in his cop mode now—just-the-facts-ma'am tone of voice. "OK, gentlemen. Thank you for your time." He begins to move down the beach.

"Hey! Wait a minute. Is that all?" I shout after him.

Bourgois stops, back still to us. He speaks over his shoulder, "Yes, well, as you can see, there may not be any need for further investigation. I don't want to take any more of your time this evening. Thank you for your cooperation." The formality, the lack of emotion in his voice is chilling.

"No need! What are you talking about? Someone blew up that boat, Chief."

He half turns to us. "What makes you think that, Riley?"

"When I towed it in today, the fuel tank was empty. This is no bilge explosion. Look at it. Looks like the Fourth of July, for Christ's sake."

"I never said it was the bilge. Things blow up for lots of reasons." He is walking slowly back to us.

"So why did this one blow up?" The question freezes his advancement.

After a deep breath, he answers my question with a question. "Why are you so interested in this boat, Riley?" He angles his head—a look of suspicion.

"Because you aren't. You're not taking *any* interest in the boat. You seem to be treating this like it's nothing. Why is *that*?"

I can sense Alan moving back away from me, trying to distance himself from my overly aggressive attitude.

"Riley. We are investigating this incident as thoroughly as we can. You are going to have to take my word on it."

"I would, if your actions spoke as loud as your words."

"Well, as a matter of fact, I am going down the beach to ask a few questions of the people in the crowd. Perhaps they can be more helpful in answering my questions than you have been. Perhaps *they* saw something. So if you'll excuse me." Before I can respond, he spins on his heels.

I watch him trudge through the thick, soft sand, his wingtips offering little traction. Befuddled with Bourgois's actions, I turn to ask Alan what he thinks, but find my dear friend purposefully walking away, heading in the direction of his restaurant. I shake my head, bemused. *What is with these people?* I ask myself.

I decide to await the return of the mysterious red skiff in the comfort of my dive shop. As I plod through the sand toward my shop, I remember that I didn't mention the mysterious skiff to Bourgois. I stop briefly, think about going over to him to tell him about it, but decide not to. Petulant for sure, but I figure he won't receive the information graciously. He certainly hasn't taken any of my assistance with a great deal of appreciation so far. I decide to check the boat first. If there is anything important then I can tell him. Until then, screw him. If he wants to do his little investigation on his own, then fine. I'll do my thing and he can do his.

As I scramble up onto the concrete ramp outside the shop I hear a disembodied voice from the darkness on the far side of the building.

"Quite a fire."

I jump with surprise. "Who's there?"

Sam Cartier moves slowly to the edge of the shadows. The variegated light of the night only reveals contours, not details. "Wanted to talk to you about the boat you found today," Sam says quietly, but with intent.

I can only manage to stand there, profoundly thunderstruck, mouth agape like some slack-jawed hill person.

Sam continues, "But the chaos here doesn't lend itself to a conversation. I was coming up to your house when I saw the fire."

Man, oh man. Why the hell does this guy want to talk to me about this? Why does the customs and immigration officer for Isla Tortuga make a special trip down to my house to talk to me about a police matter? And besides, the damn thing is a huge hunk of charcoal now anyway. My brain is swimming.

Sam looks at me, inquisitively. "What . . . did you find on the boat? I mean, anything that would lead you to the family?"

The ambush has certainly thrown me but not off balance enough not to hear "*family*." How does he know there was a family on board? Surely everyone in the Pelican Bay area knew about the sailboat by now. Hell, this burg is small enough. Probably the whole island as well. Word spreads fast about something out of the ordinary on an island where nothing much happens but the sun coming up in the morning and going down at night. But the details would be unknown to everyone except the people at the dock when I brought the boat in. The only way Sam would know there was a family on board was for someone to tell him. Who? Bourgois?

Sam's mannerisms, his unwillingness to leave the comfort of the shadows, his desire to talk in private, suggest something else. It's more than just casual interest in an incident that is out of the ordinary for Isla Tortuga. This isn't like Sam, this direct approach. Sam is ever the politician, obtuse and smarmy. It's like talking to a recording with Sam, always that bureaucratic distance. You never really know what he is after or where he is coming from. Tonight's approach is totally out of character—too forward, direct.

This gut feeling makes me keep my own distance until I can better understand his motives. "Why so secretive Sam, popping out of the darkness like a mugger?"

"Oh, sorry." He takes a giant stride out of the shadows.

"And jeez, Sam, I didn't have much time to take a really good look. The water was pretty rough out at the point, so we just wanted to get back to the bay. Why ... do you ask?" I probe.

He answers quickly, "Oh, nothing really. Just concerned. It's a big ocean out there and I hate to see anyone get ... hurt." The word "hurt" lingers on his tongue long enough for me to notice.

"Yeah, me too. But I'm afraid that these people are not OK." I try reading his face. I can't see his eyes, because he is inching back into the shadows, his dark skin a different shade than the ash gray half-light of the waning night. I want to know what he means by "*hurt.*" Doesn't want me to get hurt? Or is it true concern for the people from the *Miss Princess*? I push him further. "I planned on coming down to your office tomorrow to ask you if you know anything about the boat. Like, do you know if it has ever put in here on the island or not? But seeing as you're here now, perhaps you can shed some light on this whole thing right now."

"Tomorrow morning, huh? That would be better. What time, do you know?"

My eyebrows furrow. Not the response I was expecting. "What?" I ask, unable to disguise my agitation.

Sam shrugs his shoulders. "I'll be there all morning." He holds his hands to me as if he is a mendicant friar.

This non sequitur conversation has me befuddled. "Well, here I am tonight, Sam. Can you save me the trip? Uh, well, did it? The *Miss Princess*?"

"Oh, clear customs with me. No, but ..." He stops short, catching himself. "Maybe we should talk tomorrow—in the morning. Yes, that would be best."

"Sam, what's going on here? You're the one that came here looking for me. Why are you here, standing in the damn dark, asking me these questions? What concern is this of yours?"

"I shouldn't talk now, Phil. Come down in the morning. I should be getting back to town. Tomorrow. I'll see you tomorrow morning."

And with that, he is gone, as quickly as he appeared, back into the darkness from which he emerged.

Holy shit. This is one weird damn island. Nobody wants to talk about anything, but they sure are willing to hint around about stuff. Everything is cloaked in this veil of mystery. As if the land will open up and swallow us whole if we dare to speak about the "secret," the taboo *Miss Princess*. It's an abandoned sailboat. What is the big deal? Find out whom it belongs to, discover what has happened to them, and find the people responsible for blowing up the boat. All interconnected, no doubt. Seems real simple to me. But somehow it has become this complicated mess. Actually, not so much complicated as obfuscated. Everyone I run into is trying to keep information away from me for some reason.

I turn back to the firefighters who are now rowing back to shore, content with the job they've done. The wreck smolders, black smoke roiling up until the wind catches it, diffusing it into the night. I plop down on my Adirondack chair outside the shop and wait for the firemen to return. I look at my watch. Well past midnight. I needed some sleep.

The *Miss Princess*, or what is left of her, sits out there like a floating campfire snuffed for the night. They might as well scuttle the thing. What a shame. A magnificent sailboat reduced to a smoldering wreck, burned damn near to the water line. Just a hull filled with ash now.

One of the sailboats in the bay trains a hand-held spotlight on the wreck. The beam works up and down the starboard side of the boat.

There it is. A red gash of paint, clear and bold against the white of the gel coat, a few feet above the water. It is clearly a rub from another boat, or perhaps a dock. No, a boat. A dock would undoubtedly leave a black mark, not red. Most, if not all the docks around these parts, use old truck tires as fenders and they leave a distinguishing black mark. A boat made that mark. I shift to the skiff the firemen are rowing in. It's red. Bright red. And on the port side is as a sizable white rub mark. Or at least I want it to be a white mark. Maybe it is there, maybe not. My heart quickens; my head bobs with recognition. Then someone grabs my shoulder.

I spin out of my chair, knocking it on its side. Don Bennett is standing behind me. That fucking mendacious grin glued to his face.

"Jesus! You scared the shit out of me!"

"Sorry," Don says firmly. "This poses a bit of a problem doesn't it?" He is looking past me and out at the smoldering wreck.

"You're damn right it does. What the hell are you doing here? Why you sneaking up on me?"

"Why *did* you sneak up on me," he says lightly.

"Fuck you, buddy! What are you doing here?" Nervous exhaustion has taken over my mouth, and my mind.

Don raises his hands in mock surrender. "Easy. I am truly sorry that I frightened you. Walking in the sand does not make much noise, and you seemed quite engaged with the boat."

I take a couple deep breaths and with forced control, repeat my question. "What are you doing here?"

"I heard all the commotion, couldn't sleep, and walked down from the resort."

I plot the route in my head. A good two miles down the road to Tortuga Beach Resort. Forty, forty-five minutes to walk that distance. Possible, but he would have needed to turn around and head back almost immediately. Get out of the bus and start walking back. "You got here fast."

"I was crossing the grounds at the resort when I heard the explosion. I came right back."

We stand, eyes fixed on one another. He grins, I glower.

I tell him, "You should direct any questions to your friend down on the beach." I toss my head toward Bourgois, who is at the water's edge, talking to the firemen.

"I don't want to interrupt him. He looks busy."

"So am I." I hop down off the ramp and onto the powdery sand. I need to get the hell out of here, deciding to head back home and wait for all the commotion on the beach to die down, and then come back for a look at the red skiff. That is the new plan made up in the last fifteen seconds. I need to get away before anyone else pops out of the shadows to pay me a visit. I don't think I can handle another surprise visit, but my subtle escape is not to be. Don freezes me in my tracks.

"Do you want to know what happened to the *Miss Princess*?"

I hate that huge, toothy grin.

# EIGHT

THE HURRICANE LANTERN LIGHTS the old man's face in warm
honey light. The light plays on his eroded face, diving into the wrinkles carved for years by the sea and the salt and the sun. He smiles
with his eyes at his guest, the son of his old friend.

This is the boy's second visit. He always listens intently, like the
words spoken in this small tin house will give him life. They are
the air that fills his lungs; they are the meat that fills his belly; they
are the blood that courses through him.

The boy sits across from him now, in silence and in the half
shadow of the lantern. They sit on a stage of sorts, the two of them,
encircled by the modest light of the flame. There is surf on this side
of the island, and it rumbles outside in a way that suggests silence.
It is the lullaby to their conversation.

"Tell me more about my father," the boy asks.

---

Don and I make our way through the receding mass of people. The crowd streams in waving columns, like ants marching back to their holes. Tired faces, that's all I see. No nervous, excited talk; just hushed voices anxious for bed. I can empathize.

We punch through the flow of people and start the long hike up the path to my house. We tramp up the hill single file, me leading, Don following, head down, watching his feet, picking his way along the rough path. He breathes in rhythm with his stride, no protest to my hurried pace. I know where the gullied washouts are, where the good erosion footholds are, and I pay no heed to Don's progress. I'm anxious to hear Don's explanation and I want to get to a private place first. I'm pressing on in a single-minded quest fueled by a blend of frustration and fury. Finally I'm going to get some answers. I try to convince myself that's all I want. I just want to know what is going on, and I can let it go.

I'm lying to myself and I know it.

The churning of adrenaline tells me so. It tells me that it is just beginning for me now. It's the same feeling I have during those obtuse afternoon conversations I have with Bill. It's the quick muscle twitch, that thunderstorm of emotion in my core that is chaotic, yet somehow magical. I feel alive. Alive in a way that can only be felt and not known. I am—I am being. Something is happening and you are in it. You may not like it, but you know you won't turn from it either.

The other side of my brain tells me I have injected myself into something that I shouldn't be involved in. I know that. I know that as much as I know it doesn't matter. I am here. I haven't left. I remain. I will remain. No reasoning will help. I don't even try to listen to my brain. This phantom being inside is clearly in control, and I don't care.

I briefly entertain the idea that it all could be piffle. Don may not know anything about the *Miss Princess* and may simply be jerking my chain. It could be some sick kind of probing again, like at dinner tonight. But again, my gut tells me to press on and I'm listening to it—only it.

We burst into the clearing in front of the house. Don stops, hands on hips, but not out of breath. That surprises me. "Nice little tropical house you have here. Very nice."

"Thank you. I'd invite you in but would rather not make a long night of it. Let's hear your story and I'll drive you home."

Long silence—longer than is necessary or comfortable. The night now has a disturbing hum to it. I try to pinpoint the sound's origin, realizing quickly that it is the sound of blood rushing through the capillaries in my ears. My heart is pumping, more from anticipation than exertion.

Don's eyes dart. He examines the turf around his feet, looks up at the breadfruit tree behind me, at the house again, back to his feet. It is as if the thoughts he is composing have suddenly slipped out of his head and are whirling about him. Owl-like, his head turns and his dark eyes fall to me. "You seem quite agitated by all this. I'm not really sure why. It's like you really don't want to be involved with this, but feel obligated to continue."

"Cut the mind games. Let's hear it." I say it low, venomous.

"OK, OK, easy now." His hands say *whoa*.

I'm not in the mood to divulge my inner child to this guy at half past midnight on the lawn of my house. I want him to either tell me what he knows, or get the hell out and let me sleep.

It strikes me suddenly that I am awfully tired, and I can't say why. It's late, but not that late. I didn't do anything particularly strenuous today, but I feel drained. A little like driving ten hours in a car. Not tired; a little hyped up, but yet, groggy and sluggish—and certainly irritable.

"I would like to tell you, Philip, but I regret that I cannot."

My shoulders slump, obviously. My head rolls, odd incongruent sounds escape because my mouth won't work yet. "You mean to tell me that you humped all the way up here and now you're not going to tell me! Shit, you're the one that brought it up at the beach! You're the one that *asked me* if I wanted to know the story!" My voice is shrill, too many octaves too high.

"I'm sorry if I misled you. I thought..."

He may be genuine in his remorse, but my anger doesn't allow me to see it.

"Well that's just bullshit, Don! Why are you and everyone else involved with this fucking boat so damn secretive about it? I don't think that I'm being too out of line for asking a few questions. If it's a big secret, or involves something that I don't need to know about, then tell me. Just tell me, that's all I want to know. This slinking around in the night, dropping innuendoes and subtle threats, and 'sorry, I regret I can't tell you,' bullshit." I spit my words, I'm so livid. I take a few seconds, a few deep breaths, to calm myself. I look up from my feet and ask, "Why did you ask if I wanted to know about the *Miss Princess*?"

"I thought that maybe I could use you. You know these waters pretty well, and I thought I could use you. But my better judgment tells me to leave well enough alone."

"*You* could use me? Leave what alone?"

"I've said too much. I'm sorry. I really shouldn't have said as much as I have. I'll be going now." Suddenly he turns and starts back down the hill.

It comes out. I don't mean it to, but it does, by reflex or shock. "Hey, wait. Don't you want a ride?"

He is over the lip of the hill. I can only see him from the chest up, like a bust sitting on the grass. "It's a long way back to the resort. If you don't mind."

I do, of course. I really just want to push the bastard down the hill. That's what my emotions are telling me to do, but my mouth says, "My truck is in the back." I start across the clearing and can see peripherally that he is following me. What am I doing? Why the hell did I offer this ride?

We walk, he on my left heel, without talking down the wide path that leads around the north end of the house and through the gumbo-limbos. I can see the clearing ahead where I park my little red Nissan pickup.

Don says from behind, "Quite a banger you have here."

I am initially confused, but quickly realize he means my well-used truck. It is rusty beyond redemption, but is as reliable as any vehicle I've ever owned.

"Shut up and get in." I turn the key and the truck fires on the second cycle.

"She purrs like a kitten."

He's right. The engine is solid. Not a tick or rumble to be found. I glower at him as a response.

I back out of the clearing onto the dirt service road. Actually, the road is a long serpentine driveway that runs up the hill behind the house.

"Did you see that?" Don asks. The headlights must have caught some movement in the undergrowth.

"See what?" I question, as I turn back around after backing.

"Something moved in the bushes over there." Don points to a clump of saw palmetto next to the clearing.

"Ah, probably an iguana. Or an agouti," I explain.

"Damn big iguana."

---

I drop Don off at the Tortuga Beach Resort. We don't say a word to each other the whole short trip down to the resort. I want to, but can't find the right words to express my thoughts. My temper has cooled to a slow boil, and I'm trying to salvage what I can from this. I'm trying not to let my frustration get the best of me and prevent me from getting what I want—answers. I don't want to risk saying anything that might put Don off completely. With a little distance of time from the confrontation on my lawn, I can see he is opening up a bit; this is the first time he has admitted involvement with the sailboat. And the "*I could use you*" line really intrigues me. I fight the urge to blurt out the obvious question. I need a little time to formulate my ideas before I move on them. I know that. And maybe, I figure, Don needs a little time to shape how he, too, is going to approach this.

Now on my return trip, I pass the road that leads off into the bush to Bill's house. With a tired grin, I think, *you're the bastard that got me into this.*

I bought Dive Tortuga on a whim. I was leafing through a dive magazine when I saw a classified ad that read:

*FOR SALE:*
*FUNKY DIVE SHOP ON THE*
*FUNKIEST LITTLE ISLAND THIS SIDE OF NIRVANA.*
*TERMS? WE GOT 'EM!*
*CALL ME. I'M OLD—YOU CAN TAKE ADVANTAGE OF ME.*

So I did. I called Bill Tomey and flew down the same week. I met Bill at the shop and we went to the Beachcomber for grouper and Hairoun and I thought, *no polyester pants here. I'll take it.* The terms were pay when I could and Bill could dive for free whenever he wanted. I flew home, sold everything I had, cashed in my mutual funds, and all the other so-called safeguards I had established to protect myself from disaster, and bought a new life on Isla Tortuga. It all seemed so perfect then. Now I wonder who is taking advantage of whom.

I drive slowly along The Road, trying not to run over any iguanas that wandered out onto the road at night to warm themselves now that the pavement is radiating all that stored energy from a day's worth of sunshine. They make a terrible crunching sound when you run over them. Worse than the sound is picking the remains out of the tires, but the vile creatures stink like an abattoir if I don't. So I drive along carefully, eye to the road for iguanas, until the turn for my "driveway." Then I gun the little pickup up the sharp incline.

The dirt drive is rough and rutted by the rain, but neither the government nor I are in a position to fix it. Periodically, when it gets real bad, I go out with a pick and shovel and try to level the worst spots. Otherwise, if I don't, the truck gets hung up on the mounds between the ruts.

I come whining up the hill and swing the truck into the clearing I opened as a parking space. God, that was a treat. Three days and two machetes only to find under all that growth a fissure as long as the proposed parking area and wide enough to swallow a tire. But nothing that two more days and several bags of cement couldn't fix.

I lean forward to turn off the ignition and I hear it just as I feel it—the slap of flesh on flesh. My head flies forward powered by a very strong hand at the base of my head. The hand presses my face against the steering wheel, my right cheek pressed into the gap between the horn and the upper curve of the wheel. I reach out spastically with my right hand to grab the person that is holding me, but the angle is too great and my arm only catches air. My futile attempt at defense brings increased pressure from the hand and I think for a moment that my head might be pushed through the wheel like garlic through a press.

"Don't fight."

I stop struggling instantly. The voice of a man—an islander, for sure. The lilt. The thickness of accent. But I don't recognize the voice. I concentrate on breathing, which is getting more and more difficult because my nostrils are pressed nearly shut and my mouth is contorted so badly that I can't open it fully to breathe.

"Do not follow this, my friend. It is none of your matter. No more warnings for you," the voice says slow and sure, as if rehearsed. No, I think, I have never heard this voice before.

There is silence, only the sounds of air being sucked through very small passages, the struggling sounds of restricted breathing. I can feel the powerful fingers pinching the tendons on the back of my neck. Then my head is raised quickly and slammed down into the steering wheel. The horn toots once, musical accompaniment for the stars and lightning bolts. A kaleidoscope of colors moves in front of my eyes. Through the pain, I hear the crunching of heavy footfalls—the man running down the dirt drive.

I sit in the truck, forehead resting on the steering wheel, and try to regain my senses. A strong metal, salty taste puddles in my mouth and I reach in and pull out bloody fingertips. I reach in again and can feel the gash in my cheek where my teeth have cut me. It is deep. The blood pool dribbles out of the corner of my mouth, both warm and cold. I just about pass out as I fumble to find the door handle. I finally find the handle and fall against the door. I pour myself out, spitting a gelatinous gob of bloody mucus on my feet. Probing the inside of my mouth with my tongue, I again find the gash in my cheek. It feels like my head is electrified when I touch the wound. From then on I decide that I will not poke at it with my tongue. Seconds later, I probe it with my tongue.

With feet like cement blocks, I stumble down the path toward the house, mumbling and spitting blood. "Motherfucker. You motherfucker."

# NINE

A TINY PALAPA HUT sits atop a small ridge of calcified coral and sand on an insignificant cay forty miles from Isla Tortuga. In it, sitting lotus position, is Bill Tomey. He is nude, drinking a Shiraz out of a large-bowl wine glass. He has a grin on his face as expansive as the night sky.

"This Rosemount is fantastic. Allie's spot on about Australian wines." He bobs his large head, the quintessential hippie bob. As if his spine is made of rubber.

The sky is black and is littered with shards of planets and suns and other celestial debris that pulse and glow before Bill's relaxed eyes. Large, curved-trunk coconut palms surround the tiny building, their fronds hissing occasionally in the variable wind. The night sky casts an ivory light tinged with powder gray on his palapa hut, which sits on the north beach of Cayo Pardo.

The Spaniards named the cay Cayo Pardo, or Brown Cay. No one knows why. The cay isn't particularly brown; it is quite green, in fact. Possibly the most lush of the cays in the island nation's chain.

Perhaps it was some homesick Spanish sailor's sense of irony. And, like a good many other things in the collection of small islands that make up the nation of Isla Tortuga, no one cares to know the reason why Cayo Pardo is named as it is, nor do they see any reason to change it now. It has always been Cayo Pardo, and will always be Cayo Pardo.

Bill runs the back of his hand across the large, thick cotton blanket that covers the floor of his dwelling from wall to wall. Looking around his small, three-sided shelter, he spies his cooler against one wall. It is a large, faded Igloo cooler, now more pink than red. It is stocked with provisions for his retreat. Next to the cooler is a case of inexpensive, but tasty, South Australian wine. There are three bottles missing, and he quickly calculates that the remaining nine will last him the remainder of his stay. After all, he will be on retreat only a couple more days, at the most. No need to stay any longer than it takes for the vision to come. See the vision, head back home. Never needed more than nine bottles before, shouldn't need more than nine this time, he figures.

"Nine. Need to look up the significance of nine. There must be a reason for only needing nine. Gotta have a book back at the ranch that can enlighten me. Jung maybe. No, maybe not. Ah hell ..."

He takes a gentle sip of his wine. It moistens his upper lip, stinging a little, until the dry skin drinks up the acidic moisture. He sets the glass down, twisting it to make a flat spot on the rug, and settles back onto his palms. He looks out over the beach and sees crabs moving in and out of their holes down close to the high-tide mark. The smooth night light casts their shadows long until the wet sand and surf swallows their dark umbrae. The crabs scuttle back along the ruffled edges of the rising tide, searching for bits of food. He wonders if crabs ever get lonely like humans sometimes do.

Bill allows his eye to wander to his boat. It is a proa. He was inspired to build the boat in this Malayan style after spending some time traveling in the Philippines. It is a fast, small boat—a canoe of sorts, with a sail and an outrigger for stability. He watches it crouch on the beach, the surf frothy behind it as the water meets a shelf of coral a few yards out to sea. The ama, or outrigger float, rises and falls gently as the wind pushes its larger companion in a vain attempt to topple it. The crab-claw sail is furled tightly. The boat is secure.

Bill feels sleepy, but fights the urge to lay his head down. He wishes he had a Buddhist monk to crack him on the back with a stick to keep his focus. Being short one Buddhist monk, he instead uncoils himself and stands. The roof of the hut is just high enough to allow him to stand upright; however, to stretch, Bill must bend at the waist and pull his shoulders up around his neck. He forms a long *L*, fingers reaching out the open side of the hut into the breeze. He steps out into the talc-like sand and stands upright, hands on forward-thrusted hips. He dashes for the water, whooping like a seven-year-old boy.

———————

I look at my bloody face in the bathroom mirror. I look like a ghoul. The fluorescent bulbs on either side of the mirror cast my face in stark, morguelike light. I reach down, grab a washcloth, and run it under cold water. I then stick it in my mouth and bite down, sluicing the water, and pink diluted blood runs down the cloth. I jut my chin forward to let the small stream trickle into the sink.

The blow to my head sent me into autopilot—stop the bleeding and assess the damage. Now that I can see the damage and am beginning to see an end to the piercing pain, I begin to come around. Start to think. I try to put the pieces of the attack together.

The guy came out of nowhere. He was waiting for me to return. "Damn big iguana" was right, as I remember Don's observation a mere twenty minutes earlier. Shit, the guy was strong. I was nothing in his hands. A doll. Sure didn't recognize the voice. Why? And what did he mean by "don't follow this"? The boat? The *Miss Princess*? What? Robbery? Questions.

I shuffle over to the sofa, cloth still plugged into my mouth, and survey the room. Nothing looks tampered with. Nothing seems touched. Lamps still on tables, cushions not cut open, bed is not overturned. Nothing like the ransacking that you see in the movies. Clearly not robbery, and I knew intuitively that it wasn't before I even inspected the house.

His warning clearly told his intent. My attacker delivered a rather personal message in a very personal way. If he wanted to rob me, he had plenty of time to clean out the place when I took Don back to the resort. I knew what he meant by "don't follow this." There was only one explanation, but I didn't want to believe it. Didn't want to believe that finding an abandoned sailboat, and having the good graces to tow it in would make me a target for such a brutal attack. Sure, I poked a bit, maybe too vehemently, but surely didn't pry too much. Certainly not enough to get my face smashed in.

"What a helluva day," I mumble aloud. "Quiet little island, my ass. This place is plain crazy. I don't need this. I didn't come down here to get involved in shit like this. A big old dude tells me not to mess with the *Miss Princess*, that's good enough for me. I'm out."

A well-reasoned conclusion, considering that the pain in my head has shifted from piercing to throbbing. I flop down on the sofa, and massage my temples. It does little good.

I pull the washcloth out of my mouth, turn and throw it at the sink in the bathroom. I miss. The cloth unfolds and plops to the tile, the best sinkerball I've ever thrown. I shake my head, pull myself to my feet, and make my way, groaning, to bed.

# TEN

I DREAM ABOUT THE lions again.

This time, I feed with them. In that surreal state of being both participant and observer, I can see myself on my haunches next to the lions, but I don't see my face thrust into the open belly of the fish. But I know what I'm doing and I'm not revolted by it. It seems natural, in a way. Certainly the lions aren't disturbed by my presence. My observer self stands like a waiter and watches the feast that never ends. The fish seems to always have more and more to give our hungry mouths.

I open my eyes. Morning, barely. Above me on the mosquito netting is a small gecko I know, his sticky toes holding him away from the netting. A breeze through the louvered window stirs his perch and he rocks back and forth like a tourist in a hammock.

"Good morning, Speedy."

I sit up, and I'm instantly reminded of last night. My face feels like a mushy pumpkin. I look up and the animal cocks its head and looks down, its black eye swiveling, searching me. I must be quite a sight to him. We sit there looking at one another until the glow of the sun crawls over the spine of the island, washing the room in tangerine light.

I avoid the bathroom mirror. I know what I look like. My face was smashed in before.

It kept me up most of the night, thinking of the accident back in St. Paul. The girl, the kiss, what she said. It wasn't that I was haunted by it, but I was troubled. The familiar pains in my head—the once-broken bones again injured—brought back the accident as clearly as if it happened yesterday.

Despite my best efforts, I can't help but syncretize the attack last night with the accident in St. Paul. For a reason I can't fathom, they seemed linked. Maybe it is the way my jaw hurts, or the jelly puffiness around my eye that makes me think that this is my justice for trying to run from the pure tragedy I caused back in the States.

"What do you think, Speedy?" I look up into the netting, but he is gone.

---

It's seven o'clock and I stand at the edge of the clearing, looking below me to the bay. In the water sits the shell of the *Miss Princess*, still tethered to the mooring buoy. Her mast has fallen over and leans into the water, the lower half bent in refraction. There are other bits and pieces of rubble on the bottom of the bay, jagged black holes in the clear water.

I look at my Seamaster and know Don won't be at the shop for a couple hours—might as well head down to the Beachcomber for breakfast.

I run involuntarily down the path to The Road, gravity and momentum working all too well this morning. The bouncing does my face no good. It's visibly throbbing under my right eye.

When I hit the sand, I remember the mysterious red boat—the impromptu fireboat from last night. I look over to where the boat should be. It's gone. No surprise there. After the whipping I took last night, I know that I will never see that boat again. I knew that skiff was involved, but that information is of no benefit now. I'm finished with the whole damn thing. Alan was right. Leave it alone. Let the police handle it.

I look out to the *Miss Princess*; her hull streams minute trails of smoke in the quiet morning. Surprisingly, all the sailboats in the bay are quiet. Not one generator running or sailor on deck readying his boat for sail. Too much late night excitement, it seems. Everyone is sleeping in. Everyone but me.

I think about Manolin. Was he here last night, part of the crowd? For an instant, I think that the red skiff is his and that he is a part of this whole fiasco. But just as quickly, I dismiss the notion.

That's what I can do today, I tell myself. While Chubby takes Don out for some tune-up dives (Don can't expect me to dive in this condition), I can run over to Windwardside to talk to Manolin. Learn his story.

I can see in the window of my mind all of those marlins sitting outside my shop. I now have them displayed on a long rattan-and-glass table in my living room. The little wooden creatures have a timeless look to them, frozen in time, swimming in a way on the glass. They are jumbled on the table in no particular fashion. It seems more natural that way, like they are really swimming through the ocean. I can't imagine them not being there, they fit so well.

I move to the water's edge to where Manolin was standing a couple days ago. I half expect Poncy, our local mutt dog, to come bounding up to me. He doesn't. He too is sleeping in. The sea feels cold this morning. I can feel the low sun on my back, but I shiver and I wonder again about Manolin's story.

I clearly don't understand this man. I seem to have a mental wall that is insoluble for me. It's like a dream I had once.

I was walking down a corridor, the walls on either side doorless. The wall in front of me had a door, but no handle. I could see the shape, the outline of the door in the wall, but there was no means to open that door. So I stood there mystified, hoping that something would come to me, or someone on the other side would open the door for me. I grew increasingly frustrated, to the point of wanting to turn back and sprint down that long, empty hallway. But I didn't. I stood there staring at the door waiting for something to happen.

It surprises me that this is still important to me—this man's story. I roll my shoulders, unable to understand even myself today.

I start down the beach in the direction of the Beachcomber, hoping to find Alan awake so I can scrounge some breakfast. Alan doesn't serve breakfast to the public, but he enjoys having me over to share the morning and a couple eggs and coffee. Two bachelors staring at one another across the table like a married couple of fifty years. It's a nice way to start the day, most days. But I wasn't looking forward to our little engagement this morning. Alan will not like the condition of my face. I should have looked in the mirror this morning to make sure it didn't look too bad. I now can only imagine what it might look like. Alan will be full of questions that I didn't have the energy to answer this morning.

I slog dispiritedly through the sand, erasing the footprints of all those voyeurs from last night. Man, the beach is quiet this morning, I observe. Just as I reach the steps leading to the Beachcomber, I hear my name.

"Phil!"

I turn to see Don Bennett standing on the concrete ramp leading from Dive Tortuga.

"Phil! Wait!"

Don wears midnight blue swim trunks and a plain white V-neck T-shirt. He has a bath towel from the resort thrown around his neck. He carries a pair of fins, a mask, and snorkel. I watch him muscle through the deep sand in his booties, only a little out of breath.

"Couldn't sleep. Thought I'd take a look at the sailboat," Don says, anticipating the question. Then he takes in my face. "What the hell happened to you?"

"I'll tell you over breakfast." I turn and start up the steps, completely rebuffing Don's transparent attempt to include me in the *Miss Princess* saga. I know he has something to do with the sailboat but I don't care anymore.

Out of the corner of my eye, I see Don staring at me all the way up the path. He is clearly looking for me to explain my beaten and swollen face, but I don't feel the need to explain. Not to him anyway. Besides, there will be plenty of time for that. Alan will surely ask the same questions, and I don't want to explain it twice. We hit the patio and Don can contain himself no longer.

"Dammit, man. Who did this to you? You didn't get this tripping over a bed post." Don's eyes speak volumes. Wide, unblinking, darting. Sincere eyes, it appears to me. But again, I don't care.

"Alan will want to know, too. I'm too tired to go through it twice. Can we just sit down and eat and I'll explain it all?" I ask, quietly, gloomily.

Don nods and we saddle up on the same stools we occupied the night before. The grating of the stool legs on the wood floor brings Alan out from the kitchen, wiping his hands on the apron around his waist. He takes one look at my face and freezes, shakes his head. "I'll get us some coffee," he says, as he spins back into the kitchen.

I can smell the eggs and chorizo cooking in the open kitchen, the smell of strong coffee overpowering it on occasion, and I'm glad that I can still smell. Especially considering the beating my nose took. I sit there, at the little six-stool bar, chin gently in hand, gazing into the mirror in front of me. This is the first time this morning that I've taken a look at myself. I look like I went fifteen rounds with Mike Tyson. My face is puffy on the right side, but my eyesight is not obstructed. That surprises me, because my right eyelid is a pallet of purples and reds. The eye looks like a blinking beet. My mouth aches. With my tongue, I inspect the slit in my cheek. It's healing over, now a ridge of flesh that rubs against my teeth as I move my jaw back and forth. It doesn't feel like anything is broken, but I'm not sure. I recall that I thought I hadn't broken anything in the St. Paul accident, but breaking out a windshield with your noggin will likely result in a cracked something or other. In that accident, I dislocated my jaw and cracked a cheekbone. At the time, those injuries didn't feel terribly bad. I had other things on my mind.

This situation isn't quite as severe, but I check my cheekbone anyway. I wince involuntarily, unable to probe with much enthusiasm because of the swelling.

Alan comes out of the kitchen carrying three empty mugs and a French press full of steaming coffee. He avoids eye contact with me, saying, "Breakfast is about done, and then I want to know what the hell happened. Don. Good morning. How do you like your eggs?"

"Good morning, thank you. Over easy, if you please."

"Not a problem." He returns to the kitchen.

Don and I sit quietly, listening to the island awake. Various birds call to one another, some close, some just barely audible. A goat bleats on the other side of the cluster of casuarinas that flank the restaurant. I can barely make out the clink-clang of its bell.

Still looking into the mirror, I say, "This hurts like a son of a bitch."

"I imagine so," Don agrees.

Alan arrives with three plates, one each in his left and right hands, the third on his right forearm.

"Let's hear it, slugger," he mocks.

As we eat, I explain in detail the attack from the night before. Al and Don listen, not saying a word until I finish.

Then Don says flatly, "It was that big iguana."

Alan looks at him quizzically, "Come again? Iguana?"

Then I explain the sound Don heard in the scrub last night. Alan sits patiently with a look on his face much like a father might have that is listening to the excuses of his teenage son who has gotten himself in trouble at school. It's an "I told you so" look on his face. I don't have the patience or energy to defend myself. Besides, I am beginning to agree with him. He could very well be correct about getting too involved in island matters, and at this point I don't give a good damn whether I find out what happened to the *Miss Princess* or not. I'm ready to let this thing go this morning.

I look over at Don, who is raking his fork through the remains of the yolk of his egg.

"There are some bad people running around," Alan said. "You should tell Bourgois about this. You should really report this. He would want to know."

I'm incredulous. I know Bourgois isn't interested in anything I have to say. For all I know, Bourgois is behind all this—trying to teach me who is boss in this burg.

"Don't you think, Don? I mean, you know him. He would want to know about this," Alan continues.

Don nods. He is still working the eggs, but now the tip of his tongue is massaging the inside of his lower lip. He appears lost to us in his concentration. "I'll have a go at him this morning. See if I can get him to investigate," he says flatly, with resolution.

"No need to on my account. I'm taking everyone's advice—yours, Alan, Bourgois's, and the gorilla's from last night. I'm staying clear."

"No. It's important that Charles knows about this. Violence like this shouldn't go unpunished." Don's voice is dull.

"Yesterday I got the distinct impression Bourgois didn't want me involved. He'll probably say I deserved this."

"I sincerely doubt that. Charles is my friend. I know him. He would want to know."

"He didn't want to know anything about this." I pull the pacifier from my pocket and delicately place it on the counter in front of him. It surprises even me that I'm carrying it—but Don recoils back from the object like it might bite him. "What, Don? You disturbed by pacifiers—or just this particular pacifier?"

Don doesn't answer; just continues to stare at the object on the bar.

"Well, your reaction tells me you are in this up to your eyeballs. But look, Don. Let's drop it. I'm 'off the case' so to speak. Don't tell Bourgois—I don't need any more headaches than the one that big boy gave me last night. Here, take the damn thing. It sure seems important to you."

Don picks up the pacifier, revolves his heavy chin toward me. He opens his mouth to speak, but doesn't. Instead, he lowers his gaze and shakes his head.

# ELEVEN

THE BOY AND THE old man sit silently in the shack. The night's conversation hangs in the cool mist above their heads. The boy looks up, perhaps to relive the words spoken, but he is taken with the exposed beams. They remind him of human ribs. They both support and protect and he is in the core of it now, sitting like a vital organ, watching the sun slither through the latticework opening at the gable end of the shack. It is like a throat, this opening, first sipping then gulping down sunlight, drinking the warmth of the coming day. The mist retreats into the shadowy corners, chased by the building light. The boy rubs his heart and his eyes drop to the old man sitting across from him. The old man's smile is expansive.

"Walk with me to the beach, son, and we will welcome the new day. Then we will eat."

The boy nods. "My father was a good man."

"Yes."

Don and I stroll along the water's edge toward Dive Tortuga, our eventual destination. It's only a little after nine o'clock, but I know the day is going to be a scorcher. There is no wind to speak of; the water in the bay looks semi-solid, undulating like blue-green gelatin. I move a little to my right into ankle-deep water, my Teva sandals slipping out from under my feet, twisting my ankle. I wince and a flush of irritation warps me.

The sun has that crackling feeling to it, ovenlike. On most days it feels good on the skin, that tension-sucking, diaphoretic heat.

Not today.

It irritates me.

It's a hot shower on a sunburnt back.

I interlace my fingers and make a visor for my face, turning away from the heat, favoring my right side. I look longingly at the shade of the shop some thirty yards away.

"It is such a horrible waste," Don says, throwing his head horselike toward the *Miss Princess*.

"Yes it is, but hey!" I say, with forced conviviality, "You're a tourist here on our fair island. A visitor for a few short days to a small Caribbean island that is trying to crawl out from under hundreds of years of rule into the twentieth century. So the place still has a little heart to it. A few blemishes maybe, like say, blown-up sailboats. But tourism is just budding here, so you have to expect less than perfection. Anyway, you won't find the dolled-up, phony, touristy crap here on little Isla Tortuga that you find on other Caribbean islands. So just enjoy. Have a few drinks, maybe look a little too long at the topless ladies sunning on their boats. Who cares, right? You're on vacation, or is it 'holiday' for you? Enjoy our little slice of paradise. I can assure you, this is the most excitement that this little burg has seen in many a year. This is our quota of bad goings-on. The rest of your stay should be pleasantly boring."

Don catches my obvious sarcasm. He walks in silence, looking at my feet.

We are at the front door of the dive shop now and I start the long, frustrating search for my keys, thinking, *I've got to get me some new shorts or do something with these keys.* I like to wear cargo shorts with lots of pockets because I like to have everything I need with me. But that practice of carrying everything with you can be a nuisance as much as it is a convenience. It can take me several passes through my pockets to find what I'm looking for.

I pull out the keys—a jumble of skeleton keys, broken keys, and keys I can't remember what they're for—that are bound together with a short hunk of yellow nylon rope. I flip through them and find the key that unlocks the huge padlock that secures the front door. It clicks open and I flip the hasp and push the door open.

Just as I reach for the bolt that secures the large main window, it hits me. Don notices my start.

"What?"

"It's nine thirty. Chubby is always here at nine. Always."

"Does he have a key?"

I shake my head no. "But that wouldn't make a difference."

"Well, perhaps he found the shop locked and wandered off somewhere. Maybe to get some breakfast," Don says.

I correct him. "No, even when the shop is closed he always sits here waiting for me. Or he sits out on the dock, fishing."

We both look simultaneously down the cement walkway and out to the dock. No one. Just the *Tortuga One* slumbering on her lines. And beyond it, I notice sailors readying their crafts for the day and talking from boat to boat. Their conversations are animated with hand gestures, probably talking about the fireworks of last night.

"Perhaps he slept in," Don offers.

Don doesn't understand. Chubby is the most punctual person I know. He is never late. Never. Not in the six months I've been on Isla Tortuga, nor during the time that he worked for Bill when Bill owned the shop. I remember Bill telling me, on more than one occasion, that Chubby is always on time every morning, willing to work, without fail. He's right. Chubby is the same type of worker for me.

And after what happened to me last night, I am uncomfortable with this digression from the norm. I hypothesize that if they got to me, maybe they got to Chubby, too. He was with me when I towed the *Miss Princess* in. They, whoever "they" is, might also see him as a threat. In their minds, he might have seen something and would need to be taken care of.

But he is a fifteen-year-old boy. What harm could he do? Nothing, of course, but I can't pass off the notion that he might be a target, too. I decide to give him a few minutes to see if he shows. If not, then I'll go looking for him.

I enter the shop cautiously, not knowing what or whom I might find. I am happy to see that everything is as I left it the day before. I push open the big front window to find the morning has not gotten any cooler. Having just crested over the spine of the island, the sun casts long shadows down the hill. I hear the sound of a coconut fall into the sand with a whump. The sound makes me turn my head impulsively and I instantly hate my nervousness. I can hear the increased traffic on The Road, a sure sign that the island is awake and ready to go to work—as much as Isla Tortuga can be ready to go to work. These are all sights and sounds I've heard a hundred times before, but today they seem niggling. I want silence and solitude. For an instant, I consider tromping back up the hill to the comfort of my bed. But instead, with crossed forearms on the sill of the window, I look out over the beach and bay, and begin my impatient wait for my young captain's arrival.

I forget about Don until he moves into the shop and starts poking around the equipment and merchandise hanging on the walls. He picks up a mask and tries it on. He reads the back of a package from a light stick used on night dives. He seems content to wait as long as necessary. I watch this with side-slanted eyes.

A pelican's call brings my eyes back to the water of the bay. Squinting, I let my eyes blur out of focus as the sunlight reflects off the sandy bottom back through the gin-clear water, tinting it a soft cyan. That soft, welcoming color gives way immediately to a hard cobalt just outside the mouth of the bay and out over the wall and trench that surrounds the island. The island does, in fact, sit on a large plateau. If you drained the water from around the island, Isla Tortuga would look like an upside-down ice cream cone sitting on a table. The plateau that the island sits on drops off suddenly into the Tortuga Channel, which reaches depths of over three thousand feet at its maximum. All along the edge of the plateau are pinnacles, spires that rise, at times, to within feet of the surface. Huge clouds of fish congregate at these pinnacles, including some very large gatherings of sharks. The pinnacles make for spectacular diving and I take most of my customers to them.

When I first came to Isla Tortuga, I couldn't believe such wonderful, untouched diving could still remain in the Caribbean. Why hadn't more people discovered this spot? Why did millions pack the Caymans to see tame rays swim around in turbid water? Sure the walls are nice, if you could get a shop to let you dive them properly. And Cozumel. Again the walls, but more dive boats than fish at times, and the time-share guys are a major nuisance. I thought if people were willing to make a little effort, they could dive some of the most spectacular spots in the world, unmolested by the usual annoyances of mainstream vacation destinations.

But Bill Tomey thought the same thing when he set up shop here almost thirty years ago. Little has changed since then. I once schemed on how I could attract more divers to my little hunk of the Caribbean. But after six months of scheming, trying different tactics, I've resigned myself to the reality that only a handful of the millions of divers that travel annually for their sport will come to Isla Tortuga. I would get only the adventurous or the jaded. The ones that had been to Grand Cayman and knew the potential that lay in the Caribbean if they could only find someplace that didn't have a Hard Rock Cafe or Planet Hollywood. And don't get me started on Carlos'n Charlie's.

My eyes shift back to Don. He is now standing outside on the ramp, fingers intertwined on his head, gazing out over the bay. I can only see the back of his head, but I presume by his posture that he is daydreaming as I am. Don shakes his head, just a slight toss. I lean a bit farther out the window, hoping to catch a glimpse of Don's face. I can lean out only far enough to see the back quarter of his face. His broad eyebrows are dancing, deep in thought. I wonder what he is thinking, but hold my tongue. I don't want to open up the floodgate. Silence is what I desire most right now.

He must have sensed my gaze because he quickly swivels his head and catches my eye. I look away, reflexively, demonstrating my guilt. When I swing my eyes back to his, I find a broad smile on his face—a cat-that-caught-the-canary smile. Not really knowing why, I smile, too.

"Want to do some diving? Some wreck diving?" Don says, turning full to me.

"No. In fact I don't want you hanging around here at all. I'm done with this, remember?"

"I meant the *Miss Princess.*" He tosses his head toward the burnt-out boat.

"Why the hell would I want to do that? Didn't I just tell you not thirty minutes ago that I'm done with this whole thing? That damn boat has been nothing but one big pain in the ass for me. In fact, I hope your buddy Charles comes and hauls that thing away. Scuttles it deep."

Don looks at me blankly. Without a word, he slips past me into the shop, and makes his way to the counter on the back wall of the shop. Underneath it is the small refrigerator, humming quietly.

"Do you have any water?" he asks.

"You don't take hints very well, do you?"

He opens the refrigerator with a jerk. Looking past him I can see a half-eaten roti, two Coca-Colas, and a jug of water sitting on the top shelf. Looks familiar. Don pulls the jug of water out and looks around the shop absently.

"Do you have a glass?"

I stare at him, mouth slightly agape in stunned, silent protest.

He tilts his head, resigned to the apparent crudeness of the situation, and swills right from the jug.

Silence again. Long silence. Just the occasional sound of muffled swallows of water. I have never met a person so comfortable with staring as this Don Bennett. I've known this guy for about twelve hours, had dinner and breakfast with him, and he has said about seventeen words to me. Although, with all this staring, I sense that words are superfluous. We seem to be able to communicate through our eyes and body language. I guess most people do, but this, to me, is a particularly heightened example. I don't find this synergistic thinking particularly comforting. It isn't a soul mate kind of thing. It is kind of spooky, in fact.

I sense that the man means me harm, but I have no proof why. He's made no aggressive moves toward me but there is just something about his bearing that I don't quite like.

Don walks over to the rough-built, bright periwinkle table where I stack the dive shop's souvenir T-shirts. The shirts are a simple design but I spent a couple extra dollars on them. Over the left breast is silk-screened the words "Dive Tortuga" and "Grateful Diver." On the back, again silk-screened, is an impressionistic drawing of the Dive Tortuga shop in all its full-color glory. I went with only a few colors for the shirts but opted for a higher quality shirt and silk-screen. They sell pretty well and I make a decent profit off them. They are also a staple of my wardrobe. I have several in all the colors I carry.

Don pushes aside the stack of black T-shirts and sits down gingerly, the legs of the table wobbling a bit under his weight. "Can I sit atop this thing? It won't break under me, will it?" he asks, clearly trying to lighten the mood in the room.

"It'll hold," I answer lifelessly. His tone is too carefree and I don't like it. I'm put off by this flippant attitude.

I look at my watch. Where the hell is that boy?

———

It's a quarter after ten and still no Chubby. I leave Don sitting on the dock, shirtless. He explains that he wants to catch some sun and if he gets too hot he'll jump in the water and cool off. I shrug, knowing that his pasty white skin will be a painful pink when I return, and I don't really care.

I don't want to hike back up the hill to get my truck so I opt to ride the dive shop's bike down The Road to Chubby's house. The bike is one of those cruisers you might see on Venice Beach in California, or the Boardwalk in New Jersey. The model with fat, fat tires, handles that curve up to the hands, and only one speed. Not the best arrangement on a hilly island and I'm already regretting my decision as I push the damn thing up the drive to The Road. Sweat soaks my shirt. I'm not looking forward to chugging along on this thing in the building heat.

Chubby lives with his mother. She is a large woman with cottage cheese thighs, hams for calves, and full, ripe watermelon breasts with enough Caribbean warmth to cook those ingredients into the most satisfying stew. I've met her several times, but only casually. I don't even know her name. She is Mrs. Patois to me. I see her frequently at the bakery where she works because the bakery is located on a back street a block over from the customs office, Sam Cartier's office. I deal with him more frequently than I would like so I run into Mrs. Patois often. She always gives me a sugar cookie when I stop in and we engage in casual conversation, exchange pleasantries. I think she likes me and I've made it very clear to her about my fondness for Chubby.

Being a fatherless only child, Chubby is inordinately mothered. Chubby has told me he doesn't like the overpowering attention that his mother throws at him with all her immense weight, but I know she is a good woman and provides adequately for him. He never goes hungry and his house is better furnished than mine. Of course, the one key thing that is missing in the boy's life is his father. I think Chubby's mother sees me as the boy's surrogate father. It's a role I don't relish and don't encourage. I like the kid, but I don't want to be his father. I'm his friend, and his boss.

I ride the fat-tired bike down the undulating Road; the wheels sound like they are slowly melting as I pedal along the hot pavement. I round the northern point of the mouth to Pelican Bay and look over my shoulder at the water below. I think I see Don sitting on the pier, white skin glowing against the molten water and sun bleached pier. I could be wrong—the febrile light of late morning is exploding off everything in eye-stinging shards. At this curve, The Road turns sharply inland and downhill and I welcome the chance to coast a bit. The bike picks up speed and I open my mouth wide to catch the racing air. I can feel the moisture on my skin evaporating, cooling me.

Chubby's house is at the bottom of the hill on the island side of The Road, all told, about three miles from the dive shop. It is a little white clapboard house with chickens scratching around the foundation and a goat tied off to a tree. Jerry, the goat, has eaten everything within its length of rope.

I coast up and slide off the bike, then I see the police car parked across The Road from the house. I grimace, knowing this is not a good sign. I have the urge to flee. I want to turn my bike around and pedal back to Pelican Bay. I want to pedal back fast and hard so that time will itself roll back. If I pedal far enough and hard enough, maybe none of this will even happen. Maybe Chubby and I don't find the *Miss Princess* at all.

I walk the bike up to, then lean it against, an old wagon, long past its usable life. Jerry watches me. His pupils are but slits. The yellow-green irises look catlike to me. I take a couple hesitant steps to the open front door and rap on the frame.

"Hello!"

No answer. I can hear voices inside the house but my eyes can't adjust. The contrast between the bright sunshine outside and the dark room I'm looking into makes it nearly impossible to see any detail inside the house. I knock again, but I stop halfway through the third knock and step inside slowly. I follow the voices down a narrow hall to the back of the house. I pass through a sitting room filled with furniture that looks like it came from a French parlor many, many years ago. I then pass a lacy, sky-blue bedroom—Mrs. Patois's. Finally I come to a small room where I can hear voices talking behind a half-closed door. It's a man's deep voice and Chubby's mother. I know the man's voice, but I listen, wanting to know if there is anyone else in the room. I wait several minutes but those are the only voices I hear. I decide to knock on the door, causing the voices to fall silent. The door flies open and standing in front of me is Chief Bourgois. We startle one another and I take a step back, instinctively, regaining my personal space. Bourgois composes himself quickly and smiles, those white teeth flashing bright.

"Good morning, Riley. What brings you here?" he inquires. I sense a tone of both surprise and annoyance. I can tell he doesn't want me here. I puff with indignation.

Chubby's mother steps into the doorway, easing Bourgois out of the way. She's been crying and is on the verge of starting again. "Have you seen my boy, my Christopher?"

"No, ma'am. That's why I'm here. He was late for work and he's never late for work. I thought maybe he forgot he worked today. I kind of need him."

"He didn't come home last night," she explains, the tears flowing again.

I reach out and squeeze her hand, and she folds into me, sobbing. I underestimate her weight, making me take a half step back for support. I turn my eyes to Bourgois.

"Do you know what happened to Chub ... Christopher?"

"No. We do not know where Christopher is. In fact, after speaking with Mrs. Patois, I was planning on speaking to you."

"Like I was saying, I don't know where he is either. He was late for work. He's never late for work. I got worried."

He is looking at me funny, studying me. It's my smashed-up face.

"Worried?" Bourgois said, cocking his head slightly. "Why worried, Riley?"

I look down at Mrs. Patois, at her wet face. She looks up at me with wide, red eyes, hanging on our every word. She looks at me like a child looks at a magician. It's as if she believes that we can bring her son back to her with the utterance of the right word. Poof. Magic. Chubby reappears from behind the curtain. I want desperately to be able to do that—to bring her son to her. She clearly loves her boy. She is trying her best to remain composed but her fleshy hands are trembling. I try to soften my anxiety, and hers. "Worried is the wrong word. Perhaps concerned is better."

It starts unexpectedly. I feel trapped, enclosed. The two large black people staring at me, the heat of the house, the damn chickens in the back and then the walls begin to move. They are getting closer; everything is closing in on me. The walls, Bourgois, Mrs. Patois—all lean in on me. I hear myself breathing, round mouth blowing a muted whistle. My heart beats in my throat. It won't let me swallow. I reach up to push it back down to its proper place and my neck is slimy with sweat. My legs are rubbery. I reach out for the wall and miss. Bourgois reaches out and takes my elbow to steady me, but I need more than that. My eyes roll like a frightened horse. Just before I black out I see Manolin standing next to Chubby's bed. A small wooden marlin sits on his open palm. I crumple to the floor.

---

The next thing I remember is lying in a small twin bed looking up at the circle of wood that supports the mosquito netting. My eyes follow the fabric's cone shape down to the bed. The netting is pulled to the side and I can hear their voices.

"Do you think he hurt his face when he fell?" she poses.

"No, I don't think so. His face was bruised when he arrived here."

I lay there, listening to the two people talk, catching only bits of the whispering conversation because the chickens are making a heck of a racket outside.

These fainting spells were supposed to go away, but they hadn't completely. The doctor back in Minnesota said that my brain received quite a blow. The most severe concussion he had ever seen, and that there is no doubt some internal damage. They performed numerous MRIs on me and found my brain to be in good condition, but there were some dark areas around my cerebellum that could be the cause of blackouts. They would have to run more tests to be sure. I didn't wait around long enough to find out just what the doctors had in mind for me.

"You're awake. That's good. May I take you to a doctor or the hospital? Your face looks quite bruised." Bourgois is standing over me, looking down like a man looking down a well.

I answer meekly, "No. I'll be fine. I had an incident some months ago and hit my head. It happens to me sometimes."

Bourgois nods, still looking down the well. "What happened to your face, Riley?"

I don't know what to say. I look up at him, blinking.

"Another incident?" Bourgois offers with his wry smile.

"Another incident," I say, pushing myself up on the bed. I swing my legs down, testing their strength. Wobbly, but they will hold. I'm not looking forward to riding back to Pelican Bay on that damn bike and for an instant I think of asking Bourgois. No, I would rather keel over and fall into the sea than have Bourgois give me a ride home. I stand, with the large black man extending his hand, offering to help.

"Really, I'm fine. I've got to get back to the shop. Your friend is waiting to go diving."

Bourgois offers, "May I give you a ride back to your shop?"

"No, no. Please go look for Chubby ... Christopher. I don't have any idea where he might be, but he can't be far. It is a small island, after all."

"You're right, Riley. He will show up soon enough. He will be just fine."

I nod and shuffle out past Bourgois into the dark hallway. As I amble down the corridor, I notice Mrs. Patois in her room at the beginning of the hall.

"Goodbye, Mrs. Patois. Chief Bourgois will find Christopher. Or he will show up soon enough. And if he does, please tell him to stop by the shop when he can. OK?"

She looks up, teary eyed, "Goodbye, Mr. Riley. I will."

The sight of her sitting on the edge of that bed incites me. Why only rough me up but take the boy? It doesn't make sense. What threat is a teenage boy?

I don't have a good feeling about this. Bourgois hasn't a clue what is going on. Everything is so innocent to him. Quiet little island. No problems. Let everything lie. Make no trouble. I have no intentions of telling him what has happened to me. He would simply use the attack as proof that I should stay out of the situation. Leave it to the professionals, he would say. Yeah, right.

I walk quickly through the parlor, out the front door. I step down hard onto the crushed shell path that leads out to The Road. The white-hot sun hits me like a club.

# TWELVE

Tony's chinos are wet at the knees from kneeling in the moist sand, but he now sits and his bum is soaked through, underwear and all. A sharp, pyramid-shaped rock sits between his feet. It is covered with wisps of coconut husks. For the thousandth time this blistering morning, he slams the coconut down on the rock. The coconut only bounces off, this time hitting Tony in the knee.

"Bloody hell!"

He looks quickly at Martha and Sophie, but they are listless in the half shade a couple trees down and they apparently do not hear his outburst.

He seethes.

*What a worthless woman*, he thinks. *Always the drama queen. Tears, tears, and more tears—that's all she offers. You come over and bash this coconut for a couple hours, you slag.*

Martha catches his dead-eyed stare and he recovers. He pushes himself up, brushes the seat of his pants as he heads for the jungle. "I'm going for a slash."

Martha looks after him blankly.

---

I lean the bike against the back wall of the shop and pause momentarily in the shade, trying to slow the tornado in my head. Sweat soaks my shirt, hair matted to my forehead. I don't know what's happening to me. The heat down here has never gotten to me like this. I need a drink of water so I make my way around the building, one hand against the wall so that I don't fall down like some drunk.

I get to the front corner of the shop and see a wet Don sitting on the end of the pier by the *Tortuga One*. He pulls a fin off his right foot and rests it with its mate on top of a snorkel and mask.

Don sees me out of the corner of his eye, pushes himself up, and makes his way toward me, his eyes searching me. "What's up? Did you find your friend?" he shouts.

I don't answer but toddle into the shop and up to the refrigerator with unerring determination. I pull the jug out and finish the remaining half gallon, still breathing like a man with a broken nose. I close the refrigerator, turn, and lean heavily against the shelf and wall.

Don stands in the doorway, arms akimbo. "You didn't find your friend?"

"No. He's missing. Did you find anything on the boat?"

He ignores my question. "You may not believe me, but I'm genuinely concerned for your friend's safety."

"You know, I doubt that. It's that fucking sailboat out there that's caused all this. And you and Bourgois are involved with that boat in some way or another, whether or not either of you want to admit it to me. But I don't care; I don't want to know your connection with the damn boat. I don't give a damn. I just want Chubby to be OK. The kid doesn't know a thing, so if you have any pull in this situation, you'll fix this now. You'll get Chubby out of this."

"You've got it wrong, Phil. We never intended to get anyone hurt here. We never intended to include you or Chubby or anyone else for that matter."

"Then what was last night? You were going to tell me about the *Miss Princess*."

"It was a mistake. I know that now. I knew it this morning when I saw your face."

"Well like I said, whatever the hell is going on, I don't care. My concern now is Chubby." I drop the empty water jug in the trash and push my way past him. I stride with purpose down the ramp toward my boat.

"Where are you going?" Don demands.

"Bourgois doesn't care what happens to Chubby so I'm going to look for him myself."

With more effort than it should take, I step up onto the gunwale of the *Tortuga One*, drop with a thud behind the wheel, slide the thick black key into the ignition switch, and turn it. An electric *wha, wha, wha* greets me as the starters turn over and over. Then *woom*, the engines start. Gray-white smoke burps out of the cold engines and drifts with the wind, clinging to the surface of the water.

"Phil, I would really like to know where you are going. It's important." Don is standing next to the boat now, his pink skin pulsing like ebbing coals.

I ignore him and undo the dock lines.

The ride back from Chubby's house was a long, hot, sweaty, sticky ride of remorse. A ride of regret for what I got Chubby into.

The only conclusion I can come to is that my unintelligible need to haul in that sailboat has put a young boy in jeopardy, an innocent fifteen-year-old boy. It is my fault. Shit. Shit! I should have left well enough alone. Should have left that fucking boat right where it was. Let the ever calm and mannered Bourgois pick it up.

I need to get up to Andrews' Bay to see if anyone up there knows anything about the *Miss Princess*. That sailboat is where all this began and it's where I need to begin if I'm ever going to unravel this snake ball. I may be new to the island, but water people stick together and Andrews' Bay is the home port for the local fishermen on the island. If anyone knows anything about an abandoned sailboat, someone there will. And, unlike Bourgois, they will tell me; I am one of them.

I crank the wheel hard to port and tap the throttles and the *Tortuga One* edges away from the dock. Don looks on, hands stuffed in pockets.

I swing the boat around. The mouth of the bay appears like a gun sight from this low angle with the cliffs reaching up on either side. Aiming the boat directly for the mouth, I edge the twin throttles ahead and the boat starts to canter along like I'm on horseback. I pick my way through the two sailboats that remain in the bay and after clearing them push up the throttles to half speed, the boat still in the hole but rising up, just about on plane, then I punch it. The boat hops up onto the surface of the water as if breaking free from an imaginary tether, gliding effortlessly up on plane.

I stand at the center console behind the windscreen, feet wide for balance. The wind whips my hair, my legs take the irregular jolts when the boat slaps on the water. I fly through the mouth of Pelican Bay as if charging out of an old fort, then cut sharply north, the boat effortlessly leaning on its side, the Yamahas rumbling astern. Behind me, the twin props churn the dark, smooth water into a white froth. I'm glad the water is smooth. I need to run full out.

The wind screams in my ears. The flapping of the wind muffles the sound of the engines and the paper-tearing sound of the boat slicing through the water.

Riding full out in an open boat can be hypnotizing, in a way. The constant menagerie of sounds seems, in an odd way, to isolate you from them. You sense that they're there, clearly picking each out, but they remain only in the background. I often think of it in the same vein as a symphony. If you listen closely, you can hear the oboe, but it is all the instruments coming together, making the whole that produces the impact. And, because conversation is next to impossible, running top speed in an open boat stimulates introspection.

This time I ponder Manolin, yet again.

Just before the blackout I saw him. I saw him standing next to Chubby's bed with one of those small wooden fish. I've always been of the mind that dreams and visions are just a response to something physical happening in the brain. In this case, the stress of the blistering bike ride caused some circuit to fail and the image of Manolin was produced.

Bill Tomey would argue otherwise.

Bill would maintain that my explanation lacks imagination. That there is more to this world than we can perceive with our limited faculties. Bill argues that we only see what we are prepared to see— he got that quote from some guy named Waldo or some such thing. I can't remember whom. Bill counsels that the world is not arranged intellectually. You need to *feel* it. Not necessarily in an emotional sense, but to let yourself be and experience and not try to explain everything in concrete terms. Maybe I could if I went off someplace, got naked, and drank myself silly. I don't understand aestheticians.

I run hard past the mouth of St. Christopher Bay, the fjordlike bay that serves the capital city.

The first settlers to Isla Tortuga were shipwrecked Spanish sailors. Their ship, a man-o-war, was blown way off course in a storm. The ship was heading home to Spain from somewhere in Central America when, unable to find a safe harbor, it ran aground on a series of pinnacles just off of what today is Andrews' Bay. Most of the men somehow survived the horrible trashing they must have taken on that exposed face of the island and they fought their way into the interior through some rather thick jungle growth. When they reached the top of what is Mt. Soufiere today, the lay of the land below them reminded them of a turtle. Thus, Isla Tortuga. I have no idea how they could have thought the island looked like a turtle; the island in no way looks like a turtle. More like a cone party hat than a turtle. But somehow, the name more or less stuck, even as the island changed hands between the various European colonialists. Virtually every country in Europe gave it a try on Isla Tortuga. Typically, they brought their slaves to the island to harvest the bananas and nutmeg and other spices that grew abundantly in the fertile volcanic soil.

But eventually the English, the final "owners" of Isla Tortuga, could no longer see the profit of holding on to a colony that drew more resources than it provided, and gave the inhabitants their independence, under one condition: Isla Tortuga could be free just as long as the British could still get well below market prices for the bananas that their countrymen now liked so much on their porridge.

Thus, Isla Tortuga was let loose on the world like a twelve-year-old runaway that has no idea of what the world can really be like. The current government, placed in power by the British, had to learn quickly and has employed its version of democratic rule. But the de facto result is that most of the citizens of the tiny island nation simply go about their business with little to no regard for the government. The government, more or less, operates in a vacuum, implementing policies and attempting to bring the nation into the twenty-first century, with little input from the people they govern. The populace would prefer to grow their crops, fish the sea, and raise their children; live their lives as Tortugans, plain and simple.

Because of their ambivalence to their government, the capital city of St. Christopher is relegated to being a collection of government buildings, warehouses, a few churches, and an occasional gift shop. Of course there is the rare restaurant that caters to the odd tourist that happens through town, but for the most part, it is a government town. Ahead I can see the breakwater that protects Andrews' Bay.

Andrews' Bay is a slight misnomer. It's not a true bay but rather the product of a very ambitious British engineer who retired to the island some forty years ago. The engineer, Charles Andrews, quickly sized up the harbor situation on the island and realized there was no true working harbor. There were, of course, the docks at St. Christopher; however, they were built with the sole mission of serving only large ocean-going freighters and vessels of that kind. There is Pelican Bay that offers safe harborage to only a handful of boats and it has no facilities for them if they do decide to anchor there. Andrews surmised that rather than put marina facilities in at Pelican Bay where he was limited by space, he would build his own bay. Thus, Andrews' Bay.

In reality, Andrews' Bay is an indentation in the lee side of the island with a massive breakwater. The indentation was God's contribution; the breakwater was Andrews'. The concept Andrews came up with was pretty simple, but the task to implement it could only be described as Herculean. The accounts of the project tell of an intense operation of making five-foot-square blocks of solid concrete on shore, then hoisting them on a barge that then placed them on the sandy bottom in about forty feet of water. The completed breakwater is thirty feet across at the water's surface and pyramids out to seventy feet at the bottom. There are over four thousand blocks that make up the Mayan-pyramid-looking wall. Just building blocks really, but big blocks to be sure. Luckily, the bottom is flat and fairly solid where Andrews decided to build, so the wall has held together pretty good. The coral that grows on the wall has helped keep it together by acting as a bonding agent for the blocks, almost welding them together. Additionally, there aren't many storms that hit the island from the east, so the wall isn't tested often. Andrews' achievement, which took a mere two years to build, still stands, and will probably continue to stand as long as the island exists.

I pass around the point where the breakwater meets shore, thinking about what I am going to do and say after I tie off. Not a clue. Just start asking around and see what comes up. Play it by ear. Someone must know something. It is clear to me that I need to start asking questions in order to start figuring out what is going on. I have far too many questions and far too little information. Far too little.

I round the open end of the breakwater and the vast expanse of the bay reveals itself. There is a good half mile of water to run across before I get up to the docks. From my vantage point, I see only familiar sailboats or cruisers docked. Slow season for sure. Not to say I've ever seen it full, even at the peak of cruising season, but this was extraordinarily quiet. I scan the lineup of boats tied off in the marina hoping to recognize one or two. I see Doddy Bertram's boat.

Doddy is an old-time fisherman, now turned water taxi driver. He's long to the island and knew Chubby's father well. There is no one on the island who knows these waters better. He's the perfect person to start with. I vector over toward his small purple skiff, deciding to tie off on the other side of the finger dock from his boat. Mind made up, I continue my scan of the bay and out of the corner of my eye I spot a boat anchored out near the breakwater. I missed it when I wheeled into the bay because it was back over my shoulder. Plus, there was no reason for it to be there. There was plenty of room at the docks. No need to anchor a hundred yards out and have to shuttle in on a skiff.

It's a style of boat that I've never seen before. Wide beam, about thirty-five to forty feet long—pretty good-sized boat. A cruiser built a little like a Chris-Craft but more vertical. It's in horrible shape. I figure it must be an islander's boat. There is no way anyone in their right mind would challenge the open seas in that thing. From a distance, the hull color looks ruddy brown, but then I realized it is rust. Must be a steel-hull boat. The superstructure is no better. Even from an ever-increasing distance, I can tell that it too is sorely in need of a few coats of paint. The bleached wood of the super-structure shows through the flaking red paint and forms the pre-dominant color scheme—something like a very bad diaper rash.

I'm so preoccupied with the odd boat out in the bay that when I turn to see how close I am to Doddy's boat, I have to pull back immediately on the throttles to keep from running over the little boat and dock. As I do, my boat succumbs to gravity and promptly settles down in the water. I idle up to the quiet, wobbly dock and secure the boat stem and stern.

"Paddy mon!"

I cringe with recognition. Doddy. He's calling me by my island name. Just as Christopher is Chubby, I'm Paddy. With a last name like Riley, it meant I was Irish, no matter that I explained to him it should be O'Riley if I am Irish. He doesn't care. He likes the name.

I look up, smiling. Doddy is swinging down the dock, small fuel jugs half full, one in each hand. "You need some help, old man?"

Doddy is as black a man as I have ever met—blacker than coal, blacker than tar, blacker than the darkest night. His hair is a brilliant silver gray cut short, but still full. It might be the deep, deep wrinkles, but the skin on his face looks thick. As if all those years out on the water—the wind and the salt spray—have callused his face into an animated piece of beef jerky. When he smiles, his face fractures into a million fissures.

"I'm OK der, Paddy. Wha bring you up dis way? You loss?" He laughs. You can hear the age in his laugh, the loose vocal cords, the easy cough of air from his lungs. He strides to his boat and he slides the fuel containers across the jetty, one, then the other, like he is rolling two bowling balls. Effortless. He's done it forty thousand times. He knows just how much effort to put into them to get them to slide just to the stern of his boat.

I walk quickly up to him, extending my hand. "You look good, old man."

"Beata dan you. Wha got at you, Paddy?"

"My face? Just a little accident." His yellow stippled eyes search me, find me sufficiently well, albeit bruised.

"Have you seen Chubby in the past couple of days, Doddy?"

In fits and starts, a smile grows on his face, remembering the boy. "No. No. Haven't seen young Chubby in days. No need for him to be 'round here. Slow 'round here des days. Summer ya know."

"I hear you there. Been slow for me, too."

Doddy asks, "Chubby missing?"

"Yeah. He never came home last night. I'm beginning to worry about the kid."

"One night and you worry? Worse dan a momma." He laughs his laugh.

"Yeah, well. Maybe so, Doddy, but I sure would like to find him. It's not like him to wander off like this."

"Sorry, Paddy. Haven't seen de boy in days. Like I said. But de boy gettin' older. Find himself a girl-girl and have a little fun. Too much fun maybe. Forget ta come home." He gives me a feinted couple jabs like an old boxer.

I nod that I understand, that I get what he is implying. I try to keep on subject. "Awful quiet around here. Anyone else around that might have seen him?"

"Paddy mon, luk 'round ju. Ain't nutin' goin' 'round here. Hells bells, it so damn hot taday dat de boys up in de shade just tryin' to keep from meltin' into de sand. Dem black boys just a puddle den—be like findin' oil in desert, huh?" He finds that very funny.

I have to smile, too. "Yeah, it does seem unusually quiet around here. Kinda strange. Maybe it's the heat, but the whole island seems to be freaking out." A pall seemed to hang over the area—an air of desertion or abandonment. I know the boats tied up at the docks are working boats based on the island and I wonder where their owners are. I didn't get up to Andrews' Bay all that often, but I don't

141

recall ever seeing the bay so quiet. Old man Andrews would be disappointed. Build a magnificent harbor and no one uses it.

"You know wha strange? Dat boat strange." Doddy points out to the hulk anchored by the breakwater. "Come in here 'bout two days go. Don't want no service. I ask. Couple of down island boys. Not Tortugans. Don't know where from or where to. Just kinda sit out der."

"Not Tortugans?" I'm incredulous. "They hit the open water in that?"

"She look worse de closer you get, Paddy."

"Do they come ashore? For provisions, say?"

"When I talked to dem, dey say dey got enough. Dey say dey ain't gonna be here dat long. Dat what dey say." Doddy shrugs.

"Two aboard, huh?" I ask.

"Yup," he answers with a twist of his head for effect.

We stand silently, looking out at the derelict boat. I break the silence. "You haven't seen Cartier around, have you? He hasn't been up here today, has he?"

"Nah, Paddy. We call him when we need dat skinny boy. Like I say, too slow dis time year. No need to be sitting here waiting for somebody for customs. We don't need dat boy sniffin' 'round here."

"I ran into him last night. He said that he wanted to see me today," I explain to Doddy. "By the way, you don't know anything about a sailboat by the name of *Miss Princess*? Forty-foot Beneteau. Pretty new."

"Sorry, Paddy. I not much help fo you taday. Only new boat be dat rus bucket out der. I'd know you know dat. No boat come to de Isla without ol' Doddy knowin' it."

"That's why I came looking for you, old man."

I look around. I see no one else in the area. The place is totally empty, quiet. I don't even hear the water against the pilings nor the ever-present hum of machines that one always hears at a marina. Nothing.

I decide that Andrews' Bay has given me all the information that it can—nothing. "Doddy, thank you. Good to see you." I extend my hand and he jabs his hand out and we shake, his grip belying his age.

"I'll keep a look for Chubby boy. He show up soon 'nuph." Doddy moves toward his boat.

I swing into my boat, undo the dock lines. The air is so calm that the boat lounges there, relaxed. I shove the *Tortuga One* away from the dock and with a fluid motion, I turn and give a quick twist to the key, fire the warm engines. I slide her into reverse and gurgle back away from the dock.

Once the bow is clear, I cut the wheel hard to port and bump the throttles forward. Straight in front of me is the rusting hulk. Curiosity gets the better of me, and I decide to take a pass by her.

It doesn't take me long to motor out to it. Doddy was right, I quickly discover. The boat does look worse the closer you get to it. I approach her from astern and with a bit of imagination, I can read the faded and flaked name.

*Steel Drum.*

"Yeah. Sure is," I think aloud.

Idling along her port side, I try to imagine just how this boat was built. It looks like the hull is maybe an old Bertram or Chris-Craft, but the hull is steel. I've never seen any small craft like this with a steel hull in this part of the Caribbean. She has a nice wide beam, maybe ten feet, which offers plenty of deck space for the wood superstructure.

The superstructure is clearly homemade and very lightly built. The builder used scrap pieces of lumber and tacked them together to make a boxlike structure about three-quarters the length of the boat, or about thirty feet. Looking at it, I flash back to my childhood. The damn thing looks just like a fort my friends and I made out in the woods when I was twelve. The structure must serve as the pilothouse. From my vantage point, riding a couple feet lower than deck level, I can only see up through the windows in the superstructure, so I can't see everything. But I can tell there's a good deal of room behind the helm. The structure must serve a dual function—pilothouse and galley, perhaps.

There is no visible sign of modern navigational equipment. No radar, no radio antenna. My guess would be that these guys don't even have a compass. My conclusion: coastal cruiser only. The boat couldn't, or shouldn't, make any open water crossings. The boat has to be from around here. No one in his right mind would come across the ocean in this. Although, I had to admit, I'd never seen it before. And neither had Doddy. And this is a boat that one remembers.

I turn the *Tortuga One* around slowly, watching the *Steel Drum* the whole while.

Satisfied, I lean on the throttles and I bounce up onto plane. I point the bow just a little wide so we can sweep around the point of the breakwater and stay close to shore on the outside.

As I start my turn, I take one last look over my shoulder at the *Steel Drum*. There, on her rear deck, stand two black men. I'm too far away to make out any distinctive features, but I can tell that one is larger than the other. It startles me a bit to realize that I was being watched the whole time. Or maybe it is a twinge of guilt for snooping.

I reach down and grab the binoculars that are under the console. I hastily raise them to my eyes. Huge rocks. I jerk back from the binoculars with surprise. The breakwater. I'm skimming past the point of the wall, bounding along in the open water. I half consider turning around for a second peek at the *Steel Drum*, but decide against it. I crank the wheel hard and point toward St. Christopher.

# THIRTEEN

I sprawl flat on my stomach in a cluster of saw palmetto behind my house. The path leading to the clearing that serves as the parking pad for my truck runs perpendicular to me five feet in front of my cramping body. My weight restricts my breathing and for the past twenty minutes a stone or stick under my left side has been jabbing into my waist. I think I'm being crucified. But that's too grim and I quickly put it from my mind.

I've been lying in this same position since dusk. I wanted to get settled in well before anyone could see me setting my trap.

I have a feeling that someone might be paying me a visit again tonight and I want surprise on *my* side this time. I can't definitively answer my own question of why I think my attacker will return. It just seems he will. Instinct, perhaps.

---

Bill Tomey sits on the beach watching the sun set behind the diffusion of cumulus clouds. He is totally naked, sitting cross-legged on a towel, smoking a Cuaba, a Cheshire Cat grin on his face. *A mango, a glass of wine, a good hunk of fish, and a really good Cuban cigar. That's all a guy needs. Maybe an occasional SCUBA dive to refocus the ego, but that's about it*, he muses.

He puffs on the cigar, cheeks concave with deep inhalations, the *figuardo* shape comfortable in his hand. "You gonna smoke a cigar, then smoke a cigar," he pronounces to the sunset. The sun dips below the horizon with a flash of green and he starts. "Cool drugs. The mysterious green flash. Yeah …"

He settles back, enjoys his cigar. Fragrant blue smoke rolls from his mouth but is quickly torn apart on the evening breeze. "Riley could learn to like this, if he would just idle down."

---

Lying in the scrub I find I have plenty of time to go over it again. I can't come up with an explanation for the happenings of the past twenty-four hours other than a rather paranoid one. That suspicious explanation is that Cartier is involved in my attack and Chubby's disappearance. I build the marginally plausible scenario that Cartier came to talk to me last night as a ploy, or perhaps as the scout, for the guy that smashed my face in. It is possible that Cartier knew about the *Miss Princess*—knew her story in detail. He *is* the customs officer for the island. If anyone would know if the sailboat landed on the island, he would. And he would be the one to clear the paperwork path to make invisible whatever clandestine activity the sailboat was a part of. He would be the man to have on your side if you wanted to blow up a boat and crush a guy's face.

And kidnap Chubby.

He could make it all go away—on paper anyhow.

147

And Don Bennett did tell me they didn't want to hurt anyone. It wasn't their intention to involve anyone from the island. It sounds to me like I accidentally stumbled into a deal between Don, Bourgois, and Cartier—and botched it for them.

I had to go.

Chubby had to go.

Sure, and little green men told them to do it. It's a crazy notion except that I can't discount it by the facts at hand.

That, without question, is the biggest problem I have—no information. Despite all my efforts in the capital today, I'm no better off in terms of getting closer to understanding the last twenty-four hours. The island has shut its doors to me. And, to continue the bad analogy, I don't have the keys.

Restless, I reach out and pull the twenty-nine-ounce Louisville Slugger baseball bat just a little closer to me. The bat is a Rod Carew special. It has his name burned into the wood, although you can barely make it out through the dents and scratches and chunks missing. The bat makes a nice mallet at the shop for persuading all kinds of stubborn objects, and it will make a nice persuader tonight. Light, easy to handle, and made of hickory. I envision for the thirtieth time tonight the bat catching its target square on the head and the sound it will make—a dull, thick crack, like a limb breaking in the wind. In my mind, I know I need to rehearse the act in order to do the act, and the vision of the man crumbling under my blow both sickens and excites me. My belly warbles with the conflicting emotions.

It helps to balance those emotions when I remember that I'm waiting for the messenger from last night. He will want to come back and redeliver the message that the *Miss Princess* is none of my business. I fortify myself by remembering my bloodied face. And

I steel myself by remembering that Chubby is missing, and that *is* my business.

Not being especially practiced in hunting with a baseball bat in the Caribbean, I didn't think of wearing long pants and a long sleeve shirt to ward off the insects. As the night slips along, the more skilled hunters of this island, the mosquitoes, hone in on my warmth. The night was young when I came out, and the bugs typically aren't a problem until later in the evening. It is later in the evening now, and the bloodsuckers are having a buffet dinner on the backs of my legs. I don't dare move too much, fearing that any movement will be at the wrong time and I will be discovered, hiding in the sparse under-growth. So I lay quietly taking it, thinking of how welted my legs will be in the morning. To take my mind off of the itching, I rehearse one more time what I will do when that person comes down that path.

I will wait until he passes, then leap up and with one swing, catch the man on the back of the head. Surely he will go down with one blow, won't he? I hope so. I want it to be quick.

But what if there is more than one person? Maybe the guy knows that surprising me will not be so easy the second time. Hell, I'm thinking too much. I'll just go with the flow. These damn mosqui-toes!

I squeeze my eyes shut trying to squeeze out the burning itch that now entirely covers the backs of both legs, especially the soft skin behind my knees.

I'm seriously contemplating pushing myself up and running for the house when I hear a sound from behind. I freeze mid-breath, my lungs full of air, that stone or stick piercing my side. Is it a lizard? No, there it is again. Too large. Sounds heavy. I can almost feel the vibrations through the ground beneath me. Footfalls in desiccated leaves across small stone rubble, moving slow. I turn my head slowly, my swollen face aching. But I can't see anything. I roll very slowly over onto my back, gripping the bat in both hands close to my chest. I look out over my feet and standing to my left, about fifteen feet from me, one hand on a tree, leaning out to look at the back patio, is the silhouette of a large man. Jesus, he snuck right up on me! My heart races. The asshole didn't come down the path!

I fight the urge to jump up and charge the man, to relieve the building tension in my chest that works to freeze my muscles. I watch the man's dreadlocks swing lazily as he moves his head around, looking to see if anyone is home. Trying to see if there is any movement in or around the house. The man stands there for what seems like minutes, then creeps forward, walking cautiously, eyes always on the house in front of him. Intuitively, he picks his knees up high to clear the palmettos and scrub that reach for his feet.

I breathe shallowly, watching the man with wide white eyes. I calculate that he will pass about five feet from my outstretched legs and I wonder if I can get up in time to surprise him before he is able to defend himself. I look for a weapon on the man, but see none. Perhaps he has a knife, but he's not carrying anything in his hands.

The man is now mere feet from me and I formulate a quick alternate plan. It will have to work. I have to surprise him because I'm clearly no match physically for this man one-on-one. He must be six foot three and a solid two twenty-five. If I don't at least stun him with the first blow, he will easily crush me with his hands. I know. My aching face is proof.

The man moves past my feet and I sit bolt upright, and with a short backswing, whack him behind the right knee with old Rod Carew. The end of the bat barely reaches him, but he drops like a tree hacked through on one side, his knee giving out. He lets out a short, sharp "ah!" as he hits the ground, rolls on his side cradling his knee. I scramble to my knees, bring the bat over my head like an ax, and bring it down on the man's head. I rush the swing and my aim is poor, but nevertheless, the bat bounces off his skull like rock skipping off water. He unfolds into the scrub like a thick blanket.

I pant like a dog, adrenaline surges through me. I hear a sound coming from near the clearing and I instinctively flop back into the cover of the brush.

He didn't come alone.

I lay there, watching the path, ears scanning the area for sound. Nothing. The sound never repeats. The man is alone.

I look over at the intruder, lying on his side, legs twisted. Blood trickles from the crown of his head, and in the canopy-filtered moonlight, I can see the blood start to pool by his ear. I lay there on my side thinking how easy it was. Two swings. What, three seconds? Now what?

I push myself up and stand over the man like the African hunter over his elephant. I pull my mini Maglite out of my pocket and train it on his face. He is about twenty-five to thirty, large flat nose, yellow teeth, and dreadlocks now scattered with dirt and leaves and blood. I don't know him, nor have I ever seen him at Andrews' Bay or anywhere in the capital. I pan the light over the rest of his body. I see no weapons—except, perhaps, his size. I can tell by the rise and fall of his chest that he is breathing.

After wading through the brush to the patio and finding some old dock lines, I bind his hands and feet. Like a cat dragging its kill to a safer place, I drag my prey by the armpits into the house.

# FOURTEEN

I PULL THE MAN up the three stairs, heels bouncing, through the doorway into the living room. Judging by the ache in my arms and the shortness of breath, I'm pretty accurate about the man's weight. He has to be at least 225 pounds. I let the man drop, his hands, tied behind his back, force him on his side.

In the good light of the house, I look the man over thoroughly. He wears worn, grimy, tan slacks. An inexpensive brand made more of polyester than of cotton. No belt. He wears cheap bathroom flip-flops, but one is missing, probably out back in the scrub. His plain gray T-shirt is stained with blood from his shoulder down to his colossal chest. I inspect his hands. They are hands that have seen hard work. Gnarled, split, ashen hands. Hands of a construction worker. Hands of a seaman. Like my friend Doddy's hands, they are huge, like thick pieces of dried meat. I nod. This is my attacker from last night.

I hog-tie the man, foot bindings to hand bindings, then go to the kitchen to get a towel to place on his head. The blood is not coagulating, the cut too deep. I didn't think I hit him that hard, but a closer look proves otherwise. His scalp is split about two inches and nearly to the skull. Only stitches will close the wound, but a cold towel might stem the bleeding. I return to the kitchen and wet the towel, then wrap it gently around the man's head like a turban.

Squatting in front of him, I consider his face again. I try to place the man, in an effort to be sure that I don't know him or haven't met him sometime, someplace.

I don't know him.

Is the man from Isla Tortuga? Perhaps a neighboring island? The dreadlocks say Jamaican to me, but Jamaica is a thousand miles north of here. Don't get many Jamaicans down this way. He could be off one of the freighters, but that doesn't explain the *Miss Princess*. A hired hitman, perhaps? I imagine for the right price you could hire a guy off one of the itinerant ships to do a little dirty work for you. But who, then? This guy does not look like the mastermind behind any great scheme.

I contemplate throwing some cold water on his face, like they do in the movies, but decide against it. I'll just wait until the man comes to, hoping that will be soon.

I make a third trip into the kitchen and grab a beer out of my little refrigerator and wander back out into the living room to wait out the man's induced slumber. I hit the guy pretty hard; the gash in his head proves that. A feeling of panic bubbles up in me. What if I killed the guy? Or he could have a concussion or be in a coma. Maybe I put him in a permanent coma! I never meant to harm the guy. Not seriously anyway. Just wanted an advantage. And it will be very difficult for him to answer my questions if he never wakes up.

I take a long pull from the bottle and wipe the sticky sweat off my forehead with my bare forearm. That only makes me hotter. The night is tropical, still, and moist. My shirt is soaked with nervous perspiration, clinging in odd ridges. The moist night air is like a feeding lion's breath.

I nudge the man in the back with my toe. "You awake?" I ask with too much quiver in my voice. The man stirs, and I step over him and kneel down in front of his face.

His eyes open and close robotlike, like someone is trying to start his engine but the battery is weak. He squirms, feeling the rope that binds his hands and feet. His whirling eyes can't focus on the man kneeling in front of him leaning on a bottle of beer.

I say thickly, "How does it feel, asshole?"

The man squints with pain. I sense that he wants to reach up and cradle his aching head, but his bound hands won't allow it.

"Who are you? What is your name?" I sit down in front of the man, legs crossed.

He doesn't, or can't, respond. He lies there, eyes wide and lids flicking up and down, testifying to his pain.

"I've got a lot of questions, so you better start talking now or we'll be here all night."

"You've made a big mistake, mon," the man slurs.

"You Jamaican?" I question. I've never been good with accents.

The man doesn't answer. He looks around at his surroundings, what little he can see. The wet towel that I wrapped around his head slides off and plops on the floor behind his head.

I stare at the man. He struggles to understand his situation. His reaction is like a caged animal, eyes moving, looking for a way to escape. Battling to focus on anything other than the bass drum pounding in his head. I can't see the man's hands, but he is squirming, and I know he is testing the ropes.

"They're tight. You're going nowhere until you tell me what you are doing here. Why you smashed my face in last night, and where the hell my friend is. Understand?"

His eyes are cold. No fear, no concern. He is calm and unemotional, like a machine or a hunter animal. He simply lies there, looking around. Abruptly, his eyes plunge into me. Those black eyes set on a web of red veins that crisscross the sclera. I can feel the force of them settling me back on my haunches.

I know then that it will be a formidable task getting any information out of this guy. He is a good soldier for the general that hired him. Name, rank, and serial number kind of guy—that's all I'll get out of this guy. So now what?

I never considered that the guy wouldn't talk. Surprise a guy and club him on the head, haul him into strange surroundings, and you figure he might just say something. I hadn't figured on anything else, primarily because I've never done this type of thing before. I try to think of cop shows I've seen, or books I've read. I've read many a mystery book, and they always seem to know what to do. What would Doc Ford do now? Or Travis McGee? Shit, those guys wouldn't be in this kind of mess. They would be in total control. I'm not.

The irony.

That pisses me off the most. That the man tied up in front of me—the man spilling blood all over my living room—is the one in control. He is the one with the information that I need. I can kick him to death and that will only succeed in completely screwing me good and proper. That *really* pisses me off.

I can smell the guy now. Spicy. Earthy. Bloody. I hear the creak of his struggles against the lines that bind him. It sounds like a boat's fender rubbing on a dock.

I glare at the man, trying to intimidate him. Trying to show him that I'm the one in control. He just gapes back. He knows. Somehow he knows that I'm helpless without some way to break him. And that could take a long, long time. Time that I don't have.

Then he grunts a chuckle. "Now whas you gonna do, mon? Maybe sake me to the cops?" He laughs again. It's a deep laugh this time, from his belly, forced, and yet oddly sincere.

I pick up on "cops." Why did he say that? Did he want me to? Did he want me to take him in? Shit! Are the cops involved and he knows that taking him there will in reality free him?

The idea that he knows Bourgois bangs around in my head as loud as a marble in a tin bucket. Is my crazy theory correct? Are Don, Bourgois, Cartier, and this hulk all involved in the *Miss Princess*?

I try to calm myself down. Earlier I didn't want to give my idea much credence. It was *too* paranoid, *too* conspiratorial. It was a stretch. Or was it? This is a little Caribbean island with a very short track record of democratic rule. It is certainly possible. Stranger things happen in this part of the world, and I haven't been on the island that long to judge how corrupt the government might be.

In an effort to compose myself, I look away from him and sigh, a very deep sigh. It is meant to communicate that I'm finished screwing around with this motley guy. That I'm growing impatient. "No cops. This is between me and you." I say it low, almost inaudible, to my left knee.

"I a cus you up and feed you to the caimans, for sure."

Caimans? There aren't any caimans on Isla Tortuga. Nor Jamaica, if I remember correctly. South America, or Florida maybe. Was this guy American? No. That didn't make sense. South America, then. Guyana or maybe Brazil or Venezuela.

"You muss wan to die, my friend. You do not know wha you have fallen inso." He whistle-spits his *T*s badly and it is beginning to bother me. I wonder if I knocked out a tooth when I clubbed him out back.

I say, in my newly acquired Mafioso character, "You are right. That is why you are here. To tell me just what I've gotten myself into and how I can get myself out of it."

"I'm not going to help you. I'm going to kill you." He answers slowly.

The only thing that I know for sure is that this man lying on my floor, bleeding a false halo onto my white tile is my only link to the answers I need. I will have to make this man talk. I turn slowly to him and pin him with lazy eyes. "You will answer my questions, because if you don't, then I have no need for you. If that is the case, then we will go for a boat ride—and you'll go for a swim."

That straightens his grin. He looks at me blankly and I sense that he believes me. For the first time since his regaining consciousness, I feel the tide turning for me. He must realize that a guy that is willing to clock him and tie him up just might be capable of throwing him into the sea to let the sharks feed on his sinking body. And in my current emotional state, he just might be right. Yes, I can see it in the flicker of his eyelids. Concern.

I pour it on, slowly and softly. "Who's gonna kill who, my friend?"

He struggles even more now, desperate to be free of the ropes that bind him. To run from this man that sits across from him.

The man with the purple eye that glints the right shade of resolve to do just what he says.

The power is thick in me. It is good to now know that I'm in control, but it feels cold somehow. It's the memory of standing over a broken-winged bird that you hit with a slingshot when you were a boy. I extend my right leg and jab the man in his stomach. He woofs and stops wriggling. I tell him, "Stop fighting it. I tie good knots."

He does because I do. He lolls his head back to me.

I continue, "You need to tell me all you know. It is the only way that I can see letting you live."

The man ponders that. I can tell he is trying to put some thoughts together. I almost hear the internal argument. Do I tell this guy and he lets me go? Or does he kill me anyhow?

A sound draws my attention away from the man. A faint "oh-we, oh-we." A siren? The sound increases in intensity. I can tell it is coming down The Road from St. Christopher, heading south. It is definitely a siren. Probably an ambulance, but I can't be sure. I can't get a fix on it. The sound is bouncing off the pavement and being sucked up by the thick foliage of the jungle, until the remains are finally spit out to skip off the water. Then the sound is at a point in the road near the Beachcomber and I know it is an ambulance, moving fast.

I stand up quickly. My knee knocks over my half-full beer, the liquid foaming toward my captive. I hurdle him and sprint out to the edge of the overlook where I can see The Road below and Pelican Bay beyond. There it goes, lights flashing. An ambulance speeds down The Road past my dive shop and disappears around a bend, its flashing lights reflecting dull off the cement. I wonder where it is going when suddenly the faint "oh-we" stops. Through the canopy of coconut palms I can see the muted flashing of the ambulance lights.

The ambulance has stopped at the Tortuga Beach Resort. My eyebrows register an eighth-inch curl of curiosity.

*Huh*, I wonder.

Then it hits me.

Allie.

# FIFTEEN

I RUN BACK INTO the house to find that my bundle has somehow gotten up on his knees, but is very tipsy. With a firm shove of my foot, I topple him, first onto his back with a crunching sound and cry, then onto his left side, back to me. I check his knots and they are secure.

I have to think of a way to secure this guy to something while I'm down at the resort. He will certainly try to get away, and the knots will only hold so long before he is able to work them loose enough to slip out of them. I've used all of the rope I have at the house to bind his hands. There is more at the shop, but that's too far away. I rack my brain trying to come up with something, but I can't think of anything to fasten him with, let alone what I'm going to attach him to. In frustration, I decide to just dump him outside. Not the best solution, but at least if someone comes looking for him, they will be less likely to find him.

When I grab him by the armpits to drag him outside, he howls like I stuck a hot coal down his pants. This big man can make a good deal of noise. Fortunately, my house is fairly isolated and I'm reasonably sure no one will be able to hear him. With great effort, and no cooperation from the huge howling man, I manage to get him deep into the scrub just north of the path that leads out to my truck. It's an area overgrown with vines and stubby scrub, real primordial. No one will find him here.

I drop him with a dull thud and run back into the living room to grab the wet towel. After retrieving it I tie the towel around the man's mouth, gagging him. I clamber through the underbrush to my truck, grab the canvas tarp that's folded in the bed, and thrash back to my prize 225-pound blubbering hitman. He looks up at me like a man about to be buried alive when I unfold the tarp and cover him up.

Just as I'm about to make my way once again through the thick vegetation, a flash of caution makes me pull the tarp back and check the ropes. They are as tight as when I first tied them. They will have to hold until I get back from the resort. I toss the tarp back over him and batter my way to my truck.

---

When I get to the Tortuga Beach Resort, the ambulance drivers are putting someone into the back of the old converted van. They have an oxygen mask over the victim's bloody, mushy, face. A blanket covers the rest of the body, hiding any other possible injuries. I push my way up to the back of the ambulance, but a tall, wiry paramedic shoves me aside and slams the twin doors. The wiry paramedic runs to the open driver's door and I try to look in through the back window of the van. Before I get a decent look, the van speeds away, throwing sand and gravel.

"Riley?"

I spin to the voice. It's Allie.

She waves me to her and I wonder if I'm seeing a ghost. People mill around us, pass between us, as if in slow motion. I don't trust my eyes until she speaks again.

"It's Don. He's going to be fine, they say."

I trudge to her. "I thought it was you."

"Me? Why me? What happened to you?" She is referring to my face.

"That's why I thought it was you. I got the shit kicked out of me last night and they came back for me again tonight. I thought they were going for all my friends."

"All your friends? Did someone else get hurt, too? Alan and Bill are safe—tell me they are safe." She reaches out and holds my wrist.

"No. They're fine. I think. But Chubby is missing." I can't look at her. If I look at her, she might disappear but if she keeps talking everything will be all right.

"Missing? Since when? Riley, you don't sound so good. You sound strange."

"Chubby didn't show up for work this morning. Not like him at all. I went to his house and Bourgois and Mrs. Patois—Chubby's mother—were there. They told me that he never came home last night. There's something wrong and I know he is in trouble. It's the sailboat."

"The sailboat down at your shop? Don Bennett mentioned something about that."

I reach out and grip her shoulders. "What did he say? What did he say?" I shout.

"Riley!" She shakes free, takes a step back. "He only mentioned that you towed in a sailboat. Nothing more than that."

I step past her deeper into the lawn. I can feel her eyes on me. I turn and ask, "Can I see Don's bungalow?"

She nods toward a bungalow and we walk, quickly, to a brightly lit unit that sits off from the others. It is also the closest bungalow to the beach and I know it to be the best unit she rents, often reserved for special guests.

Looking through the doorway, I can see that all the lights in the little building are on. My eyes flex, trying to adjust from the dark night to the brightness of the cottage.

"This is Mr. Bennett's—Don's—cottage," Allie offers, tossing her head toward the building. "You know him, right? He spoke about you. Actually, he asked a lot of questions about you. Was very curious. Where you came from. Stuff like that."

"Yeah, I bet. He asked me the same questions. What happened here?"

"Another guest found him laying about here." She points to an area just outside the door. "He—the other guest—was coming back from a walk on the beach and found him. He was very badly beaten, Philly. And stabbed in the side. Very bad. This is very bad."

There is a large stain of dark blood smeared over the threshold. Black blood. Blood from the deepest part of the body. A gut wound must bleed the richest, darkest blood, I imagine.

I can see that Allie is very shaken. She has every right to be. This type of stuff never happens on Isla Tortuga, let alone at the Beach Resort. This resort is no flophouse, no drifter's cheap digs. The resort is the best hotel on the island, and Allie is one hell of a manager.

163

I let her know it wasn't her fault. "There was nothing you could have done," I say consolingly.

Allie looks at me quizzically. "What?"

I instantly know I read her wrong. I thought she was worried about her hotel's reputation, but she is worried about her guest. I quickly change the subject to cover my mistake. "Can I take a look?" Without waiting for a reply, I walk into the bungalow.

The one-room cottage is appointed in typical Caribbean decor. Bamboo-framed oil paintings of sea birds and fish hang on the walls. A wicker fan serves as a headboard for the bed. Nice lacy mosquito netting drapes from a brass ring suspended above the bed. All very nice and clean and well taken care of, but yet, not quite what you would find at a five star hotel in the United States or Europe.

I find it interesting how tourists find adequate, if not at times inadequate, accommodations charming when they travel to the Caribbean. They would never stay in a hotel in Cleveland that had bamboo-framed art on the wall, yet here, it somehow works for them. It's the suspension of false standards to perpetuate the illusion of a great, adventurous, Caribbean holiday.

I assumed Don was inside the bungalow when he was attacked, but that theory is quickly put into question. I don't see any blood in the bungalow. The blood is on the threshold and smeared inward. Like he was coming from the outside, not going out.

"Allie. Is there any blood inside the bungalow?"

"I don't know. I don't think so. But it's all over out here," she answers, pointing around her feet.

"I'm sorry. I guess I don't understand. He wasn't attacked in the room?"

"No. On the beach. The police said maybe a mugging gone bad."

"The police are here? Where are they now? On the beach?"

"They left already. They called Chief Bourgois and took off. Said they had a possible suspect already."

I'm dumbstruck. What does this mean? Are the four conspirators turning on each other? Allie snaps me out of it.

"You all right, Phil?"

I nod unconvincingly. "Did they say anything else? The police?"

Allie is still outside, not wanting to put herself into the scene. "They came and went pretty quickly. Like they knew what had happened before they even got here. Didn't look around much at all. They left just before the ambulance left. Right when you pulled up, actually."

I say, "I didn't see them on The Road."

"I don't know what to tell you. They left just before you got here."

"Bourgois wasn't here, then?"

"No. Just a couple of kids, young guys, you know? I've seen them around, but I don't think I know their names."

I turn my attention back to the room, but still address Allie. "Did they take anything? Fingerprints or anything?"

Allie replies, "No, but they did look around outside a bit."

I turn back to her, make the short trip across the room, and step down the two stairs from the tiny porch to the lawn. "Where? Where did they look?" I ask, as I brush past her.

She shouts after me. "The beach . . ." but I'm already walking in that direction. She jogs to catch up with me.

The beach. Yes, the beach. It is the most logical route of escape. The Isla Tortuga Beach Resort sits on the longest stretch of beach on the island. Only thick jungle and scrub lies between Pelican Bay and the huge banyan tree that marks the beginning of the property at the northern end of the resort. From there it is a beautiful, undulating beach of snow-white sand that ends with a jumble of rocks marking the southern end nearly two miles away.

At the edge of the lawn where it meets the sand, I look up and down the dark beach for any clues. I move to my left just as Allie catches up to me. We walk to the south, Allie slightly behind me, both of us looking down at the sand.

There they are.

Footprints in the dry sand. Someone was running—a tall guy with long legs, judging by the distance between the steps. The lawn is eroding, leaving the beach about eighteen inches below the lawn. I jump down from the lip of the lawn to the sand and under my weight I sink up to my ankles in the powdered coral. The sand feels course as it works its way through my sandals and between my toes.

"Wait here, OK?" I tell Allie. I walk cautiously to the trail of footprints, squat down, examine them. They are merely holes in the sand. Small explosion holes made by a running man. The footprints offer no other clue than that they are heading south in a hurry.

"Ramon raked the beach at dusk. These are new. Or some guest was out for an evening run." Allie hadn't heeded my request and followed me down to the footprints. She also came to the same conclusion about the footprints.

I step over the footprints toward the water. "You said that the police looked at these."

"I said that they came down to the beach. Looked around for a while. That's what I said."

"They saw these, then." I point to a second set of footprints closer to the water in the damp sand. These prints were clearly made by a

166

man in dress shoes. The smooth imprint of a leather sole and the textured imprint of a man-made heel are clearly visible. "There were two men here tonight."

Allie's eyes widen. "Poor Don didn't have a chance. Two guys."

"I don't think that two guys attacked Don. This guy here, near the water, was standing. Look, the prints move right back up to the lawn. They didn't run off together. It was like this second guy was watching."

"Like a lookout," Allie suggests.

My eyes follow the diagonal line of the second set of footprints until they meet the lawn. I let my eyes follow an imaginary path as if the man had stayed a straight course. The proposed path leads up to The Road and to a small bar, the Lime 'N Pub.

————————

The Lime 'N Pub sits on the ocean side of The Road just a quarter mile from the turnoff to Allie's resort. It is *the* spot for people that live in Calliaqua, a village on the hill above the resort. They come to the Lime 'N Pub to socialize and listen to local bands and musicians. The music is eclectic—often in the same night. Soft early in the evening, louder as the night progresses.

It is a private establishment not connected to the resort. Even though the club is not far from the resort, not many of Allie's guests frequent the place—at least not more than once. If they do wander in, they don't stay long. On more than one occasion I've seen the treatment a non-villager receives. Typically, the bar hushes as the locals slant their gaze at the outsiders, like shy schoolchildren looking at their teachers. You can feel the eyes of the people boring into your back, and the stillness, the silence, is suffocating. After that kind of treatment, the idle tourist hurries back to the Resort after a quick gin and tonic and a nod to the shuffling bartender. I hate the place because of that. It is the only bar on the island that I feel uncomfortable in.

When I first arrived on the island, I stopped in for a beer on separate occasions because it's quite close to my house, and I was trying to get to know my new neighbors. I was trying to build some friendships other than the ones that come easily among the expatriates on the island. But after sitting by myself at the bar talking at the bartender and having him respond in grunts and maybe if I was particularly witty, three-word answers, I gave up. I gave up and the Beachcomber became my watering hole.

So considering my past treatment, I don't expect to get much information out of anyone inside. Thinking that Allie might have better luck, I pull her aside and ask her to be the intermediary. "I'm not the most welcome person here for some reason. Do you mind asking the questions? Just ask if they saw anyone come up from the beach," I whisper.

Allie has a casual way about her that puts anyone and everyone at ease the minute they meet her. She is almost always smiling or laughing, enjoying her life and everyone in it. And she isn't shy. She saunters up to the bar and raises her hand, as if asking permission of a teacher to speak. "Excuse me. I'm sorry to bother your evening, but I was wondering if anyone was down on the beach tonight. Or saw anyone down on the beach." She asks it smiling from ear to ear, looking around the room like she just told the funniest joke known to man and is waiting for everyone to get the punch line.

The customers look at one another and at Allie, talking quickly to one another, but no one knows much because no one was down to the beach tonight. They've been in the bar most of the night except for the short time when the ambulance came. Then they were outside, watching the excitement. But no one was on the beach. They were unified on that fact.

So I make up a lie, hoping to inspire some individual thinking, "Well, we found a nice watch out on the beach. Just wondering if anyone lost it."

Everyone checks their wrists. All watches present and accounted for.

The bartender offers, "Well, I don't know if he was at the beach or no, but that must be Sam Cartier's watch. He'd be the only one with a nice watch 'round here." He laughs, looking around to see if his customers get the little jibe.

They do and shoot little jibes back, everyone a bit tipsy and having a good time. All of them seem a little jazzed with the newfound excitement on Isla Tortuga. One patron, a middle-aged lady with cornrow hair and wearing a gingham dress, says, "First a boat blow up, then a big fight. Boy, what going on here? Some kind of bad obeah goin' on here." That renewed the chatter in the bar, but the noise clouded to a murmur in my ears. All I hear is the bartender's voice saying Sam Cartier was here. At the Lime 'N Pub. Tonight.

---

Slowly, stoically, Allie and I walk back to the resort, following the curve of The Road.

Cartier was here tonight? Why? The only logical explanation is that he is the linchpin to my whole theory. Doing that, it all starts to make sense. It's like building a puzzle, with the pieces scattered all over the table. Once I start putting a few pieces together, and the more pieces that I can fit into the puzzle, the clearer the puzzle becomes. Bourgois, Cartier, Don, the *Miss Princess*—pieces that fit together. This thing, whatever the hell it is, is pretty big, at least by Isla Tortuga standards. That is, if my theory is correct.

We are back at the turnoff to the resort. My truck is lurking in the shadows off to the side. The scene is eerily quiet now compared to what it was only a half hour ago when the ambulance was spinning away and the all the people were milling around.

We pause on the gravel road, both of us looking down at our feet, both trying to figure out what to say or do next, when, with a visual flash, I remember the man tied up in the bushes behind my house.

"Shit!"

"What? What's wrong?" Allie reaches out and takes my elbow.

"I need to get back home."

"And I should go clean up Don's bungalow. Do you think the police will mind? They seem like they have all they want."

"I think they do, too," I say, with a curl in the corner of my mouth.

"What do you mean by that? You sound awfully strange and suspicious tonight, Phil. Do you know something that I don't? Do you have some idea what went on here? It sure seems like you do."

Something tells me to lie. Or maybe it isn't a lie. My theory is an evolving one. I'm not sure I have all the pieces of that puzzle put together well enough to give a firm opinion on anything that has happened in the last two days. I study my feet and offer, "No. It's just been a long night. Sounds like you'll be up late tonight. Do you mind if I give you a call later? I might need your help."

"With what?"

I'm moving to my truck, drawing her along. "This is really going to sound suspicious, crazy in fact, but I'm not sure yet. I just might need your help is all."

"Yeah. Sure. I guess. I'll give you a hand if I can," she says with no hint of hesitation, no suggestion of resentment. Her response surprises me. I expect more of a protest, more of an inquisition, but I'm happy not to get one.

I'm in the truck now, leaning out the open window. I owe her an explanation. My heart tells me to give her the information that I have so that she might have some idea why her best bungalow is streaked in blood, but I know I don't have the time, or the words. So I say instead, "Thanks. I appreciate it. Be careful."

"You too."

And in my side mirror, I watch her watch me drive away.

# SIXTEEN

"He didn't have to leave. People would understand."

"Yes, some would understand. Not all."

The old man and the boy sit on stools outside the door of the shack. The hurricane lantern glows on the table behind them and they are silhouettes in its light.

Below on the beach, the thunderous surf from last night is but a soft rolling thud tonight. Storms get tired, too, and yesterday's storm has spent itself out. Curved like those limpid waves, the boy droops on the stool, elbows on knees, and watches a moth crawl across the top of his bare foot.

The moth makes the short flight across to the old man's foot and the old man's wise eyes drop to watch the creature explore his talonlike toes. He smiles.

"He didn't mean to do it. It was an accident. People see that, don't they?"

"*Sí, un accidente*. But a child died and your father was ... *melancólico*. Sad." The old man relied on his Spanish when he tired. He wanted to measure his words so he measured them in Spanish and then served them in English.

"But my father was a good man. Right?"

"Yes. Your father was a good man."

"Thank you, Manolin. Thank you for telling me about him."

---

I need a beer.

I just want to sit on the deck of my dive shop, drink a couple beers, and will these crazy last two days away.

If only it worked that way. Maybe if I click my heels together three times I'll be transported back to Kansas.

I'm tired.

I'm at the trunk road that leads up behind my house and I must refocus on my bundle in the scrub. I have a sinking feeling that my tightly bound package won't be there. I can almost see the empty ropes resting in the moonlight.

And I know what that means.

The big man in the bushes is my only tangible link to this whole mess. I need him to explain what is going on and who is involved. If he isn't still squirming under the tarp, that means I'm at square one again. Or more accurately, out of the game altogether.

As I wheel into park, a rush of panic billows up in me. I mutter to myself, "You're missing everything. You have got to get a better handle on this thing or you and Chubby will end up dead."

If he's not already.

I turn off the truck. The only sound in the night is the *click, click* of the cooling engine. I half expect to hear Rasta man struggling in the dark even though I realize it's impossible from here. He's too deep in the brush.

I swing the door open, leave it open, and carefully pick my way through the scrub and palmetto to where I left him. The moon is three-quarters, waxing, the night still and clear. Through the tangle of campeachy limbs, the small clearing looks gray as a dead porpoise. The night, the foliage, and the scrub coral rock ground absorb all the colors. A breeze whips up, shuffles the leaves, and makes me squint my eyes. A small night creature scurries unseen through the underbrush.

I see the ropes first. They are piled neatly into a small mound in the center of the tiny clearing. No man. Instinctively, I hunch over to make myself smaller. My ears ring with rushing blood; I can hear nothing else. From my crouch, I scan the area, spinning slowly. To my right, draped across a saw palmetto, is the turban towel I used as a gag. It hangs on the bush like it was laid out to dry. It is so quiet. So damn quiet. Too damn quiet. I roll up my shoulders, waiting for the reciprocal blow to the head from a very pissed-off Rasta dude. Hours pass, it seems, no blow. I relax a bit, head coming out of its shell. Still hunched over, I slide my way through the growth to my house.

———————

I cut down the hillside and down to the beach, making my way through the tangle of brush that grows down the side of the hill to The Road. I keep off worn paths in an effort to avoid all contact. I cut across The Road and follow the border of frangipani and sand until I come to the back of the shop. The beach smells like day-old fish.

A clang—a very loud clang—from inside the shop paralyzes me. It sounds like a tool hitting concrete. Someone dropped something. I move quietly to the front window and pry up one of the louvers. I detect a small amount of light coming from inside, probably from the workshop. I jump down off the porch, the sand cool on my ankles. Like a thief, I move around to the other side of the building into the shadows. I slip along the southern side and I'm met with a glow of light from the window that ventilates the workshop.

High on the wall, the window is a three-foot, horizontal slit. It can't be six inches high, well designed to offer air but no access for a would-be burglar. I want to jump and pull myself up to peek in the window, but the window is too high. No way I can reach it jumping out of the soft sand under my feet. Besides, the light just went out.

I move to the front corner of the building and await the departure of whoever is in my dive shop at twelve midnight. I hear singing, or humming, coming from inside. It's a merengue tune I know, but I can't remember the name of it. The front door swings open and Callie emerges. I collapse against the wall of the building, wondering why the hell he is still at the shop at this hour. Surprised at how quickly it comes to me, I remember that the compressor is still down and that Callie was probably working on it.

I feel like rushing out and grabbing him and asking him for his help, but when I peek around the corner, he is already gone. I move delicately to the back of the building just as Callie walks past me. I again flatten against the wall, hoping the shadows hide me, because they are all I have. Callie is only ten feet from me but he is too delighted with himself to see me. He just whistles and bobs his head as he trudges along the sand and scrub line until I lose sight of him in the shadows of the stand of coconut palms.

I hustle to the front door of the shop and smile at the padlock that dangles, unlocked, in the hasp. I pull the lock out and slide inside the shop.

Without turning on the lights, I feel my way to the workroom at the back of the store. There, I find a spare dive light hanging on the wall on its lanyard. I click it on. The swinging brightness startles me momentarily. I wonder if it is too bright. They might be watching me. I didn't come down the path from my house because I thought they might be waiting for me. It was a struggle getting through the underbrush on the steep hill, and I didn't want to ruin the effort by giving myself away too easily.

As my eyes adjust, I conclude that the light isn't too bright, and that I need the light anyhow, too bright or not. But to be safe, I stop the slow swing of the light, take a shortie wetsuit off a hanger, and hook it over one of the exposed rafters in front of the slit window above the compressor. I'm reasonably sure that no one has followed me to the shop but I can't be certain. No need to take any chances and I don't want any more surprises.

I look down at the compressor. My guess was right, that's what Callie was doing. The compressor is put back together—filters, gauges, and belts all back in place. Callie even cleaned up the outside of the green beast. It looks like a new machine. If I get through this, I've got to give that kid a raise.

I turn my attention back to what I tumbled down the hill for. I need a pair of hand-held marine radios that are stowed in the secured storage locker at the back of the workshop. I dive both hands into my pockets and this time find the mass of keys on the first try. I flip through the jumble and find the small key that unlocks the gray metal locker, reach in, and pull out two Motorola radios and the waterproof bags that hold them. I scan the small room for some-thing to carry them in and find nothing, so I stuff them into the large cargo pockets of my shorts. Finally, the shorts come in handy. Prematurely, I click off the dive light and have to make my way by feel out to the front door.

---

I watch as Allie waits in her car in the shadow of a large mango tree at the base of Mt. Soufiere where The Road cuts directly back through the grassy interior of the island to the capital. Her little Nissan is parked exactly where I told her to be, just on the outskirts of Wells Corner.

Wells Corner is a small farming town in the foothills of Mt. Soufiere. It is, literally, a town where the streets have no names. It's a small, sleepy village on the west side of the spine of Isla Tortuga, with little clapboard houses with gingerbread fretwork and bone-white fences scattered well off The Road up into the side of the mountain. The entire town of perhaps a hundred goes to bed at sundown, so it is a perfect place for Allie and I to meet unnoticed. I told her that she should be careful not to be followed and if she is, then to forget about meeting me. Just turn around and go home and I would handle it myself.

I didn't tell her what to do if *I* didn't show up. I was supposed to meet her twenty minutes ago, but I need to be sure she is alone.

My paranoia is in full bloom. I tell myself that paranoia is a good thing. That maybe I need to be suspicious so that I won't miss something that might get me killed. From now on, I will stay cau-tious and alive, because things are serious now. Whatever is going on between the conspirators is clearly falling apart. What else explains Don's attack? Random mugging? Not on Isla Tortuga. Plus, there is Cartier's mysterious appearance both nights—the sailboat fire and tonight on the beach when Don was attacked and nearly killed. It looks like Cartier's cleaning up loose ends.

I don't want to be a loose end.

That's why I need to get into his office—tonight.

But I wasn't ready to tell Allie that quite yet. Honestly, I didn't think she would believe me. I only told her that I suspect the attack on Don had something to do with me. Would she be willing to drive me into St. Christopher to check on some things? I hoped she would accept my cryptic explanation, but half expected her to say no. That half was wrong.

When I called her from my house before I went down to the shop to get the radios, she was very receptive. There was a bit of a lull on the other end of the line when I asked her to meet me in Wells Corner, but she didn't ask a single question. Just said she wanted to help in any way she could.

But for the last five minutes, she looked like she was about to bolt. She would lean forward over the dash to look both ways down The Road, then check her watch, then shake her head. I decide that I've made her wait long enough. Keeping to the shadows, I creep to her car.

She shakes her head, disgusted, as I slip into the seat beside her. "I've been sitting in this car for a half hour now, listening to the damn mossies honing in. Where the hell you been, Riley?"

"Sorry. Had to make sure you were alone. That no one followed you."

"You've been our there all the time? You bastard! Why did you leave me sitting here? I was worried." Allie's Australian accent is very evident when she's angry.

"Wow, Allie. I'm sorry. Really. I needed to be sure that you weren't followed. Really. I'm sorry. I really appreciate you helping me. I'm not sure who else I could count on to do this," I say, sincerely contrite.

She immediately calms to a simmer. "No one is stupid enough to come out at one in the morning except me. So why the hell am I here, Riley?"

That didn't take long. I throw my brain into gear trying to quickly come up with a plausible explanation for these late night covert activities. Fortunately, she didn't probe further. She says instead, "No one followed me. Jesus, the island is dead this time of night. Not a single light on in Windwardside when I came through it."

Attempting to steer the conversation to safer ground I add, "I didn't see any lights either. The south end of the island is pretty quiet this time of night."

"Well, you've got some explaining to do. And you can tell me all of it while we drive in. And I mean all of it."

I'm not getting away that easily. She fires the engine, and I watch the condensation fog from the exhaust roll south down The Road.

We drive in silence through Wells Corner. The little hamlet is as quiet as a graveyard. The overhead power lines look like a deserted spider web, draped through trees, drooping off tilting poles. We pass a powder-blue tin house with a dirt yard. It has a seven-foot rail fence that corrals three or four goats. Their heads are stuck through the fence and they watch us pass as if on swivels. We make the sharp right-angle turn and head toward St. Christopher.

Allie breaks the silence. "So what *exactly* is going on?"

I look over at her. She is concentrating on the undulating road, one hand on the steering wheel, the other on the gearshift. She leaves the car in third gear as we pull up and down the many small hills, making our way to the capital. I study her face in the electric light of the dashboard.

It is a round face. Full cheeks and a small, round chin. Eyes, green eyes made greener by the dash lights, set wide on her face, framing a long, thin nose. Allie is the kind of woman that you don't look twice at on the street, plain and unremarkable. Yet, there is a presence about her when you are in her company. You sense something. Not a sexual longing, but certainly a desire to know her. The first time I met her I felt it. Inner strength is the only thing that adequately describes it. Intensity and strength. When she looks over at me for the answer to her question, I see it again. She is focused, alert, intent.

It makes me want to spill it all to her. Like when you were a boy and your mother asked you why you were crying and you wanted to tell her all your troubles.

But I can't. Not yet.

"I wish I knew. I've stuck my nose into a hornets' nest and now they're stinging everyone in sight." Including a fifteen-year-old boy with a mother at home, crying on the edge of her son's bed, praying for his safe return.

She retorts, "Don't give me that. Tell me. Why are we going to St. Christopher in the middle of the night?"

"I'm serious, Allie. I don't think I can give you an explanation that will satisfy you. I just need you to trust me and understand that I'll tell you when I know."

There is a considerable silence, not only in time but in weight. In the fractured light I can see her thinking. Her eyes narrow then return to normal as they shift from object to object within the car. I look down at her left hand that rests on the shifter between us. She twists the shift knob, knuckles white, until it breaks free on its threads. With the pad of her middle finger, she spins it on the stick until it wobbles. Then she spins it back on tight.

"When I first met you, Phil, I wasn't attracted to you, *per se*. Not physically anyhow, although you're not unattractive. Average build, six foot, one-eighty, I'd guess. You're certainly in decent shape. Not a hard body, but reasonably toned. Long fingers not unaccustomed to work, but not gnarled, rough, and short fingered. I like that in a man. All of my past experiences were with men with hard hands. Hands more like tools than parts of a body. You're a nice mix. Not a soft man like an accountant or school principal, but not a hard man like a lumberjack or outback cowboy either. I decided right then that I would like to get to know you better. Not romantically, understand. Just that I find you very interesting. I thought you would be a nice addition to the collection of expats on the island.

"So you see, or maybe I'm not making myself very clear here, but I consider us friends. I considered us friends from day one. And in my book, a friend can tell another friend why the hell he dragged her out into the night to circumnavigate the island." Slowly, she rolls her head toward me, fixing me with her stare.

"Whew, Allie. I'm not sure what to say. I consider us friends, too, but I'm not lying to you or keeping anything from you. I'm really, really not sure what's going on here. Dead dog serious. I'm just not sure."

"OK, then. You sound sincere about that, although I'm not buying it completely. So answer the question about St. Christopher. Why now, and who are you going to see at this time of night and in so secretive a manner?"

"Hopefully nobody. I'm hoping Cartier isn't in his office."

"Cartier?" She is incredulous. "Why Cartier?"

"Because I think he's involved in Don's attack tonight."

I surprise myself, and Allie, with my candor. The comment locks the look of disbelief on her face.

I don't know why I said it. I've been trying so hard to keep it in, not to involve her. Maybe I said it because I'm tired, letting my guard down because my mind is overloaded with data that won't compute. Or maybe I'm unwittingly asking for help by looking for that ever-objective mind to help me understand how a good deed like towing a boat to safety can spiral downward so quickly.

"You think just because Cartier was at the Lime 'N Pub he is involved in Don's knifing?"

"There's more, but I have to admit, it sounds insane. That's why I need to get to his office and see if my theory is true."

"What do you expect to find? The bloody knife?"

I look at her and I can see it in her eyes. The tone of her voice tells me she is going to pull over right now—hell, she might not even stop—and throw me out if I give her my theory.

"That's where the friendship comes in. That's where the trust comes in. You have to believe me that I have a good reason for all this. I'm not crazy and I wouldn't drag you out here if it weren't for a very good reason."

Allie nods. Not a nod of affirmation. More a nod of *yes, I'm listening.*

I continue my argument, "I'm not sure what it is, but I don't trust many people. I need to be able to trust you, Allie. I need you to believe in me."

Allie shifts the car into fourth gear with emphasis. The Road is leveling out as we pass out of the foothills of Mt. Soufiere and plane down toward St. Christopher.

I know Allie knows Cartier. Everyone with connections to the outside world knows Cartier. If they want to get anything onto the island, it has to pass through his office. I also know she dislikes that situation. Over a couple of beers she once told me it felt to her like someone looking through her chest of drawers. Snooping into her private affairs. Cartier knows exactly what she orders for her resort and how much she pays for it. It isn't like there is some huge bureaucratic office with hundreds of clerks where a person's items can be lost among the masses. There simply isn't enough traffic going through the island to warrant another officer. Cartier is it and he oversees everything that comes to and goes from the island.

I also know she doesn't dislike the guy, just the situation. He is a bit odd, she thinks. Shifty is the way she described him, but not the kind of guy that would have a hand in stabbing a man. He is too passive for that. Maybe skim some money or property off the top—white-collar stuff but certainly not blue-collar rough stuff. Then she says exactly what I'm thinking. "Cartier doesn't seem like the type, Phil."

I have to agree, but the guy I clubbed in my back yard was not Tortugan, so Cartier would have had to stamp his passport if he is on the island legally. And if the *Miss Princess* did make landfall on the island, it would have to clear customs at Andrews' Bay with Cartier.

Then there was last night. Cartier acted fairly odd when the *Miss Princess* blew up. And the final coincidence that puts Cartier squarely in my bull's-eye is his presence at the resort when Don was attacked. Cartier's presence and its attendant results. I have to believe that he knows something and I hope and pray that he's kept some sort of record of it all.

"I can't argue with you, Allie. I never saw it in him either. But there are some things that lead me to believe what I believe. Again, I'm sorry to keep saying this, but you've got to trust me."

"Why the hell do I have to trust you? Why don't you just tell me what you're thinking?"

"Because, to be honest, you'd think I was stark-raving mad."

"I think that already," she says with a smile, a modest effort to relieve the tension and put me in a less reticent mood.

"Nice try," I say with as much finality as I can generate. I want the interrogation to end now.

"Did Cartier give you that nice shiner, too?"

I involuntarily reach up and pat under my eye. It is still tender and mushy. "You're a sharp girl, Allie my dear. I'll leave it at that."

She is quiet, apparently trying to put the fragments of information together in her mind. I see her mouth the word "why." She looks over at me. "What is he up to, then? Smuggling? Drugs?"

"I don't know. But it is something so important that they're not willing to take any chances of anyone finding out about their operation. They've moved so quickly. Hell, I brought the *Miss Princess* in just yesterday."

"They? The *Miss Princess*? Is that the boat that caught fire last night? The one at your dive shop?"

Again, I have said too much. It will lead to more and more questions until eventually I will have to spill it all to her. Thankfully, the lights of St. Christopher appear in the windshield. "Slow down," I say, pointing at the city lights.

The city is asleep. Only the streetlights are on and the occasional forgotten lamp in a window of a house. That's a good sign. We'll be able to get into town without anyone seeing us.

I point at the spire that rises above the rooftops. "Park next to St. Matthews. It's very dark there and it is only a few blocks away from Cartier's office." I reach into my pocket and pull out one of the radios and turn it on. The static hiss tells me it is fully charged and working. "Here, take this radio with you, but keep the volume down."

I hand the radio to her. She looks at it, feels its weight. "What the hell is this, Riley?"

"I'll click in a series of three short clicks, three times. That means I want to talk to you. Cartier's office is only a couple of blocks from the church. The radios should easily reach. Got it?"

Allie's lip curls. "What are you going to do? And what the hell am I supposed to do?"

I ignore the question, because once again, I have no answer. "When we get up to the corner, let me out. I'll hike it from here."

Allie slows the car at the intersection of San Miguel Boulevard and St. Matthews Street. I grin. What an island. Can't decide if it's Spanish or English. I reach out and lightly punch Allie's knee. I say, "Thank you. I'll signal you as soon as I can."

"Riley, stop. This is insane." She thrusts the radio at me. "I can't be a part of this. It doesn't make any sense. You are jumping to conclusions—making decisions without any information. You can't do this." When I don't take the radio back, she sets it next to me on the seat. "Let's go back to your place and figure this out. Let's stop and think about this."

I look over at her and see that her face is passionate, pleading. I know she won't help and I equally know that I won't be able to convince her.

"I'm sorry Allie, I have to do this."

With that, I slip out of the car and immediately duck between two stone houses. A dog barks once but not at me. I press myself against a wall and wait. But wait for what? Somewhere inside me I guess I hope that Allie will follow me, so I wait.

I only have to wait a few minutes before I hear Allie accelerate down the street, that bubbling exhaust sound of her Nissan bouncing off the stone walls until it is lost to me. I look down at the now impotent radio in my hand. I shove it in the large side pocket along my left thigh, like sliding a gun into its holster.

When I look up, I see the spire of St. Matthews, and I flash on Manolin and our short chase through the streets of the capital and then to my truck and the wooden marlins. I think to myself, *am I chasing ghosts again?*

# SEVENTEEN

SOPHIE HASN'T LEFT HER mother's arms since they left Grenada. Even as they were provisioning the sailboat—the boat he named after his daughter—she clung like a monkey baby to Martha. And as Tony watches her now, in the light of a thousand stars, on this beach, with their empty stomachs, with mouths of sand, the girl writhes against her mother and the bloody woman doesn't complain.

Tony shakes his head in disbelief.

He doesn't understand his little girl that never speaks and his wife that has no inner strength. Their weakness offends him and frustration and anger well up. He wishes he were rid of them. He could make it without them. He could … do anything if they weren't sitting there, huddled together like waifs from the East End. He pledges that if this scheme really works out, he'll leave them. He nods as if confirming his plan, but when Sophie looks over at him with eyes full of fear, he quickly looks away, guilty.

I work my way between homes, through vacant lots, startling pets and goats and chickens, stepping in what I hope is mud more often than I want, until I finally come to the end of Upper Bay Street. Upper Bay is the main street in town and all the official offices of the government are on it. The street typifies the architecture of the capital. Stone. Gray stone buildings that meet gray stone sidewalks that meet gray cobblestone streets just wide enough for four skinny goats. It feels eighteenth century British: dark, damp, solid, and immovable. Even the chill is present, and it is running down my back.

Sam Cartier's office sits midway down the block. Maybe it is the streetlights or maybe just the ambient light of the night, but I think I see a light on in the street level office.

I lope across the street like a Neanderthal man, bent low, arms swinging. I reach the side of the street the offices are on and hug the buildings.

I freeze. There is a figure standing in a large display window looking my direction. Then I realize it's only a mannequin in a dress shop. I move cautiously past the window and the female mannequin wearing a batik dress of green and blue.

I'm only ten yards from the front door of Cartier's office when the door opens and Sam Cartier steps out onto the sidewalk. Like a deer hoping that the hunter won't see him standing in the middle of a hay field, I stand motionless. And Cartier doesn't. He moves quickly to his car and pulls out a satchel, spins on his heels, and half jogs back through the open door, slamming it behind him.

Cartier was only thirty feet away, close enough to smell the fear pumping from me. I back up slowly, ball of foot to heel, not taking my eyes off of the door, right hand on the wall, feeling my way back, very slowly. My right hand slides off the hard, rough stone of

Cartier's office and into thin air. I discover that my hand has found a small gap that runs between Cartier's office and the dress shop with the vigilant mannequin. The gap is about four feet wide and leads directly back to the service alley behind the buildings on Upper Bay Street. I turn down the gap.

I'm at the back of the buildings now, peeking up and down the service alley. It's deserted. I slink cautiously, very quietly, to the rear of Cartier's office. I try it, but it's locked. I lean back, scanning the back wall, eyes moving up until I see only stars and wispy silver clouds. There are no windows on the back of the building. I stand at the door, hand on the doorknob, and think, *what the hell am I doing here? I'm a damn SCUBA diver, not a detective.* But there is no one else to turn to—I'm it. I can't trust the police and there are no other law enforcement agencies to turn to for assistance. No FBI or ATF agents on little Isla Tortuga. Just Phil Riley, dive shop owner. I smile sarcastically as I build the mental image of myself in a fedora and dive mask, greeting a damsel in distress in the back room of my dive shop. Frosted glass door with my name stenciled on it and all.

The rattling at the back door brings me back to the moment and sends me scurrying like a rat back into the gap. I look down the narrow passageway. It's too long to run down. Cartier might see or hear me. I stand there momentarily, thinking, flat against the damp stone wall of the dress shop.

The back door opens with a quick squeak—salt air on steel hinges—and I hear muffled voices. Cartier is not alone. The voices become clearer as they exit the back door. One is clearly Cartier. The lispy way he holds his *S*s too long. Another is my escaped prisoner. Those *T*s. The third voice I don't recognize. He has the same general tone as my attacker, but he sounds bigger. Like his chest is a bass drum. But the two are probably from the same country. Guyana, had I decided?

I drop to the ground, belly flat, arms at my side like I'm midpushup.

The voices pause at the back door. I can't see the men, but I can tell by how their voices bounce off the walls of the alley that Cartier is probably still in the doorway and the other two men are in the alley. I listen.

Cartier says, "I will get rid of the papers about the boat, Cephus. Don't worry."

Cephus replies, "That is good, mon." It's my attacker, my bundle of joy in the bushes. I grin. *Hi, Cephus, how's your head?*

Drum Chest speaks. "We be at the boat. Making ready to leave this fugging eye-land."

Cartier says, "Then we are done. This is over. No more."

"No more with *you*, mon. You are out of it," Cephus retorts.

The two men walk right past me too quickly for me to get a good look at them. They don't see me prostrate on the black cobblestones in the black walkway. They are making no haste in returning to "the boat." I wondered what boat that could be. Maybe they were anchored off the coast somewhere. No, as the realization slowly builds.

They are at Andrews' Bay. The men are too confident in their moves to anchor out of the harbor. Besides, they have Sam Cartier to cover them. Yes, they are at Andrews' Bay. They are on the boat anchored out away from the docks. The *Steel Drum*.

I hear the sound of a car starting, a small engine *barroom* sound and a bad muffler echoing through the wet cobblestone streets of St. Christopher. The Doppler sound of a car speeding away.

Cartier's door closes, those same squeaky hinges. He must have watched the men walk down the alley and only went back in when he knew they were gone. Cartier must trust them as much as I do.

I have a decision to make. Go to Cartier and find out what is going on, or go after the men and try to stop them. They probably have Chubby on board their boat, if they haven't killed him already. I didn't want to think of that possibility. I try to focus on what I can do if Chubby is alive.

So the boat makes the most sense. But there are two of them, and possibly more on board the boat. I can't risk an attack without some further information, but I will have to get that information fast. The men are only a few minutes from the harbor and can be under way in under an hour. That's why Cartier has got to tell me it all very quickly.

I opt for the blitz approach. Hit Cartier while he is unaware and maybe I can throw him off balance. Besides, time is of the essence and I can't let the *Steel Drum* get out to sea.

Mustering as much bravado as I can, I push myself up and shuffle to the back door of Cartier's office. I try the knob again. It's locked. I'm standing there, fiddling with the doorknob when it opens. I look down at my now empty hand and then look up into the face of the very surprised Sam Cartier. He has an armful of papers in one hand, the opposite knob in the other.

I react. I lower my shoulder and bowl him over, the two of us tumbling back into the office. Cartier's pile of papers explodes in a waterfall of white and manila as he slams into the file cabinets that line the back wall of the office. I spin off of Cartier and land in the middle of the room, but scramble to my feet before Cartier can regain his. I grab the smaller man and drag him into the main office, kicking the back door closed with my toe as I pass it.

As I drag Cartier by his shirtfront, he asks, stunned, "What the hell are you doing, Riley?"

I respond, adrenaline venom in my voice, "I don't have the time to fuck with you, Sam. I need to know where Chubby is!"

"Who?"

"You know who I'm talking about. My divemaster. Chubby, Christopher."

Clearly, Cartier is stunned speechless. He looks up at me with the eyes of a child just caught reaching into the cookie jar. His lack of response infuriates me. I throw him to the floor and straddle his chest. Still nothing from him. Just shock and confusion flowing from his wide eyes.

"Tell me where Chubby is!" I scream as I grip his thin neck and slam his head on the floor. Once. Then two quick bounces. "Tell me!" Once more, real hard. Too hard. His eyes glaze. I release my grip, recoiling in shock at my brutality. He goes limp, crumpling to the floor.

Oh God, I killed him.

I lean over him, ear to mouth. He is breathing. I throw my leg over him like I'm getting off a horse and sit next to him, leaning back on my arms for support. I cross my ankles, an insincere gesture of relaxation, and look down at him. He is out, as they say, like a light. Just that easy. Now what?

I look over at the scattered papers peering from around the corner by the back door. Cartier was carrying those when we surprised each other at the back door. I crawl over to them on my knees and push them together in a pile and while sitting on my heels, I tilt the papers toward the ivory light of the desk lamp. They are official documents, all pertaining to the *Steel Drum*. Manifests, passport records, other immigration forms and documents—with only two names mentioned in the papers. Cephus Greaves and Willy Avers. Cephus I know well. Barrel Chest must be Willy. I look through the entire haphazard stack. There is nothing about the *Miss Princess* or Chubby.

After seeing them, I wonder what I was expecting to find. There really isn't much information included in the stack. Just form documents telling when and where and how much in nice neat little boxes. Not much to go on, but it proves a connection, and that is the best I can hope for right now. I roll the papers into a tube and stick them in my pants. I tie Cartier up with the only cordage I can find, the telephone line, and I stuff him into the bathroom.

------------

I walk out the back door of the office into the stillness of the late night. There is a different kind of animal that awakes after midnight. It's a desperate animal hunting. It's an animal that knows no fear, knows its nature, knows why and what it must do.

Who am I kidding? I wish I had that animal in me. My face pulses, nerves firing randomly.

I turn down the dark passageway leading to Upper Bay Street. I'm frustrated at how poorly the Cartier "interrogation" went. No solid information from the papers where Chubby might be, or what Cartier and the men are involved in. Clearly that's what's going on. Cartier is working with these two guys on some sort of deal and he was heading out the back door to destroy the papers that would prove his involvement. That's what Cartier said to Cephus. "I'll take care of the papers." Well, the papers are in my pocket now.

I can't believe this is happening. How in the hell am I going to do this?

I'm planning this as I go. Consequently, I have no firm strategy on what to do next. My only hope is that Cephus and Willy are still at Andrews' Bay when I arrive. My little tumble with Cartier took very little time, only minutes, so surely they are still prepping the boat for departure.

It dawns on me that I've been doing that far too often these past few days—hoping for things to be a certain way because I have no control over the situation, how it really is. Things, events, keep coming at me and I'm fending them off as best I can. After all, I'm only a dive shop owner, not James Bond, so I'm winging this as I go and so far it's going pretty mediocre. But I'm still going, and that isn't all bad. Things are happening too fast and I don't have the luxury to stop and make a real plan. I don't have the time to deliberate my options. Actually, in my twisted logic, that's probably for the best. If I had time to think about how crazy all this is I probably wouldn't be doing any of it.

I stand at the entrance to the passageway, remaining in the shadows. I need to get to Andrews' Bay quickly. I look over at Cartier's car parked at the curb and smirk. I stroll up to it and find the passenger-side window rolled down. I stick my head in and the keys are sitting in the ignition switch. Is my luck turning for the better or worse?

# EIGHTEEN

How the hell am I going to get out to the *Steel Drum*?

During my short drive out to the bay, I come to the conclusion that Cephus and Willy have Chubby aboard, probably tucked below deck somewhere. It's the only conclusion that makes sense in this thing that doesn't make much sense.

I need a good plan that won't endanger him, or me. I have a seed of an idea but the details are still sketchy. It isn't the best idea, I have to admit. In fact it's pretty crazy, but it just might work. But there are also a lot of things that can go wrong, and I'll need some luck if I'm going to pull it off. To truly work, the plan requires two people, but I don't see Allie helping—she wouldn't help earlier—so she sure as hell isn't going to help me with this. Alan? No, his reaction on the beach the night of the fire gives me my answer. There is no way I can convince someone else to help me with so little time to waste. It looks like I'll have to make it work alone. Through the windshield, the gray water of the bay folds out in front of me.

I take a dead-end road that I know winds up to the top of the bluff overlooking the bay. From that vantage point, some two hundred feet directly above the *Steel Drum*, I can get a better look at what is happening down in the bay. After that, I pray for inspiration.

I chug up the rutted road in Cartier's underpowered sedan. When I reach the peak of the hill, I pull the car over as close as I can to the inadequate guardrail—pilings, connected by wound steel cable, that are driven into the ground that, in reality, would only slow a vehicle before it went tumbling over the edge. I clamber under the guardrail on my belly until my face emerges over the brim. Looking straight down, I can see the *Steel Drum*. Her stern is swung toward shore, her bow pointing into the evening sea breeze.

I wish I had my binoculars but they are back on the *Tortuga One*. The night strikes me as exceptionally dark despite being cloudless, the stars shining bright in the ink sky, yet the stars don't supply enough light to really make out any detail. I can't tell if anyone is on deck or if the boat is running or not. I concentrate on the pilothouse, hoping to find some movement that'll clue me in to something, anything.

From this vantage point, it is clear Cephus and Willy have planned ahead. They don't want any surprise visitors—anchoring out in the middle of the bay assures that. They are a good quarter mile out from the dock and about fifty yards from the breakwater, tight to shore under me, but looking down that sheer wall, there is no way of getting down it unless I magically turn into a mountain goat. There is no sure way to get out to them undetected.

---

Don Bennett reclines in his hospital bed, hands gripping the sheet covering his legs. The pain that he feels in his stomach doesn't compare in intensity to the frustration he feels about how badly he has bungled his job. "I'm a bodger of the highest order," he says aloud to himself, through clenched teeth.

A slice of light pierces the dark room as the door opens a crack, hesitates, and then opens fully to reveal Charles Bourgois, his face lit by the bright fluorescent lights in the hallway. Bourgois looks in at his old friend with a look of both relief and anger. It's a father's look when his son finally comes home two hours after curfew.

"Hello, Charles. So nice to see you again," Don says, forcing amiability.

"Don't give me that. What the hell happened?" Bourgois replies, moving into the room, hand sliding off the door, allowing it to swing shut behind him. He is back to business.

"Get the bad guys and bring back the boss. That's my job. It shouldn't have been so difficult. These guys are amateurs after all. Not like those barking rebels of the Revolutionary Armed Forces of Colombia who have terrorized the company's oil workers and fields for months now. *They* are organized and truly deadly. These two guys just read the paper and thought, what a wonderful way to make some quick money.

"It was my mission as head of security for British Petroleum to ensure the safe return of Tony and his family. They were supposed to be on a nice, quiet sailing holiday in the Caribbean. Trying to get away, for a time, from the sticky heat of Cupiagua, Colombia, and spend some quiet time with his wife and child. Hell, he even named the boat after his little Sophie. It has all gone so terribly wrong, Charles. A real clanger."

"I see that. But the doctors say *you'll* be fine."

"Yes. The bastard slid it in just right. Just nicked the lung."

Sensing a lengthy conversation, Bourgois pulls a chair bedside. "Tell me what happened."

———

I see it before I hear it. Even without their running lights on, I see the telltale seething of the water astern. The *Steel Drum* is powering up. The boat turns slowly, bow swinging toward the mouth of the bay.

They're moving, but I have to control my urge to rush back to Cartier's car and follow them. I need to see which way they go. I need to let them get out of the bay and see which direction they turn. I wait long minutes and now they've made the mouth of the bay and are making the wide turn around the breakwater. So south it is, boys.

———

"He surprised me. An innocent knock on the door and the next thing I know I've got a knife in my stomach and I'm bleeding all over the place. I thought it was Cartier knocking. That's why I let my guard down. I had no idea that it would be anyone else," Don explains.

"He didn't say anything, or do anything else?" Bourgois asks.

"One stick to the belly, and that was it. Not enough, my friend?"

Bourgois ignores the quip. "Cartier never showed up, huh?"

"I was a bit busy. Thank God for that little man with the pocketful of shells or I would have bled to death on that stoop."

"I've got a call in to Cartier." The chief looks at his watch, tongue working lower lip with concern. "He should be calling any moment now."

"And my attacker? Connected to all this, of course."

"You said that Riley was beaten pretty bad. I wouldn't be surprised. They seem awfully rough—aggressive, in fact. I'm not sure why they are lashing out like this.

"And before you ask, I've got the airport covered, although there isn't a plane leaving until morning. I've also got some men down at Andrews' Bay watching the *Steel Drum.*"

"They wouldn't leave without the money."

"I'm not sure what these guys are going to do next. That's why we need Cartier. They're his relatives. He might have some insight into how these fellows think."

Wincing, Don pushes himself more upright. "I have not handled this as I would have liked. I don't like to include the local authorities in my business. It has never been to my benefit to do so in Colombia, and if it weren't for our relationship, I wouldn't have this time. What I'm saying, before you get defensive, is that I'm unsure of Cartier."

Mechanically, the chief looks at his watch. "I'm beginning to wonder, myself." Bourgois shifts in his seat and pulls his radio out of its holster. "Joseph? You read me?"

A moment of static, then, "Yes, Chief. I read you."

"Where are you?"

"Just pulling up to Cartier's office."

———

Chubby Patois slips quietly into his house, barefoot, flip-flops in hand. He knows his mother will be upset. She's been so protective since his father left, not wanting to lose her boy, too. He thought of her when he was with Manolin and what she might be thinking. That her son, like her husband, would go away one day never to be seen again. He didn't want to hurt her, but he needed answers. Manolin was unable to give answers, but he was able to explain.

He hears his mother rise from her bed, the springs squeaking as they again find their shape. Her silhouette appears in the doorway, holding a handkerchief to her nose. She stops momentarily as her eyes adjust, making sure she sees what she think she sees. She breaks down and Chubby goes to her.

"I'm sorry, Momma. I'm sorry."

She hugs and rocks and cries without an ill word, grateful for her dear son's return. Chubby lets her rock him, like he's a baby, a baby as tall as her, until she is finished. Then she holds him away to be sure it truly is him, and smiles. "Are you hungry, Christopher?"

"Yes, Momma, I am."

She leads him into the dark kitchen at the rear of the house and sits him down at the small wood table. Chubby watches her move about the kitchen, from icebox to cupboard to the table and back around the circuit again.

Chubby's mind wanders. He remembers riding the bus north past Pelican Bay and Dive Tortuga and seeing Boss Riley out by *Tortuga One*, tossing in gear. He wonders what Boss Riley is doing with the boat this time of night. Probably a night dive, that's the only reason he can think of, but it's awful late for a night dive. *Guess I'll ask him in the morning—I hope he isn't too mad about today*, Chubby muses.

His attention is drawn back to the kitchen by the sound of a plate set before him.

"I'm sorry it's cold. I could heat it if you like." His mother refers to the plate of cold snapper, rice, and potatoes that sits in front of him.

"No, Momma. This is just fine." He feels something in his pocket and he slowly pulls it out, keeping his hand below the tabletop. He unfolds his hand and smiles at the tiny wooden marlin in his palm.

# NINETEEN

I TOSS THE LAST of the gear that I'll need into the *Tortuga One* and step back on the dock to survey the pile of gear behind the center console seat. I force myself to concentrate on the task and not the logic of my plan because logic doesn't matter now.

I *have* to try.

I have to try because if I don't it will be like last time and I'm tired of running—I'm so tired of hiding. I may think I'm doing this for Chubby, but I know I'm doing it for myself, too. Yes, I know that now and I guess I've always known it, from the beginning. That's why I couldn't let the *Miss Princess* go—especially after the pacifier.

Time to face the past.

Time to make things right—at least for the future since I can't change the past. Now I sound like them. Yeah, I know what the shrinks would say about my dreams of fish and lions on the plains of Africa.

For the tenth time, I run through my mental checklist: buoyancy compensator, an eighty-cubic-inch aluminum tank, mask, fins, wetsuit, regulator, dive computer and gauges, a pony bottle—a little air for Chubby—and most importantly, two lift bags. Keep it simple.

"I'm ready," I pronounce aloud, with as much confidence as I can muster, considering the weight of the hour, the lack of sleep, and the complete lack of confidence in my weak plan.

I step into the boat and hit the toggle switch to lower the outboards. They whine down, silently piercing the water. I turn the ignition and the twin Yamahas fire, cold. The noise is intense as it pinballs around the tiny bay. I look over at the two sailboats that remain in the bay. I wonder, momentarily, if the noise will wake them. It's a silly concern.

I toss off both stern and bow lines and pull in the fenders. I crank the wheel and the boat slogs away from the dock, and as I let the engines warm I step astern to put my gear in order.

Unexpectedly, I feel the boat dip slightly and I turn to see a brown pelican sitting on the bow of the boat, head turned toward me, wings held away, ready to take flight again if needed. I didn't hear it coming in over the noise of the engine—and it's a big healthy juvenile with what I would guess to be a five-foot wingspan. We watch each other for a few minutes, the boat slowly rotating in the water, the background of Pelican Bay sliding behind the big bird like a movie reel. Slowly it opens and closes its mouth, as if it's whispering something to me.

"You want to come with me, friend? I'm going fishing."

———————

Joseph steps out of his patrol car in front of Sam Cartier's office. He looks through the window into the dark office. He can make out the forms of a desk and cabinets but nothing else from his limited vantage point.

Something tells him to be cautious. Maybe it was his chief's tone of voice. Maybe it is the strange goings-on lately. He can't remember the last time there was so much commotion on the island. In fact, he has to admit, there's never been so much tumult. Certainly not in the five years he's been on the force.

He slides over to the front door, tries it. Locked. He cups his hands around his face and peers through the clean glass—nothing but the same desk and cabinets, but now much clearer. He hears a noise. It sounds like it's coming from the back room, from behind a small wall that juts out from behind Cartier's desk. He has been to Cartier's office many times and knows the storage room is behind that wall through an open doorway. His eyes drop to Cartier's desk. Something is wrong, not quite right, because usually it's immaculate. Neat stacks of papers, the two fountain pens in their holders, and a black desk phone perched on the right-hand side of the desk, always the same, without fail.

That's it. No phone. The deputy scans the area around the desk and his eyes find the phone. It's sitting under the desk, partially in view, overturned, the receiver off the cradle and somewhere in the shadows of the desk. As he puzzles over the phone, two bound feet protrude out from behind the wall. They urge the owner along, heels pulling a body like a caterpillar. Joseph watches the body inch into view. Cartier.

Joseph takes a half step back and then puts his shoulder to the door, popping it open like a dry twig snapping. He rushes to Cartier and pulls the gag out of his mouth, looks into the bleary, dilated eyes. Cartier wets the areas of his mouth covered by the gag. The name "Riley" stumbles from his mouth.

---

Martha and Sophie are alone and the woman doesn't know where Tony is. He left without a word. Just stood up and plodded down the beach in the same direction he always goes and turned into the jungle at the same spot he always turns. But he has been gone too long this time, and worry battles the thirst and hunger that come in waves now that they are in their third night on this island. She knows her daughter is starving because she herself is starving. That and her child's whimpers tell her that she must find food. But her husband has proven inept at gathering food and she has been unable to forage herself because she can't pry her little girl from her side. This incessant hugging has become like a snake constricting its prey, slowly squeezing the breath out of her. She tries again to set the child down, but is met by a grasping so strong it surprises Martha and she relaxes, letting the child cling. Where does this child get the strength?

"Soph, honey. I need to find us some food. I need for you to let go of me and walk with me as we search out some food. Can you do that for me? You must be starving, love. Aren't you starving?"

The girl relaxes, eases back from her mother and meets her stare. "Mum. Home? Home?"

"I know, love. I want to go home, too."

"Dada's mates? Boat?"

This stops Martha short, the implication of her daughter's question too incongruous to believe. "What do you mean, Soph, daddy's friends?"

The little girl slowly nods her head.

I squint out over my course and let the apparent wind whip me awake. I'm running without lights at about thirty knots down the leeward coast of the island. I pass Hell's Gate at the southern end of the island and that's where I see the outline of a boat against Cayo de Tiburon, a mostly low, flat cay that is part of the chain of small islands that make up the nation of Isla Tortuga. Even at this distance, I recognize the unmistakable superstructure of the cabin. I know it's the *Steel Drum*.

I caught up to it very quickly. I thought they would be running harder, attempting to put some distance between them and Isla Tortuga. I smile a straight smile. My luck *is* turning, perhaps—and perhaps for the better.

I move my hand to the throttles and the engines take on a slightly lower growl as I back down a bit. The water is relatively flat so it's possible that the *Steel Drum* might hear me approach, especially if they are not running full out, as it appears they are not, and their engines don't hide the approach of another boat. It's important to get in front of them undetected because surprise is the only way of stopping the boat. I judge my distance to be sufficient that they won't hear me so I punch the boat back up to thirty knots, maybe more, and point her toward Cayo de Tiburon.

Cayo de Tiburon is a totally uninhabited, small, flat island of scrub and sand. The Spaniards named it after the large promontory at the northern edge of the island that bears a striking resemblance to a dorsal fin of a shark. The huge rock is sixty or seventy feet tall and can be seen from Isla Tortuga on a clear day. I aim straight for the fin, using it as a bearing.

I rehearse the plan again in my head: Get out in front of the *Steel Drum* and cut the engines and drift, waiting for it to come to us. Then I drop in the water on SCUBA and wait for the boat to pass overhead. As it does, send up lift bags into the props to stop it. Pretty simple plan—that's full of holes.

The first problem with the plan is that I can't be sure the *Steel Drum* will pass over me. I will have to get in the water early enough so I can swim away from the boat unseen but not too early so that I can't predict with some confidence the course of the *Steel Drum*.

Then, even *if* I'm able to lay in wait along their course, how can I be sure when to send up the lift bags into the props? And, will the props even catch the bags, and will the bags be enough to stop the boat? Then, of course, if all goes well up until then, and the *Steel Drum* does stop, how will I get on board and get Chubby off the boat?

There are too many questions swimming around in my head and the answers will have to come in the trying. So I tell myself, *Tackle them one at a time*. The first problem is how to get in front of the *Steel Drum* without them seeing me.

Cayo de Tiburon is about four miles long and about a mile wide at its waist, so I figure I can reach the southern end of Tiburon on the far east side at about the same time the *Steel Drum* reaches the southern end on the west side. Maybe not at the exact time but too close for me to cut across the southern end and be far enough in front of the *Steel Drum* to set my trap. I'll have to run farther south, but that means running out of sight of the *Steel Drum*, so there is a good possibility that I will lose the boat if I get too far ahead. And because I still have no idea where they are going, they might change course suddenly and head west, or east, or back north.

So I think of landfalls where they might run but they are all too far. Even on the course they're running, there is nothing but a chain of small, sandy islands until they hit Trinidad and Tobago some three hundred miles south. Again I come back to the conclusion that I'll have to wait and see and adjust to their actions while trying to keep them in sight as much as possible.

And there is morning to contend with. I have about two more hours of solid darkness to work with. In the daylight the chances of the plan succeeding are greatly diminished. I have to be in the water before dawn breaks bright and revealing at 5:30 a.m.

I plot the chain of tiny islands that are scattered south of Cayo de Tiburon. There are many and I calculate that if I run dark down the east coast of Tiburon and keep east of the smattering of islands that follow, I can run undetected for miles. I'll point the boat so I'll run about a mile offshore on the windward side of Tiburon and from there I can pick a heading. Perfect. Step one complete. Unfortunately, it's the easiest step.

Here I am flying along the water at night chasing a boat going who knows where with who knows what on it and with no real clue on what I'm going to do when I finally catch that boat. It all seems so very odd. Like it isn't really my life—like it's a dream. But the ache in my bones and the goose bumps from the blasting wind-chill of night air tell me it's no dream.

Then concern breaks from its shackles and starts to kick around in my head, trying to escape. It's as if I'm wandering around a dark, unfamiliar room, trying to find the light switch, then suddenly, someone across the room flips the switch and the light illuminates just how totally off base I really am.

I want to convince myself that this little adventure makes absolutely no sense and there is no reason whatsoever for me to be running after this boat. It isn't my job to be the rescuer of this boy. I'm not Chubby's father.

Furthermore, I don't owe the island anything. Certainly the locals are ambivalent to *my* existence. In their eyes, I'm just another expatriate looking for paradise. They would think nothing of it if I didn't go after the boy. Chubby would be just another lost boy eaten up by the big, cruel world. More reason, they would argue, to stay shut off from the twenty-first century that threatens to bowl them over like a late summer hurricane. I know they wouldn't even think to question the authorities, and the knowledge that the police and government officials might be involved wouldn't surprise or anger them anyway.

And I know they know nothing about my past. I've told no one.

But all the arguments are unconvincing. There may be concerns, but there is no doubt about what I must do.

# TWENTY

BOURGOIS STANDS WITH HIS back to the wheel of Isla Tortuga's only police boat, a thirty-foot Tiara. Joseph and Claude, the captain of the boat, lean against the transom, ankles crossed.

"OK, Joseph, what happened at Cartier's office?" Bourgois asks.

"After I got Cartier untied and calmed down enough to tell me exactly what happened, he said that he went down to the Tortuga Beach Resort to speak with Mr. Bennett, but never got to the man's room. Cartier said he saw Willy charge out of Mr. Bennett's cottage and run down the beach toward him. Cartier said he feared he would be discovered for the "double agent" that he was, but Willy was glad to see him. Willy said that he needed Cartier to give him a ride back to town. Cartier didn't know what to do, so he did what the man said. But as they were driving back into St. Christopher, they saw Phil Riley's truck parked alongside the road by the resort. They decided to stop at Riley's house to check on Cephus. They found Cephus tied up in Riley's back yard. They untied him and

210

all three drove back to St. Christopher—straight back to Cartier's office.

"There, Cartier said, Cephus and Willy decided that things were getting too complicated around Isla Tortuga, and that they should head back to Trinidad that night, without the ransom money. They left in a hurry and Cartier was about to call you, Chief, when he heard a noise at the back door. He went to investigate, thinking it might be Cephus and Willy returning, but instead found Phil Riley standing there. Cartier said that Riley immediately pounced on him and they struggled. Cartier said that he was getting the better of Riley, but he must have somehow hit his head in the struggle and was knocked unconscious. The next thing Cartier remembered was waking up bound in telephone cable."

"Where is Cartier now?"

"I dropped him at the hospital before I came down here to meet you."

"Very good. Let's get going, gentlemen."

Bourgois watches Joseph and Claude scramble around the stern, readying the boat for departure. He twitches his head, irritated at the thought of Riley.

And he ruminates.

*It's amazing how all this got away from me so quickly. Maybe it's the erratic behavior of the kidnappers that caused all this trouble, and that is puzzling. This was supposed to be a simple exchange of money for people. After the exchange, we'd follow the two Trinidadians and arrest them. All very easy. All very straightforward. I didn't count on them getting so spooked and aggressive. Why attack Don and Riley? What did they have to fear from them? It makes no sense. Now they are fleeing and we have to run most of the night and into the morning to catch up to them. But we have no choice now. We need to get the men in custody, as they are the only ones that know where the Whites are.*

*I hope Cartier is correct and their forty-six foot beast of a boat is plodding along on one engine. That the other engine threw a rod and the men couldn't fix it. Actually, Cephus and Willy are more likely to sink than outrun us. The* Steel Drum *is barely seaworthy by all accounts.*

"Untie the lines!" he shouts, and spins around to face forward, drumming his fingers on the wheel, impatient to get on with it. He leans lightly on the captain's chair behind him and feels the holster of his forty-five-caliber Colt clunk heavily against the seat. The heel of his palm drops on the weapon and he thinks, *I've never had to use this. I hope I don't have to tonight.*

———————

"I'm a man of means, by no means, boomp, boomp, king of the road." Bill Tomey loves to sing. He knows he has a terrible voice, but sings anyway. It is the right of every man to sing, he's often proclaimed.

He sits in his palapa hut, nude, drinking an Australian Merlot that he would say has a nice finish if he were asked. He looks west, trying to guess the time. Early morning for sure. Still very dark.

A small green lizard scuttles into view just outside the door of the hut. "Riley!" Bill shouts involuntarily. He smiles at his intuition. "Always scurrying around without any idea of what you're going to do next. Patience, my friend. Let it come to you. Let life come to you. Be aware and watch and wait. Not everything needs to be gone after. Life will come to you. Now shoo." He waves the back of his hand at the lizard, but the animal just cocks its head and stares unblinking. "Just like Riley."

He takes a quick sip of wine, and settles back, lower back bending, relaxed.

It's "The Night of the Vision," as he calls it. The second night of no sleep. Forty-eight-plus hours of walking, swimming, eating, and drinking on this deserted desert island known to him only as Isla Viaje, the Journey Island. He had many visions here before, on "The Night of the Vision," and is confident that he will have one tonight. It does concern him, only slightly, that the vision hasn't come yet. Usually the vision comes much earlier in the evening, often only after one bottle of wine. Now he is on his second, and the vision still eludes him—and this wine has an alcohol content of 13.5 percent. He wonders, based on that fact, if he missed it—the vision. No. Impossible. How can someone miss a vision?

He throws his head back and yawns deeply, jaw creaking. When he reopens his eyes, he has a hard time focusing on the fronds above his head. They keep moving, or is it his head waving? He drops his heavy head onto his chest, eyes closed. Then he opens his eyes, raising his cannon ball head slowly. The horizon dances. Tomey smiles. Vision time.

———————

I slice across the surface of the water, Tiburon about a mile off starboard rail. I strain to see the next island in the set but can only make out what I think is the island; a dark mass on the horizon. Still too far away to be sure.

"I'll keep this heading for a while." I'm starting to talk to myself. "Do I have enough fuel?" I look at the gauge and decide that I have about two more hours of running time. That's just enough fuel to get me there and back—if there are no problems. Not totally convinced, I concentrate on keeping the boat as straight as possible to take the most direct route. I look back at my wake and find only small deviations caused by the occasional roller nudging the boat. It's good that the seas are calm now, but I know that when it comes time to implement the latter half of the plan, a nice chop would be nice. It will hide my exhaust bubbles, giving me a better chance to snag the *Steel Drum.*

I look at my Seamaster. 2:30 a.m. Two hours of solid darkness left. Plenty of time. I look up at the sky, rolling my head 180 degrees side to side. There is still not a cloud in the sky that I can see, which I take as another good sign. Rain would be a bad omen, even though rain should have no negative impact on the plan. Still, I prefer that it not rain, for the sake of morale. Why is my mind rambling like this?

I scoot past the southern end of Tiburon and look to starboard hoping not to see the *Steel Drum* chugging along opposite me, even though I know that it won't be there. The *Steel Drum* is moving exceedingly slow and I wonder if they are having engine trouble. That could be both good and bad. I can easily get in front of them if they are having trouble, but of course, if the *Steel Drum* breaks down, I could be sitting out in the middle of the Caribbean for a very long time waiting for a boat that never arrives.

I'm growing weary of all my doubts. There are so many questions, so many. With considerable effort, I force the thoughts out of my mind and concentrate on the water in front of me. *Tortuga One*'s draft is shallow but no need to risk it. I do, however, want to try to cut some distance traveled so I can conserve the fuel. I estimate that the island lying out there in the dark is about a mile out. I'll be on top of it in minutes. "Calm down, Riley, just calm down."

I've got the boat trimmed so that it feels like I'm floating across the water, and like a photograph developing, the shape of the next island in the set slowly comes into focus. In an effort to determine which island I'm looking at, I reconstruct my travels with Bill Tomey when Bill took me out on a tour of the great kingdom of Isla Tortuga.

The islands are pretty little jewels in the sapphire sea, but don't offer much more than visual interest. They are too small to inhabit, too small to really offer a nice anchorage for itinerant sailboats, and too small to offer any wildlife room to live—except maybe a wayward frigate bird.

Tomey loves them. He says, "The islands are the building blocks of a new chain of islands. They are the foundation of a great new Antilles. Give it a couple thousand years and we'll have a new Bahamas down here. You wait and see."

Of course, it will be a long wait, and I probably wouldn't be around to see it happen.

But then, neither will Suzy Lieman.

I try to keep the memory at bay. It's been bubbling just below the surface for a good week now. The restless nights and their resulting dreams of fish on the African plain, the headaches and the blackouts, the insane effort that I find myself in tonight have all conspired to let loose the memory that I've tried so hard to subdue. In the stupor of fatigue, and the rushing, battering wind, and the ache of guilt, it all floods back to me.

———

It was like a womb, the cab of my pickup. I sat there for a good fifteen minutes I'd guess, just looking at all those leaves glued to the windshield in overlapping geometry, bleeding colors, wet fibrous texture. I put my hand on the glass and was surprised to find it cool to the touch. I expected it to be warm, moist, like sliding a hand between the press of thighs on a cold night.

The truck was running and the heat was coming up and I unzipped my jacket and wiggled out of it, letting it slide off my arm onto the letter sitting on the bench seat next to me. I hit the wipers; slow first, little effect, then high, leaves pealing off in tenacious layers. I watched as a blood-red leaf, maple, clung to the passenger-side wiper, refusing to let loose as it rode the bucking bronco, back and forth, back and forth, back and forth.

"You win," I said, cutting the wipers. Reverse, right arm on the back of the bench, wheel around and then accidentally past drive to second, then bump the shifter back up to drive. *Home to the Crock-Pot*, I thought to myself, *for the first of many nights eating that stew. Did I remember to buy biscuits?*

I rode home, window open, amazed by the profusion of leaves. The street was slathered with them, curb to curb, fuscous skin for the pavement. I could feel the truck lose traction momentarily when I crossed a particularly thick layer on the road. And they were still falling—the leaves—almost racing to the ground like they couldn't get there fast enough.

I hung my head out of the window and had the odd sensation that I was one of them. The leaves didn't know why and where they were going. These leaves simply succumbed to the roulette of nature—the wind. The wind perforated the petiole, sending the leaf from its birthplace off to be recycled in a soggy mass grave under the wheels of cars and trucks and baby strollers. I, like the leaf, didn't know where I was going. I knew being laid off meant I wasn't going back to the plant on Monday, but after that, who knew? What mass grave would I be subjected to? The city smelled musty, like the underside of long-settled rock.

As I rolled down the bent street, I tried catching one of the thousands of leaves through the open window. Just as I caught one, thrilled with my prowess, I saw her out of the corner of my eye— flash of metallic red among the swirl.

"No!" I screamed, so loud that I know the people on the sidewalk heard me.

I punched the brakes just as the girl, Suzy Lieman, zoomed out into the intersection on her bike. The truck fishtailed slightly, and I could hear the tires sluing on the leaves like the street was made of mud. I saw her look over at me, expressionless, her face a mask. No horror, no surprise. Blank. Like I wasn't there. Like she wasn't there.

My truck slammed into her broadside, popping her off her bike like a champagne cork out of a bottle. She tumbled up onto the hood of the truck and slammed into the windshield, forehead smashing the glass directly in front of me, inches from me. Her face flattened into a forced squint through folded-up cheeks and safety glass, the glass webbing with the sickening sound of wet wood cracking. It looked, through the fractured glass, like she was trying to pucker up and kiss me.

I screamed and the truck hopped the center curb into the tree-lined boulevard. As the truck bounded the curb, she bounced away from the windshield and out onto the hood. The truck slammed into a huge oak and came to a smashing stop, throwing me into the windshield in the same spot where she struck. The impact of my face, pushing in the opposite direction, punched a jagged geometric hole in the windshield. My eyes were closed but I heard the slow dance of chunky safety glass slide down the hood, the sound like a hush. When the radiator screamed, my eyes bolted open in time to see a huge cloud of steam billow into the air and I smelled hot antifreeze.

Torn on the wind, the steam tumbled away, revealing Suzy sitting upright on the hood of the truck, her back against the tree. Through the fog of steam and pain and shock, it looked to me like she was sitting there taking a fall nap under a tree in the park, her head cocked, laid on her shoulder, legs at angles to one another.

The radiator finished and I could now hear an odd rhythmic pounding, intermittent and muted—smack of flesh on metal. Through blurry, bloody eyes, I tried to focus on Suzy's foot extended out in front of her on the hood. I could see that her foot was bare, the sock and shoe blown off on impact. Her foot convulsed spasmodically, the heel pounding out an incomprehensible tune. Then, as quickly, the foot stopped.

I remember the rest independently from the witnesses on the sidewalk, and apparent reality.

Suzy drew her arms to her sides, raised her cheek off her shoulder and looked directly into my eyes. Her eyes were an emerald green like the grass from some Irish tourism advertisement. A smile grew on her face. It read pure, original joy. I was barely holding on, breathing in fits due to my damaged windpipe. I saw Suzy push herself to a standing position, all the while gazing into my eyes, then step with no evidence of damage up to the cab of the truck. She quietly lowered herself to her knees directly in front of me. She was close, very close, looking through that malformed window in the windshield.

"Have you seen my shoe?" she asked gently.

I looked at her mouth as she spoke. She had the sweetest smile. Small white teeth set in two perfect rows in a small round mouth. *Innocence*, I thought, *pure innocence. You are so beautiful.* "I'm sor..." is all that I could manage to gurgle out.

I was blinking rapidly in an effort to stay conscious. *Hold on*, I thought. Lift your head. Do *something*. My right arm was wedged under the dashboard. I fingered thin wires. My left hand wasn't there—at least I had no sensation of it. I shifted my eyes and saw my left arm pointing at my crotch, broken mid-forearm.

I looked back to her, blinking quickly, and then bugging my eyes in an effort to stay focused. I could see small droplets of blood being flung from my eyelids onto her face, she was that close to me. Then she looked quickly to her side, nodded, her eyes returned to mine. Suzy reached through the opening, cupped my face and gently kissed my forehead.

"Thank you," she said. She went from me as if the leaves that rained around us were capturing pieces of her and taking her away.

———————

Full house at the hospital, so they put me in the maternity ward after I got out of ICU. I felt like a murderer sentenced to serve his punishment living with the family of the victim. Happy fathers and relatives, all smiles and boisterous humor, would come in to see the new mothers and wonder about the silent plaster guy sitting in the hall. Some would engage me, but I couldn't talk because of my windpipe, so some left in a huff, muttering, "prick." I couldn't argue with their assessment; I was the killer of what they cherished most.

Mercifully, I only spent a few days on the ward until they put me into a regular room. The room overlooked the rooftop of the cafeteria with all the mechanical equipment silently whirling four floors below. I never saw a bird.

The room faced east and the morning sun was my alarm clock. The nurses said they could draw the light-blocking curtains but I preferred the bare windows. I wanted to see out. Nothing left to look at inside.

I spent four stuporous weeks in the hospital, going to physical therapy, working the broken bones and atrophied muscles in a room filled with ancient men and women dressed in knee-length hospital gowns, fuzzy slippers, and polyester sweatpants. The room smelled like impeded death—urine, unknown medicines, dirty hair, sulfur gas. After those four weeks, they said all my physical wounds were basically healed. Continue to do my exercises and I'd be fine.

So I went home and cried for a week.

My brother found me huddled in the corner of my kitchen and I spent another week or two or three in the hospital trying to keep from exploding into a million pieces that would never be put back together again. A real-life Humpty Dumpty. At least I didn't have to go back to the rehab room. At least I don't think I did. I don't remember too much about that second trip, they dropped me out full and deep. What I do recall is that the hospital staff was nice and quite understanding. The told me that it wasn't my fault—that accidents happen.

Yeah. Sure. I killed a twelve-year-old girl. And she thanked me for it. Eventually I convinced them, somehow, that I wouldn't melt down again, so they sent me home. The second go-around was a little better. I only cried every other day.

I did a lot of sitting by my front picture window as I had developed a mild phobia of enclosed spaces. I liked to watch an albino squirrel that frequented the neighborhood. He was working diligently, preparing for the long winter that was showing itself more and more everyday. He raided the scat of the oak tree across the street, but preferred to bury his booty in my hosta bed at the corner of my house. He would catch me watching and with a look that suggested, "You don't mind, do you?" he would wait a few seconds and then vigorously dig, drop the acorn, then scamper back across the street. I enjoyed his company.

I took my perch one frosty morning and discovered him dead— just a smear of crimson and white. A murder of crows stood like pallbearers around the mess, their black bodies set against the frosty pewter pavement. Surprisingly, I couldn't manage a tear.

Death was everywhere. The hostas had turned black from the frost, the trees were naked, even the mums looked like they were ready to give it up. I drew the curtains and took up sitting at the kitchen table.

It seemed to me that I too was dying, slowly, surely. I had nothing in my life. No work to go back to. No desire to, but still no work to go back to. No family except my brother and his wife and kids, but they grew distant after my second return home. I was too much for them. I was the embodiment of death to them, I guess. I know I wasn't very good company. I was short with Jim when he came with groceries and a couple minutes of conversation. I don't blame him. He has a little girl of his own.

I tried to shake my thoughts of doom by reading—anything and everything in a vain effort to keep from rending myself in two. I read newspapers telling of sports heroes' adventures. I read magazines telling of foreign adventures. I read tabloids telling of mundane adventures. I read mystery novels—guys with a mission and all the tools to complete it. Of them all, those were the furthest from my life. True escapism. No tools in this shell to deal with killing a twelve-year-old girl. And she thanked me for it.

I couldn't get it out of my mind, the image of her on the truck. I told only my brother about my visions. He squinted at me and shook his head slightly. "You had a pretty good bang on the head," is all he could say.

It was more than that. More than I could comprehend. More than I wanted to understand. I'm not a guy that's prone to speaking about his emotions. Life is a personal journey, not a topic for a daytime talk show. Don't talk about what's inside. Deal with it on your own—figure it out on your own. Ultimately it is up to you to resolve your own questions.

The doctors said that my reticence was my defense mechanism against the "pain." Read: killing a twelve-year-old girl. They say that holding in the ache only makes the pain fester. They said that I needed to lance my anguish like a boil by letting it flow. That felt cheap to me, too easy. I could tell some guy that I don't know from Adam about what it's like to watch a twelve-year-old girl die before your eyes, but that won't make that image go away. It won't undo the damage that, like a rogue wave, washed over so many people. The Liemans lost a daughter and I lost my way along the path that seemed so clear and simple. How do words make that right again?

The accident was a kick in the teeth. I considered myself a pretty happy guy until...the incident—psychobabble word. Hell, the killing. I lived my life doing my job and doing the things that gave me joy. I loved life, really. I was at peace...I thought, maybe. Guilt threatened to drown me in tears, literally. I have never cried so much in my life. Even at my parents' funeral I was able to hold it together pretty well. I loved them dearly and miss them even more. But this was different. Little Suzy Lieman changed my life forever and I knew she had, and I had no idea how I was going to go on living. I wasn't suicidal, but I had killed a twelve-year-old girl and that would be forever with me and nothing would ever, ever be the same. I could never see anything as I had seen it before. I would never be the person I was before.

And with that realization, in a very twisted way, I felt reborn. It came to me slowly and I fought that thought. The guilt was still there, but ebbing. The feeling of being reborn began to win out more often than not. The skies were bluer, the air crisper. I hated myself for the thoughts and the smiles that would appear on my face as a cloud would shuttle across the sky. I was glad to be alive, but felt profoundly guilty to be living. I fought the conflicting feelings, trying to plague myself with guilt, attempting not to find joy in a morning snow. I struggled to find a balance.

It all came into focus one morning, in the darkness of pre-dawn, fighting another massive headache, when, smiling at the girl's face as she appeared to me through wet eyes, I knew without ever knowing why that I would never beat these feelings. They would be with me forever and that nothing could, or would, make them go away. It meant that no matter what I tried or did, I could never go back to my old life. The little girl on the bike had irreversibly changed my life, as I knew it. I needed to make a new one.

"Thank you," I whispered.

It was eleven weeks after the accident. I sold everything and moved to Isla Tortuga.

# TWENTY-ONE

BOURGOIS SITS IN THE pedestal chair next to Claude, who pilots the boat. Bourgois is sullen, still mulling over the mistakes he's made with the case. *Where did I make my first mistake? How did I let the circumstances get out of control, pushing me in directions I didn't want and couldn't have anticipated?*

*I was sloppy, no excuses. Too many years of crowd control at Carnival has made me complacent. Kidnapping doesn't happen on Isla Tortuga very often—in fact, never—so I treated a serious crime like all the other "crimes" on this island. I won't let it happen again.*

He tilts his eyes up to look at the radar screen above his head. Nothing. Nothing on the screen except the green-light sweep of the radar as it searches out in front of them. "What is the radar set for?" he asks his skipper.

Without looking, Claude answers, "Five kilometers."

"Clear night like this, we should pick them up pretty nice, I'd suspect."

With a single bob, Claude agrees. Bourgois falls back in his seat, shaking his head, ruminating about Cartier.

*Cartier's handled the situation impressively. I never thought of Sam Cartier as a man that would be up to something like this. Too skittish; too much the self-conscious bureaucrat. Too used to pushing papers and looking through codes and regulations to make sure everything was by the book. Sam is the kind of man that runs from these situations, not the kind that offers his assistance.*

"Joseph." Bourgois flicks his fingers, signaling Joseph to him. "What did you find at Riley's house?"

"He wasn't home, Chief. His truck was parked behind the cottage, but he wasn't about. I noticed that his boat wasn't tied off to pier either."

"Thank you, Joseph."

*I wonder how much Riley knows?*

---

With Sophie in tow, Martha trudges up the beach, following her husband's footprints in the sand. She needs to know if her daughter's assertions are correct. Does Tony know the men that put them ashore on this godforsaken island?

Tony's path is like a cow path, worn obvious by little variation in route. She's been following the path for a good twenty minutes now. She never realized that Tony went so far away when he wandered off.

Ahead she can see that there is an obvious angle in the path and she quickens her pace, little Sophie silently struggling to keep up. Martha stops at the elbow in the path and discovers that it veers off into the jungle, and again, with no variation in course. For the first time since watching her husband take this route for days, Martha finds it curious that he never varied his path. With her eyes, she follows the gully in the sand up to the edge of the jungle until it disappears into the play of shadows and tangled underbrush. Now she is frightened. "Tony?"

No answer, no sound except the brush of stiff tropical leaves against one another. The opening in the jungle is distinct but not large, and she is hesitant to take her daughter into the jungle without knowing what might be in the shadows. She looks down at little Sophie and finds her daughter staring wide-eyed at the opening, her small hand waving in the air as she reaches for her mother's leg. She finds the leg and pulls herself in tight, all the while staring at the slash of an opening in the jungle.

Martha scoops up her daughter and moves up the incline to the edge of the vegetation line. She cranes her head around, peering through the darkness, eager to see Tony sitting just on the other side, but all she sees is more plants and trees she doesn't recognize. But she can tell that the path does widen, so she pushes on, taking timid steps from toe to heel, creeping like some cat burglar out of a cartoon. Little Sophie is stone quiet and locked onto Martha's right hip, sitting firmly on her mother's forearm, head buried into the sweaty part of her mother's shoulder blade.

The smell of decaying vegetation hits Martha full on and she stops and notices that she is breathing through her mouth in deep, gulping breaths. The carbon dioxide and methane create a warm odor distinct from the cool, salty sea air just feet behind her. She knows she is in another world and has only walked five feet. But her eyes are adjusting and she can see a small pile of something off to the right around a switchback in the path, so she hitches Sophie higher on her hip and resumes her cat burglar walk. At the curve in the path she stops, puzzled. In front of her sits a 70-quart cooler, its lid flung open, inviting Martha to come and have a look. So she does, her bewilderment slowly giving way to anger as she realizes what the cooler means. She looks inside the cavernous cooler and finds empty water bottles and the remnants of food but nothing intact. It has all been eaten. Consumed by her husband. Her anger is now rage and with her free hand she slams the cooler lid down. The woofed explosion of sound doesn't make it far in the thick air of the interior of the cay.

Now that the lid is closed, Martha can see a large flashlight lying on the ground behind the cooler. She bends to pick it up and hefts it in her hand, feeling its weight. It's huge. Like something you'd find attached to a boat or airplane. She clicks it on and the explosion of light is almost material in nature, pushing her back a step in surprise. She pans the jungle with the light but even a light this bright can't penetrate past the overlapping trees and gap-filling undergrowth. She switches off the light and it clicks loudly as it cools.

But she turned the light off one-quarter sweep too soon. If she had panned right another few degrees she would have caught her husband standing in the shadows, watching her. She would have caught him taking a final sip from a water bottle and clicking on the marine radio in his hand.

---

The memory of the accident muddles me with emotion. I fight these emotions like I fought them in all those worthless sessions with the head doctors. The white coats didn't know what I felt. They didn't know how I should react. They only know what *most* people *should* do—not what everyone *will* do. Some things you can't talk away. Some things you find a way to live with—or not.

This rationalization has always calmed me and it does so tonight. I'm able to reconnect with the task at hand, especially since I recognize the island to my right.

It is Cayo Pardo.

I flush with adrenaline knowing that Bill is on the island. I throw my hands up in prayerful thanks and slam the throttles back to neutral, the boat bow plowing as gravity and friction conspire against momentum and force the boat to a sideslipping stop. When she settles, I bump up the throttles and point her toward shore, hoping to pick up Bill's boat or hut or tent or something that tells me he is indeed on the island.

I have to concentrate on the water in front of me because I see soft breakers roll over scattered coral mounds. My eye follows the foam from one of those small waves as it slides its way toward shore—a sheer, rocky, sandless shore. And these telltale signs indicate what I should have realized before now—that I'm on the windward side of the island and Bill won't be on this side of the island, if in fact he is on the island at all. He will be on the other side—the leeward side, the protected side—the side that the *Steel Drum* is steaming down.

Frustrated, I whip the wheel to port and to deeper water. "Now what, genius?" I'm talking to myself again.

———————

Bill Tomey waits patiently now for his vision to come. Other visions started in this manner. The dancing horizon is a good sign, and a likely place for the vision to appear. So he stares at it. Concentration, Tomey believes, brings better visions. He knows men that subscribe to letting themselves go into a state of total relaxation. That's bunk. Meditation only puts a guy to sleep. Sure, dreams are cool, but they are not *visions*, and that is what he is after. Granted, he drinks a bit to relax his inhibitions on his vision quests, but he never gets completely drunk. He just wants to open the door a crack, so to speak, to give easier access for the vision.

And come it does.

Bill squints, boring through the night air, staring at what looks like a boat floating just above the water. He recognizes the shape but can't place it. He searches his foggy mind for the answer that floats just out of reach, like the boat floating before his eyes. Try as he might, he can't come up with it. He has never seen such an odd-looking boat, homemade-looking, almost. Running at a very odd time of night. Nobody would put out this early in the morning. These big cruisers rarely do late-night crossings. He watches the boat float away, heading south, until it's just a dark shadow in the dark night, fading around the bend in the island. Then it's gone.

A floating boat, his vision. Not exactly the vision he is hoping for, but certainly a sign of something. What does it mean? He ponders the question a moment and then exclaims, "What a shitty vision."

———————

I'm picking my way down the windward coast of Cayo Pardo looking for some little hunk of beach I can nose the boat into. If I can find a safe landing spot, I know Pardo is no more than a half-mile wide and I can crash through the growth, and with any luck, I'll stumble across Bill right away when I reach the leeward side. I can't take a chance of running *Tortuga One* around the island—the *Steel Drum* is running too close to shore. I'm still convinced that surprise is my best weapon and I'm unwilling to risk giving it away so quickly or so easily.

But I'm nearly to the end of the island and still no beach that I'm comfortable with, so I whip around and head back north, with a smidge more pressure on the throttles. I need to get off this boat and find Bill. I tell myself that a perfect beach isn't necessary but I'm hesitant to just slam the boat ashore. I still need her for the second half of the plan.

The island is eerily quiet tonight. Maybe it's the calm air and gentle, almost nonexistent surf, but the place feels otherworldly. I don't belong here, it tells me. I'm not of this place and simply don't belong. The air feels thick and looks translucent tonight, here on this island; I can feel it in my chest, and the shoreline waves in and out of focus as if in a fog. I'm having a hard time catching my breath. If feels like I have a plastic bag over my head with the air inside getting moist and stale and hot. It's panic setting in and I know the feeling well and I know what to do about it.

I hit the toggle switch on the side of the throttles and hear the engines whine up, the cavitations around the props popping and gurgling like a drowning man. I point my boat toward shore and pick a spot that looks mostly free of coral and rock, and with a small burst of acceleration, nudge the boat up onto a spot of beach that is remarkably sandy.

I turn the engines off, quiet, leave the keys in the ignition, and hop off the side into knee-deep water. I can breath again.

———————

Bill Tomey trudges nude through the soft sand, wine glass in hand, down to the water's edge. He wonders if from the water's edge he can see around the point and perhaps get a second look at his very disappointing vision. "A boat in the night just isn't going to cut it," he says aloud.

He stands on a small outcropping of sharp coral looking south. He can't see the boat anymore, but that doesn't surprise him. No wonder the thing is out of sight, the damn thing was running without its lights. Odd. Dangerous, too. But, he reconsiders, it *could be* a good vision. A black ship in the black night. Pretty heavy symbolism.

But a vision of a boat is totally out of his realm of experience, as far as visions go. Typically his visions are ethereal—odd light patterns and things like that. He hasn't seen anything as concrete as a ship before. Well hell, one can't decide what his visions are going to be. Just take them and use them. A hush of wind sends a chill through a sensitive spot and he brings his knees together reflexively. A boat. Huh.

He turns gingerly on the sharp coral, stepping lightly, and is frozen by the sheer whiteness of it, like a high-beam headlight from a massive truck shining directly into his eyes. He squints, but finds he doesn't have to and relaxes his eyes. He concentrates on the light. It moves back and forth, up and down, panning his face and body. It's moving toward him, slowly, bouncing along, getting brighter, getting bigger. He can make out a figure in front of the light, maybe. He isn't sure. The light is too powerful to cast the person in silhouette, but there is an odd-shaped darkness in front of the light. A human form, it seems. A little girl? Is it a little girl? Yes, a little girl with white golden hair. Walking directly toward him with this white sun of a light glowing behind her.

His heart pounds. He begins to pant. His vision. "This is more like it," he breathes through short breaths.

"Uh, hello there," the light says, in a proper British lilt.

Tomey cocks his head. No vision has ever talked to him before. Much, much better than a floating boat. "Hello," he answers tentatively.

"Yes. Hello. We are in need of some assistance. Do you think we could trouble you?"

The light stops bouncing, points down, the white sand reflecting the light, but only enough to illuminate a woman and the small girl she holds in her arms—a small child with pale white hair.

"My daughter could use some food and water, and if you have a radio ..."

The woman's words trail off in Bill's ears. All he can think about is, *where did she go, the little girl before the light?*

# TWENTY-TWO

I RUN NORTH ALONG the rocky windward side of Cayo Pardo, taking the long way around to the other side of the cay, consciously avoiding the inevitable struggle of thrashing through the underbrush. Logically, my brain tells me I should push through right here and now because Bill could be just opposite me, but I've been running on emotion for so long I'm not sure I trust my brain anymore. So I don't stop and I don't run into the jungle; I keep hopping and scrambling along, making good time, I convince myself. *So there, Mr. Brain, I don't really need to make that left turn.*

I can hear crabs scrambling out of my way but the moon is behind the shore-hugging tree line. I can't see the crabs, but I sure seem to be able to find the cracks they scramble in. I'm forced to slow down so I don't stick a foot full into one of those cracks and break an ankle or leg. The effort has me sweat soaked and I've just begun. My Tevas aren't designed with a great deal of lateral stability, so the moist soles of my feet keep jamming out between the interwoven straps and for some damn reason I think of that Jimmy

Buffett song where he sings about a blown-out flip-flop—and perhaps he's right, it is my own damn fault. "Boy, a margarita sounds good right about now." A little confidence-boosting humor never hurts.

Off to my left, I see that the rocky shoreline gives way to a narrow stretch of protected sand—sand that must have been storm-tossed over the rocks. I bound down off the rocks and find myself sprinting full out along the sand, my legs and arms pumping as I take advantage of the comparatively firm, flat surface.

But after a quarter mile or so, the little beach ends at a six-foot wall of craggy, moonscape-looking coral. The wall is sharp as knives and so sheer that it makes me do what I've been avoiding since touching foot on the cay—turn inland.

I stop at the wall to both catch my breath and get my bearings. I look back south down the shoreline and it looks like I've been running downhill for some time because I find myself in a sloping depression and I can't see but seventy-five yards back down the beach. I can't see my boat, and I can't see the ocean, but I can hear water sloshing into the cracks and crevices behind me. I turn my attention to the jungle in front of me.

Yes, I'm definitely in a depression, or more accurately a funnel, because the tree line is about chest level and the purslane- and strumpfia-covered rock beach slopes down to my feet. But the good news is that the night sky is visible between the trunks of the scattering of trees. I convince myself that I must be at a narrow part of the island and that I'm seeing the sky on the other side of the cay—otherwise the trees would eventually overlap enough to block my view. Buoyed by this detail, I lope up the incline and into the scrub and trees, pushing my way toward the other side.

*Should I ask this man to clothe himself?* Martha has a difficult time taking her eyes off this man's bare arse even though it is hardly a beautiful arse. Not to say that he isn't in decent shape for his age, whatever that might be or mean. But his arse is an arse of an old man—pocked, wrinkly, and as white as the sand they march on.

He walks with such confidence. And he is so tall that it is difficult to keep up with him, especially with a small child on her hip. But he said he would help and instinctively she believes him. A man naked to the world is in no position to be deceitful.

They are heading north up the beach past the rock shelf where she found him standing like some weathered sculpture, wine glass held delicately. She can see their destination is a small hut set up near the tree line in a tucked-in little bay. There is a small, odd-looking boat pulled up on the beach and she is both relieved and concerned; it's possibly a way off the island, but it's also a very small boat and she was nervous on the *Miss Princess*—a modern sailboat. But she will do what is needed to help her daughter.

The big man ducks into the hut and reemerges with an uncorked bottle of wine in one hand and a half-empty bottle of water in the other. "Water or wine? And I can't turn either into the other."

It's taking me longer to punch through than I want. The tangle of vines and the crazy assortment of plants and bushes and trees makes a knee-high maze so thick that it feels like I'm wading through clutching arms sprung up from the ground. I can still see the night sky in front of me and if I could take flight I'd be on the beach by now. Frus-

236

trated, I stop in an attempt to regain some composure and perhaps come up with a better plan for getting through this mess around my ankles. I notice the pungent rot of vegetation rising from my feet and I breathe deeply through my mouth to minimize the smell.

That's when I hear it.

It's a boat and its big diesel engines rev up like it's jockeying in the water, trying to keep a position or set an anchor. The sound is coming from off to my left and not that far, so I push on in that direction, legs swinging like I'm a lifeguard running through the surf.

Unexpectedly, I come to a clearing in the undergrowth and I immediately recognize it as man-made—the machete lying next to the cooler is my first clue. This doesn't look like a Bill Tomey camp to me and the confusion throws my brain into reverse. I look back at my track as if I've passed a road sign that will explain this big cooler, empty water jugs, and a machete—but no ex-hippie.

Maybe I should ask the shocked-looking guy standing in front of me.

"Hello. My name is Phil Riley."

My formal introduction doesn't erase the shocked look—in fact it appears like it's growing into panic. "What are you doing here?"

It's a classic opening so I take it. "I was going to ask you the same question." Even my idiot grin doesn't ease his anxiety.

"No, seriously, who are you and what are you doing here on this island?"

With this second exchange I realize he's British and that triggers concern in my brain although it's a jellylike kind of concern offering no firm ground to stand on. In a combination of frustration and unease I respond, "Hey pal, I was looking for a friend and this cay is uninhabited, so my question to *you* is what the hell are *you* doing here?"

We study one another like big cats sizing up the competition and as quickly as that, he turns and bolts back down a path that leads out of the clearing. Triggered like some predator's attack response, I instinctively take chase.

When I hit the beach, I see he is already into the shallows and wading out toward a boat—the boat I heard just minutes before. He's up to his waist and the boat is still a good thirty yards out in the water, engines idling, two men on the bow working a crude, island-made anchor that looks more like a huge fishing hook than an anchor.

My head drops to the side with the realization.

It's the *Steel Drum*.

*Christ, Riley. You ran right into their arms.*

The Brit is yelling something toward the boat but I can't make it out—but Cephus and Willy drop the hook overboard and move quickly astern, heads craning, looking for the origin of the voice. Apparently Cephus has the better eyes because he sees the man in the water, now doing the front crawl out to the boat.

I stand on the beach watching all of this, not knowing what to do, but when I hear the pistol crack and Willy waving something in my direction, I know I better get moving. I didn't hear the first round hit, but the second one buries itself in the sand behind me, so I spin and duck back into the shadows behind a triangle of coconut palms.

It's clear Willy can't see me because he's lowered the pistol and is yelling ferociously at Cephus who stands there like a rock, taking the abuse. The Brit is now at the stern of the boat and I watch

Cephus and Willy watch him clamber up on the rickety swim platform. The Brit hangs on to the transom with his left hand and with his right gestures wildly in my direction. The argument seems to be going his way. Cephus nods approval and Willy writhes with every word, apparently not wanting to agree but forced to by the situation. The two men leave the Brit and move toward the pilothouse, and I turn my attention back to the man on the swim platform. It's clear that he's scanning the jungle trying to see me but when he can't, he slams his fist on the transom and I read his lips—*shit*.

Cephus and Willy are up on the roof and are hurriedly untying a wooden red-hulled skiff and I immediately recognize it from the beach the night the *Miss Princess* burned. *So that's where it went*, I think to myself.

Without a davit or any other mechanical assistance, they unceremoniously slide the skiff off the roof. It makes the long fall into the water and attempts to flee as the bow hits just right to send it skidding away from the *Steel Drum*. But it jerks around sharply and I see that a long painter attached to the bow ends in Cephus's big paw.

Willy has already clambered down from the pilothouse carrying two well-used oars and I see that Cephus is close behind, towing the skiff by its painter like a little red wagon. It's clear they mean to come ashore.

———————

"My name is Bill."

"Martha, and this is Sophie."

Bill Tomey nods like this information is confirmation of an already-held belief. "What brings you two to this out-of-the-way cay?"

Martha doesn't know how to answer. Her discovery in the clearing turns her story on its head. "I think we've been pirated."

Bill picks up on her uncertainty. "You think? You either have or haven't—been pirated, that is. Kinda like being pregnant, ya know?"

"I'm not sure how to explain this to you, Bill."

"Well, the beginning is always a good place to start."

"Yes. Yes of course. We were on a sailing holiday ..."

Bill interrupts. "We? You and your daughter—Sophie—here?"

"No, no, no. My husband just bought a sailboat and he thought it would be great fun for all of us to take a holiday and sail up to St. Vincent. But we weren't far out of Grenada when we came across this old boat and two men that needed help."

"The pirates."

"Yes."

"OK, so where is this husband of yours?"

Martha blanches at the rapid-fire questions. "I'm not sure. That's why I say I *think* I've been pirated."

"We've come full circle haven't we, Martha?"

"If you'll simply let me explain."

"I think I'll need another glass of wine for this. One minute, please."

"And if you don't mind, could you please put on some trousers?"

———

I know I have to move, so I do. No destination, no plan—I'm just moving north as quickly as I can, hoping that something comes to me, and in the meantime I'm putting distance between a bullet and my back. I'm hugging the tree line and leaving a very obvious trail for them to follow, but at this point I'm sure distance is more important than stealth.

It occurs to me that heading back to my boat is the obvious solution—and the healthiest—but that leaves Chubby back on the *Steel Drum* and wasn't that why I came out here? It then occurs to me that the boat is deserted and if I can somehow loop back behind them I can get on the boat and get Chub off without being caught. That's the new plan, now that my original surprise plan is definitely out. I duck into the jungle and quietly work my way deeper into the bush.

Something on the wind makes me stop short. A voice. A voice I recognize. Bill's voice? I spin around and through the trees, in flashes between the trunks of coconut palms, I spot the big guy striding down the beach heading south. He is walking like he always walks, with purpose, and closely behind him is a woman and child, the woman struggling to keep up. I'm speechless but I can feel my lips mouthing, *Bill?*

They are past my point of entry and I'm still standing there dumbstruck, watching their backs disappear up the beach. Finally I'm able to move and when I hit the beach I shout, perhaps a little too loud, "Bill!"

The small troupe stops instantly and spins to my voice. The woman shuttles crablike toward the brush but with a huge grin and a waggle of the head, Bill strides back toward me. He is barechested, dressed only in khakis rolled to mid-shin. With his wild hair and unshaven face, he looks like some poor shipwrecked soul. "Some freaking vision quest this has been. I thought this cay was deserted."

He's up to me now and grasps my shoulders. He shakes me as if to see if I'm real. "What the hell are you doing here? You get pirated, too?"

"What?"

Bill spins, looking for the woman. I watch her emerge from the shadows, slowly, like a phantom in the silver light. My eyes drop to the child on the woman's hip and I find that I'm surprised by her presence. I was so intent on finding Bill that the child's presence hadn't fully registered earlier when I first saw her. The girl looks at me with wide, dark eyes. She looks at me like she knows me. Her gaze unnerves me and I feel myself retreating, leaning back and then taking a step back.

"Riley, this is Martha and Sophie. We might have a problem here and I'm really glad you decided to show up when you did. I could really use your help."

I'm half listening to Bill, but mostly I lock eyes with the child. I feel compelled to look at her feet and I see one is bare. *Where is your shoe, Suzy?*

"Riley? You still with me there, buddy?" It's Bill, snapping his fingers.

I look up into Bill's smiling face and my own face feels slack and numb as if I've been shot full of Novocain.

"What the hell is with you, man? Come on. Pull yourself together. We need to get down the beach and check on Martha's husband. I think he might be hurt."

"Have you seen my husband?"

I turn to her and she is very close now. I can't look at the girl, but I feel her eyes on me. The woman's voice trips something in my mind. Her British accent turns my lethargic brain back on.

"I think so." And to Bill I say, "I don't think he's hurt."

Bill lunges for me and a microsecond later I hear it.

The gunshot.

Bill grunts and drops against me, eyes pleading, panicked, then quickly calming, resolved. I look over his shoulder and there they stand, maybe thirty yards down the beach—Cephus, Willy, and the gun-toting Brit.

I ease Bill to the sand and notice that he is hit high in the scapula just below the shoulder joint. The wound is a small black hole streaming blood down the contours of his back.

My friend looks up into my face and says, "Pirates, I presume."

# TWENTY-THREE

BILL IS SLUMPED TO the ground, lying on his side. I kneel, holding his upper body off the sand. He breathes deep and full, but not labored. The bullet missed everything vital, it seems, but man is the blood pumping out of that ragged little hole. His eyes are clear and focused.

"Riley, I need to get to the radio and call for help." Bill's voice is so calm and controlled that I stare at him in disbelief. The man just got shot and he's acting like he twisted his ankle.

"Riley. My boy. I need you to pull it together, amigo. I need you to distract them. Pull them away from me so I can get back to camp and radio. Are you following me, buddy?"

I'm coming around to what he's saying, and I nod with conviction.

"Good. Now lay me down like I'm dead."

"Get away from him." It's the Brit. The man that shot my friend who lies bleeding at my feet. He alone walks toward us—Cephus and Willy hang back and spread out, closing off the beach to the south.

"Tony! What is going on?"

"Shut up, Mart." And to me he says, "I said step away from him."

I look over at the woman and the little girl. Sophie is still focused on me, her eyes without fear. They have the look that I see in Bill's eyes—resolve. I turn my attention back to the man with the gun.

"So it's Tony, then? You never gave me your name back in the clearing. Kinda rude, I'd say, just running off like that." I try to come off cocky as I walk toward him but at an angle toward Martha and Sophie, too. I have to draw attention away from Bill.

"Stop. Stop right there. Don't come any closer. I'll shoot." He raises the gun at me.

I don't stop—don't even slow my pace—but I do fall off a bit more, heading directly toward Martha and Sophie. Martha's eyes bounce from me to Tony, not really knowing what to do and looking more confused with every passing second. But I feel electric because it's happening right now. One way or the other, I'm committed and it will or won't work out. But at least I don't have to think anymore.

"Bloody hell! I said stop!"

I'm next to Martha and Sophie now and I fight the urge to look back at Bill to see if he made it to the water. I force myself to turn to Tony and when I do, I'm surprised at how close he is. He can't be more than ten feet from us. I look past him and watch Cephus and Willy shuffle around like anxious teenagers. I'm encouraged that they are still holding back. "What do you want, Tony?"

That makes the pistol drop to his side. He looks at Martha and then at little Sophie, who now has her head buried into her mother's armpit.

"It was such a simple plan. Little backwater island—no problems, right? But some damn dive shop owner has to stick his bloody nose into it."

"How do you know who I am?"

"Those two imbeciles." He waves the gun back toward Cephus and Willy.

I look back at Cephus and we lock eyes. He stops pacing and even at this distance I can sense his rage. I bet he'd like to get another shot at me. *How's that head of yours, Cephus?* "Well I'm sorry to mess up your little plan, but you kidnapped a friend of mine."

"You mean him?"

We both turn toward Bill and I can't contain a smile but when I look back at Tony, he is anything but smiling. He can't seem to figure out how the big guy he just shot dead crawled into the ocean. He gapes at the obvious track, his eyes following the ragged trail until it meets the lapping surf then disappears. "What the ... ?"

It's all I need, that moment of confusion. I lunge for the pistol in Tony's hand and succeed in grabbing his forearm just above the wrist. I've got his arm with both hands but the distance is farther than I expected and I finish by rolling and spinning on my butt, legs swinging at Tony's knees. Somehow my left calf catches the back of his left knee and he crumbles down, felled like a tree. I slam his hand against the soft sand and amazingly the gun pops out. I look up at Martha and Sophie and shout, "Run! Go!" I throw my chin in the direction I want them to run—north toward Bill's camp. It doesn't take her long to understand, the obvious fear running through her making her cat-quick. I watch her feet throw up small sand explosions as she sprints north, little Sophie bouncing on her hip and looking back at me. I think I glimpse a smile.

But now Tony is fully aware of what's going on and is tugging his arm trying to free himself from my grasp. The third tug does the trick and he rolls away from me with a grunt.

The loss of resistance sends me tumbling backwards flat on my back. I tilt my head back and I see Cephus and Willy running upside down. I roll toward the sea. After a couple rolls I find firmer sand and in one movement roll up onto my feet just in time to be hit square in the temple by some unseen fist. The blow staggers me and now I'm ankle deep in the water and Cephus is coming after me. He is so big he blocks out the night sky. All I can see is his bloody white T-shirt, his loosely clenched fists held like a boxer, and those wide yellow eyes that read *payback*. Willy steps behind him, curious but unconcerned. Tony is on his knees sweeping the sand looking for the pistol.

Somebody once said, "Discretion is the better part of valor." So I run.

But I run south, away from Bill and away from Martha and Sophie. I need to give Bill time to get back to his shack and radio for help. I only need to give him time and I only need to stay alive.

My temple is throbbing as I sprint down the firm packed sand near the water, increasing the distance between the three men and the gun. I briefly think that I can make it out to the *Steel Drum* and get Chubby off, too, but that fantasy evaporates when I step on a rounded hunk of coral buried just below the sand and I take a running tumble, arms whirling in that classically vain attempt to keep upright. I at least have enough sense to roll into the fall and my right shoulder takes the initial jolt, but my spastic flailing has turned me

247

toward the water and I come splashing down on my ass—hard. So hard that I whip my neck and realize that in comparison, the throbbing temple wasn't so bad.

I take this unexpected break in my escape to check the boys' advancement. They are closer than I want them to be. Surprisingly, big Cephus leads the small train with Willy and then Tony following. They are too far away for me to see if Tony found the gun, but I'm not waiting to see. I stumble to my feet and struggle across the sand, directly for the scrub.

———————

"Mayday, mayday, mayday. This is Bill Tomey. I am on Cayo Pardo, thirty miles south-southeast of Isla Tortuga. I am on the northwest point of the cay. I have a gunshot wound and I need both police and medical assistance."

No response. *Shit!*

"Mayday, mayday, mayday. This is Bill Tomey. I am on Cayo Pardo, thirty miles south-southeast of Isla Tortuga. I am on the northwest point of the cay. I have a gunshot wound and I need help! Over!"

This time they respond. "Bill. This is Chief Bourgois. We read you but you are breaking up. Repeat your message. Over."

"Chief! Damn is it good to hear your voice! Some asshole shot me! Can you believe it?"

"Bill. I need you to calm down and tell me exactly where you are. Was it Cayo Pardo? Over."

"Yeah. Cayo Pardo. Northeast point. Some British dude shot me and he's got a couple island boys with him. I hope you're not alone. And by the way, how are you reading me from Isla Tortuga? You shouldn't be able to pick me up from that distance. Over."

"That's because we are only five miles from your location. Now tell me about these 'island boys.'"

---

My instinct is to run deep into the interior of the cay and hide until the sun comes up. But I don't. I'm the rabbit. I know I need to make sure they still follow me and don't double back and try to find Bill, Martha, and Sophie. So I use the relative cover of the tree line and move as quickly as I can south, running at times, stopping occasionally to check on Cephus, Willy, and that asshole Tony.

After only a few minutes, it becomes clear that they really aren't that interested in catching me as they only occasionally look my way for apparently the same reason I keep eye contact with them—they want to know where I am, too. But they stay down by the water line and continue jogging down the beach. Both of our paces have slowed considerably since we've reached this non-negotiated rolling DMZ.

Then the reason for their nonchalance becomes obvious to me when I see the red skiff off to my left. I'm not the only one trying to escape. I've got no offense at this point—all I can do is stand in the shadows and watch Cephus and Willy float the skiff off the sand as Tony stands guard. Tony found the gun. He holds it limply at his side. Cephus and Willy stand knee deep in the ocean and hold the skiff steady as Tony tumbles in over the transom, quickly scrambling into a kneeling position, gun raised like a youngster playing cowboy. Cephus steps into the little boat and nearly capsizes her but Willy lays his body on the starboard gunwale and keeps her upright. Willy shakes his head and berates the big man.

I'm left standing on the beach, looking out at the *Steel Drum*, and panic surges up in successive waves. Chubby is still out on that boat and three men who aren't above shooting to kill are rowing out to him. I realize I've just sentenced the boy to death and there isn't a damn thing I can do about it. I'm frozen with fear and I can't seem to get my eyes to blink. I just stand there, wooden as the tree I lean against, hands crossed on my chest, trying to keep my heart from exploding through.

All I can think to do is watch them row out to the *Steel Drum* as I say a silent prayer that I don't hear a gunshot when they board. It seems like hours, the waiting like standing graveside waiting for that first shovel of dirt. I step out of the shadows as the three clamber aboard and I know they can see me against the white sand. Cephus and Tony stay at the transom and look on expressionless while Willy heads into the pilothouse and fires up the engines. Without letting the engines warm, he throws the boat into forward and the *Steel Drum* lurches forward, but the bow pulls down like a horse reined in. They forgot the anchor. Then the engines idle back to neutral as Cephus and Willy scuttle forward to haul it aboard.

Tony remains at the transom looking across the water at me. I put my middle and index fingers to my eyes and then point at him. It's an underwater signal divemasters use with their clients to signal that they want the diver to look at what they are looking at. I intend it to mean that I've seen him and I won't forget him. I feel a little silly after doing it because it feels awfully melodramatic, but I want to send a message: *I've seen you and if you harm Chubby I will hunt you down and finish you.*

Tony's only response to my signal is to lower his head and it remains that way as the *Steel Drum*, now free from the bottom, makes its way out to sea.

I turn and plow headlong into the jungle repeating my plea. *Hang in there, buddy. I'm coming.*

———————

"Man, what a whacked-out night this has been. First I get shot and then the shooter's wife turns out to be a nurse and ends up bandaging my wounds. Wow."

Martha kneels behind Bill, using his folded shirt as a compress against the wound. "Not a nurse, technically—just some first aid classes. And you shouldn't drink—it thins your blood. You want your blood to coagulate."

Bill takes a pull on the bottle. "Yeah, but the bottle is open and wine never tastes the same if you re-cork it and save it for later. Ah, there they are, finally."

Martha looks over Bill's shoulder and watches a boat fall down off plane just as the big marine lamp fires on, shooting a yellow beam to the heavens. The lamp arcs down and the beam hops in fits down the beach until it lands on Bill and Martha. The light is blinding and Bill has to look away; when he does he sees Sophie standing next to him like an angel aglow in the warm, intense light. *The girl before the light?* Bill's vision swims. *Maybe the wine wasn't such a good idea.*

"Bill? Bill? This is *Tortuga One*. Bill, this is Phil."

"Did you say something, sweetheart?" Bill asks the girl.

Little Sophie turns to him but it's Martha that answers. "It's your radio. The boat must me calling. Is it your friend?"

"Yeah, that's my boy." And with that, Bill topples to the sand.

———————

251

"Hello? Hell..."

"Who is this? Where is Bill?"

"Uh, he passed..."

"I repeat: who is this? And you need to hold the button down until you finish talking."

"This is Martha. Are you Bill's friend? Are you on the boat in front of us?"

For the briefest moment terror clouds my brain before I realize the boat she is talking about can't possibly be the *Steel Drum*. But if it's not the *Steel Drum*, then who is it?

"Martha. Yes, this is Bill's friend Phil, but I'm not on the boat you are looking at so I need you to describe the boat to me. Over."

"I don't know what kind of boat it is. It is not a sailboat. Oh, a man in a uniform is jumping off the side. He is coming toward us."

*Uniform?* "Describe the uniform, Martha."

"It's blue. Shall I give him the radio? He looks official. I think he is here to help. Over."

*Over?* I look at the radio handset in my palm—Martha is getting the hang of this radio thing.

"This is Chief of Police Bourgois from Isla Tortuga. Whom am I speaking to?"

Oh no. Oh no. I stare at the handset as if it's an object from another planet. I can't believe my incredibly bad luck. Bill gets away once only to land in the grasp of the kingpin of the whole operation.

My only hope is to let Bourgois know I know. "Bourgois. This is Riley and I know what you are up to. I know you are behind all of this and if you hurt Bill I swear to God I'll kill you."

"Riley. I haven't a clue what you're talking about and we don't hold you responsible for the Cartier incident. All is forgiven, really."

"Forgiven! You forgive *me*? You and Cartier and Bennett are all in this together!"

"Riley…" And in the background I can hear Martha say something but I can't make it out. "Riley, I want you to talk to Martha White. I think she can dispel your concerns. Here she is."

"Phil? This is Martha White. Donald Bennett works for Tony, my husband. He is a family friend. He is Sophie's godfather. He couldn't possibly be involved in whatever this is."

"Bennett works for Tony? Well Tony is the fucker that shot Bill. I'm afraid, Martha, your explanation doesn't convince me. Put Bourgois back on. Now, Martha, now." Standing against the console, I stare out at the brightening eastern sky and think, *Nice husband you got there, Martha.* My mind is running on fumes and I can hear it in the constant hum in my ears. The run across the cay through all that undergrowth has slashed my legs into a patchwork of bloody and welted wounds that throb in a syncopated rhythm with my temple and neck.

"Riley. I don't know what to tell you. I mean you no harm."

"What about Chubby? What about Bill? Do you mean them any harm?" A wave nudges my boat and lifts it back down off the beach, floating it just a bit more. The bow holds on, but the stern is swinging free in the gentle surf. The lower units of the outboards bump against a rock, sending a shiver through the hull.

"Bill has a solid pulse and Martha seems to have stemmed the bleeding—he'll make it back to Isla Tortuga. And I don't know what you mean about Chubby. Chubby is Christopher Patois, correct? You call him Chubby, right?"

"You know who I'm talking about and you know why I'm out here. I'm going to get Chubby off the *Steel Drum*. And I don't have time to talk about this with you. Especially you." I hit the toggle switches and lower the outboards so that the props are just below the surface. "I don't trust you but what I do know is that if you don't take Bill back to Isla Tortuga and if anything happens to him—or Martha and Sophie—I'll know and you won't be able to run. I'll find a way to get you. I'll get you." I fire over the engines and I can't make out Bourgois's response over the noise. I toss the handset onto the console and turn off the radio. I bump the throttles into reverse and take a deep, deep breath.

# TWENTY-FOUR

I KICK WITH FIRM strokes away from the *Tortuga One*. I need to get out around the point of Sandy Hook Key and then it shouldn't be too long a swim out to intersect the *Steel Drum*. I know right where they are because just a few minutes ago I blasted by them just a few hundred yards off their port rail. Then I swung around the back side of Sandy Hook Key and tossed out my anchor. They saw me as I went by—the stunned looks on their faces told me that—but they'd never expect me to swim out to them.

My surprise plan is back on.

Using my fins, I frog kick around and begin sidestroking on my left side, to face the *Steel Drum's* path. There they are, steaming right at me just a few points off to the left.

I run through my checklist of items, making sure that I have everything. I'm not sure why, because if I don't have it now, I will have to make do without it. But I run the checklist anyway. It's comforting somehow.

Checklist complete, I look up, judging the distance between the *Steel Drum* and me. It appears, from my low angle, that it's about two miles down current. I'm drifting toward it along the reciprocal course heading.

I watch the *Steel Drum* loll toward me in the gentle night sea. I can't believe how calm the ocean is. Granted, I'm protected by the lee of the island, but the wind is eerily calm, spooky calm. While I wait, I again rehearse my plan. Those niggling thoughts find me, building like thunderheads in my mind.

I decide there is no need to submerge until the boat is well within a hundred yards. I just have to be certain that I keep low in the water so that I blend in. My black hair and black mask will not show particularly well to anyone looking ahead, especially if they are not looking for anything in the water. Surprise will be my greatest weapon— my only weapon. Tony, Cephus, and Willy will never know what hit them. I smirk at the thought. It's like I'm about to torpedo them from my U-boat. No, I'm just going to lasso a fifty-foot boat. Hardly hitting them hard, but it will be enough. Enough to make them stop and assess what happened, giving me enough time to get on the boat and get Chubby off. The *Steel Drum* is no aircraft carrier. It should be pretty easy to find Chub, I hope.

I'm bobbing lightly, letting the salt water roll up my face, when it strikes me yet again.

I am alone, very alone.

I scull with my hands, spinning 360 degrees. Being so low in the water makes the sky look immense with all those stars and planets and galactic debris. I feel like one of those small stars, one of those specks of light off away from the rest, not really connected with any system.

Then I'm nudged.

I'm dangling in the water, feet relaxed, fins hanging down. It brushed the tip of my fin. My stomach tries to escape through my throat, but finds the opening too small, and slides back down, sending electric waves through my body and out to my fingertips.

I splash my face into the water, trying to see what could have swept against me. My eyes have a tough time adjusting and focusing on anything underwater. I'm in water too deep to see bottom, so I'm looking into nothing but gray-blue nothingness. I scan the area, kicking gently to turn myself. I spin a quarter turn, when something large and blue-black glides by at about twenty feet and just about directly beneath me. My stomach makes a break for it again—a shark!

A shark? No. I watch it closely, following its path. The large shape swings back around, pushing small silver flashing fish before it. It clicks in my head. Marlin. It's difficult to see any detail in the poor light, but I can clearly see the swordlike upper jaw.

Just as I'm about to pull my face out of the water, the big hunter hits on some flying fish, scattering them. The frightened fish break past me for the surface and I watch the lucky ones sail away, flapping like mad to escape the marlin. "Wow," I can hear myself say. I watch the marlin glide by about ten feet below me. I see a small silver tail protruding from its mouth. A quick *woof*, and the tail is gone. I can't help but smile, and my mask leaks a trickle of water where the seal is broken. All too soon, the marlin is gone. I watch the fish fade like a specter into the infinite darkness.

I tilt my head out of the water and blow a puff of air out of my nose to clear the small puddle that formed at the bottom of my mask. The salt mist burns a little and it awakens me to the task at hand.

Looking over at the *Steel Drum*, I can tell it won't be long until I put my plan into action. They continue to steam directly at me as I drift like animated flotsam. I kick gently to keep in their line.

The waiting.

It passes that way for some time, me kicking to adjust, the boat bearing down on me, the wide night sky a cloak of speckled lights thrown over the gray sea.

I can see the *Steel Drum* clearly now. She is within a couple hundred yards. I let a couple puffs of air out of my buoyancy compensator, or B.C. for short, and sink until only the top of my head is out of the water, from the eyes up. I kick again, tenderly, to keep myself directly in front of them.

I scissor kick and pop out of the water to get one last look at their bearing. Straight on. Time to move.

I sink down quickly to about ten feet underwater and kick west. I instantly doubt myself, wondering if I waited too long to get moving. Would they be past me before I can get the trap laid? I instinctively stop, hopeful that the distance will be right.

The lift bag has to be inflated by dumping air into it from my backup regulator. I don't need to give it much. I just want it to go to the surface and suspend a couple ropes.

I yank the regulator out of its holder and purge air into the bag. The bag responds immediately and begins to pull me up, so I let it go and it wobbles upward, clownlike. I see small ripples as it breaks the surface.

Turning quickly 180 degrees, I swim back in the direction I came. I hear the rhythmic hum of the boat approaching me and it isn't as loud as it should be. Two screws usually make a good bit of racket underwater, especially if you are within yards of it and only a few feet underwater.

The ropes are on a spool and they trail behind me. As I swim I try to keep some tension. It's all a guessing game now. I try to figure how far I swam one way, and hope it's enough to get the bag on the other side of the boat. I spool out what I think is forty feet of line, and I'm surprised at how awkward it's getting.

By the sound of it, the *Steel Drum* is nearly on me now. I swim to the surface with the rope in hand. When I break the surface I can see that the *Steel Drum* is only thirty or forty yards from me. I need to time this right. Pull too soon, and I'll pull the bag across the bow and leave all the line on my side of the boat. Pull too late and the boat will be past me before I can get the lines up and taut enough to catch the screws. I heft the rope, checking its slack. Real hard to tell, but I guess the bow in the line is about five feet at its deepest. I look at the lift bag. It's bobbing nicely on the surface with clearly enough air to support the rope, but not enough air so that pulling the bag through the water will be difficult. Too much of the bag is underwater, causing needed drag.

I stare back at the *Steel Drum* just in time to realize that I better start pulling on the line if I'm ever going to hook the boat. I yank on the line and swim backwards on the surface, the rope between my legs. After a few kicks, I can see the bag bob from my effort, like a bobber reacts when a fish takes the hook. I peek over at the *Steel Drum,* concentrating on the water line. I focus on the bow and the pressure wake it forms. The angle is bad, but it looks like my little plan is going to work. They are heading straight for the lines. I carry on kicking and I can see the ropes come up to the surface.

Then the *Steel Drum* is in front of me. It's crossing the lines. I can feel the vibration of the ropes slide along the bottom of the boat and I pull harder. Then the ropes catch. They yank me violently, almost tearing out of my hands. Unexpectedly, the boat pulls me along behind it and I wonder when the props will catch the ropes and bog down. I swing slowly around into the wake of the boat, not quite sure what to do next.

*Shit!* Now I'm surfing behind the boat on my stomach, in the wake, swallowing water as it splashes up off my chest and throat. I roll over onto my back, still holding on to the ropes, and reach behind me to retrieve my trailing regulator. Instead of finding the regulator, I grab the fat little lift bag. I squeeze the air out and shove it between my B.C. and ribs. I'm drinking a good amount of seawater now as I again reach for my regulator. Finally, I find the bounding hose, pull the regulator to the surface, and swing it to my chest. It lands with a *whap*, compressed air burping sharply out of the purge valve. I do all of this while still waiting for the grinding halt of the props and my slow-motion water skiing to end.

Then it hits me. Why hadn't I thought of it at once? I caught the rudder. Like a navy jet catching the cable on an aircraft carrier, the *Steel Drum* has caught my rope. The boat must have a skeg keel and the rope must have skipped over the propellers and caught on the low-hanging rudder. And now I'm flopping around behind the boat in the wake, and, it occurs to me, the *Steel Drum* is going to drag me to South America if I don't do something quick.

I'm a good thirty feet from the stern of the *Steel Drum* and I begin to pull myself forward on the lines. I have to get up to the rudder and free the rope and jam something into the props to get the boat stopped. Then the *Steel Drum* starts to slow. I can hear it in the sound of the engines. I know I must be creating a tremendous drag on the boat, plus my presence is no doubt being transmitted through the rudder to the wheel. If anyone is manning the wheel—no way these guys have autopilot—then he will feel my weight and wonder what it is.

I pull frantically on the ropes until I hear the engines quickly pull down to idle. I let go and immediately submerge. I drop to fifteen feet and kick quickly to the keel of the boat.

Over my shoulder I see the explosion of light. Someone on the stern shines a light down into the water. The beam cuts through the gin-clear water in the exact point where I submerged just seconds before. The beam pans back and forth and quickly up to the very stern of the boat, feet from me. There is no way they can see me. I'm a good five feet from the props and at least ten feet from the very end of the boat. They will have to get in the water to see me, unless they have x-ray vision. My exhaust bubbles roil up in front of me, and I focus on getting my breathing under control. I watch the bubbles ascend up the starboard side of the boat and disperse as they hit the surface. I have to figure the men on the boat won't notice them. There are too few of them and the bubbles could be anything.

I pull myself together enough to realize that this is a golden opportunity to jam the props. Cephus, Willy, and Tony will get back under way as soon as they are satisfied that there isn't anything they can see, and, as if on cue, they douse the spotlight. I hear the muffled footsteps of movement on the boat. It's my sign to move. I pull myself along the keel to the screws and grasp the starboard shaft. With my left hand, I pull the deflated lift bag out of my B.C. and shove it into the port prop between two of the four blades. I then weave the ropes around the other blades of both propellers as quickly as I can.

Then they hit the throttles. I immediately let go of the shaft of the starboard prop, then look up at it, startled. It isn't turning. Curious. I look over at the port prop and it's winding up the rope like a winch on a sailboat. The port propeller is occasionally bogging, but the unseen driver somewhere topside simply pushes the throttles farther forward, succeeding only in spinning the rope onto the shaft and prop that much faster. I check around myself to ensure that I don't get entangled in the ropes. The last thing I need is to be dragged *underwater* to South America. There is less than fifteen feet of rope left when the prop finally has had enough and creaks to a slow jerking stop. The ropes on the prop and shafts look like Medusa, telling me that it will take hours to cut all that rope clear.

I hang there, hand on the keel, waiting for the driver to try his starboard engine. He doesn't. I hear the engines roll back to idle, then after a few seconds the driver shuts them off. The silence is refreshing but startling. I hadn't realized how loud the engines were until he shut them off. The silence shakes my tired brain into focus. I anticipate what they will do next.

Looking down, I still can't see the bottom in the early light of pre-dawn. I think back to when they trained the spotlight into the water. If I remember right, it didn't hit bottom either. We are about a half-mile off the coast of the small island and are probably in several hundred feet of water. They will not try to anchor.

I figure they will attempt to de-foul their props. *I* would try that first. In their minds, maybe it's something simple they can pull loose and be on their way. They will send one of them down to check it out, I deduce, but I wonder who it might be. I ready myself by hugging the underside of the boat. My stomach is flat against the starboard side, my left hand is on the keel, and my right hand holds the fifteen-foot length of rope that the prop didn't gobble up. There is only a slight bow in the line, so I judge my distance to the prop to be about eight feet. I'm like a seagoing bat hanging in an underwater cave.

My line of sight is not very good, but I know that whoever is coming down to inspect the problem will come on the port side because that's the propeller that's fouled. I will hear the person getting into the water before I see him and I want to be able to surprise him if I can. I pray that they don't have SCUBA gear. I have a pretty good hunch they won't, but they might have a mask and snorkel. Just about as bad—they can still see me clearly huddled here under their boat.

I also have a feeling they will send only one person down to check it out because the area is too small for two people to effectively work. I also know I'll need to incapacitate that person before he can get back to the surface. I have my dive knife, but I don't like the idea of that. All that blood will cause some concern topside and will send the other person into the water immediately. I also realize, at some level, that I can't do it, even after having Bill's blood on my hands. No, I can't stab a guy to death no matter how much I try to convince myself. Not that what I have in mind for the guy is any better; the outcome will be the same, but somehow it seems more clinical to me. Drowning is a bitch of a way to go, but it will buy me some much-needed time because I know that the two remaining on deck will give him some time to clear the props and won't think too much about him being down so long. That will give me time to get aboard, somehow, and get Chubby off.

I hear a slicing splash—the sound of a dive, and that emboldens me. No one would dive in the water with SCUBA gear on and probably not with a mask either, as it would rip off on impact with the water. With no mask, he will be relatively blind underwater, especially in the poor light of pre-dawn. I shift slightly on the hull so that I can see the props better and I see him come out of the gloom. He frogs toward the stern of the boat, legs and arms pulling and pushing through the water. It's Cephus. We meet again.

He is dressed only in brief-style underwear, his bare black chest as big as the carapace of a loggerhead turtle. He reaches the props quickly and immediately realizes the situation and starts working on the tangle of rope. He is between the props, his right side toward me. I'm in his peripheral vision and I can probably get to him before he knows what's happening. He yanks on the loose end of the rope and nearly tears it out of my hand. He follows the path of the rope with his eyes. He looks right at me. His white eyes bulge, trying to take in as much light as possible. He cocks his head, struggling to figure out what I am. I freeze. He's looking right at me, he must recognize what I am, my bubbles trailing away from me, my bulk. I'm in shadow, but he's only eight to ten feet from me. Surely he can make me out even without the aid of goggles or a mask.

He does.

He drops the rope and releases the shaft and kicks for the surface. I spring forward as he turns away from me and with a huge kick I'm at his feet. I grab his ankle and pull down and at the same time slip the noose of the rope onto it. Mysteriously, he goes limp and that gives me time to pull down on the rope and snug up the noose. Then he kicks for all he's worth, panicked, clearly running out of air. But the rope stops him like a leash stops a dog that runs for a car and is whipped off its feet when it reaches the bitter end.

My timing is perfect. He's almost out of air and has precious little time to figure out the simple knot on his ankle before he does indeed run out of air. I kick away from his thrashing feet and watch him pull himself down the rope to give himself some slack. His face reads pure panic. He knows he's drowning, and I know that I'm watching him drown. I swallow hard, fighting back the nausea, the million pinpricks on the back of my neck. I tuck my head into my shoulders, cowering from the sight. Did I have to do this?

In his panic, he can't get the simple knot undone. The rope is cutting into his ankle and he can't control his body enough to slip it off. He looks up at the underside of the boat and pounds on it with the flat of his fist. Then he burps a huge bubble of air and I watch his body go rigid when he swallows a lung full of water. He pounds again and I can watch no more, terrified by what I've done. I swim quickly toward the bow as I hear the last series of pounds on the hull. Then silence.

I don't look back. All I hear is the continuous stream of exhaust bubbles past my ears. I'm hyperventilating and shaking with adrenaline. I close my eyes in an effort to remain calm. *Think, Riley, think.*

The short length of rope will keep him under the boat and either Tony or Willy will have to get in the water to see him or get him untied. So I don't have much time to waste before they begin to wonder about their friend with the extraordinary ability to hold his breath.

# TWENTY-FIVE

I'M AT THE BOW of the *Steel Drum*, just under the surface. I'm hesitant to surface, not knowing what to expect when I do. Will Willy or Tony be there with a gun ready to pick me off? It's possible—unlikely, but possible—that they saw their comrade struggling underwater. But if they did, they would go into the water to investigate or help. They wouldn't go to the bow, would they? I'm thinking too damn much, wasting time.

With the blind faith of a first-time skydiver, I thrust for the surface. I break through into the atmosphere and I immediately look up to see if that anticipated gun is pointing in my face, but I am relieved to see nothing but stars in the pewter pre-dawn sky. My Seamaster reads 4:28, the sun somewhere over Africa, its radiation slowly bending around the planet. I still have some time to get Chub out with some darkness to cover us, but not much. I need to move quickly.

Through my waterlogged ears, I listen for voices or movement and hear neither, except for the ever-present creaking and groaning that every boat makes in water. As the water drains out of my ears, my hearing improves. Still nothing. No movement. Deathly silent. I don't like it. I should hear something—yelling down into the water or pacing, something. The calm of it all is unsettling, the silence reinforcing the image in my mind of Cephus's body waving in the current under the boat, and Willy and Tony leaning over the transom looking into the water wondering what happened to their friend.

And Chubby.

Chubby is aboard this boat that I cling to. Probably bound and gagged, thirsty, hungry, wondering what is going to happen to him next. He must be as scared as I am.

I hug the starboard side of the boat, training my attention on the stern. Nothing. I still hear no conversation or any movement from anywhere on the boat. I estimate that Cephus has been down for a good four minutes, maybe longer. They should be getting concerned.

The spotlight explodes at the stern of the boat, illuminating the water. They are looking for Cephus. The light scans the water immediately behind the boat but as suddenly as it when on, the light goes dark.

"Fuck!" The accent tells me it is Tony.

It takes me a second to catch my breath. I'm still shaking with adrenaline or fear—both, really. I listen for Willy to say something. Nothing but odd and unsettling silence. I want—no, need—to hear his voice to place him on the boat. I would expect excited chatter, but Tony's voice is all I hear.

I look for a way to climb aboard but there is no clear way, especially with all the gear on my back. The gunwale is at least four feet above the water and there is no way I'm going to reach it even if I bob down and kick with all my might. Even if that would work, it would make too much noise and I can't risk detection.

Hoping that the gunwale is a bit lower at the waist than at the bow, I scan astern and there it is, my boarding tool. Lolling against the side of the boat is a ratty old fender tied to the center cleat about ten or twelve feet down from where I float. It's a little too close to the stern for my liking, but it offers a place to loop my gear so that I can easily retrieve it on my escape.

Silently, I kick to the fender, unbuckle my B.C., slide out of it and stick my console through the loop of the line above the fender to secure the assembly. The unit swings with the current and I ease it, inflated side against the hull to keep it from banging. I then slip out of my fins and stuff them through the armholes of the B.C. Everything secure.

Hesitantly, I grab the wet rope of the fender and begin to pull myself up, testing the strength of the line. It holds. I ease my feet under me and onto the hull and walk up the side of the boat like Batman. I grasp the gunwale with my right hand, steadying myself and then quickly reach up with my left hand. I then pull myself up so my chest is against the boat, head and shoulders above the rail, forearms on the gunwale supporting my quivering weight. I look up and down the side deck and see no one. While continually looking astern for any sign of movement, I throw my right leg up over the gunwale and roll aboard. I wait for the sound of angry men running back to check on the noise, but no one comes. I hop gingerly into a crouch, spin, and slink forward.

My plan is to go through the front hatch and down into the front cabin area. From there, I can see out into the galley and salon area. I'm guessing that the ship is pretty standard belowdecks. It's only a guess, and probably not a very good one considering the appearance of the homemade superstructure.

I pray that they are keeping Chubby in the front cabin. It will make our escape a good deal easier. Just climb back out and get in the water before they are any the wiser.

I hunch over the hatch. It's closed. When I reach under the lip, I discover it is unlocked; in fact, it doesn't even have a hasp. Without lifting the Plexiglas, I look through the hatch into the dark cabin below. The glare is terrible and I can only see a distorted image of myself. I pull back immediately, knowing, or at least thinking, that I'm backlit and my face is a perfect silhouette in the hatch so that anyone below can see me.

I kneel there for what seems like a week thinking of my next move. I hear a noise inside the boat and see the hatch glow with light. I lean cautiously over the hatch and peer down. The light is minimal and the source is apparently coming from inside the salon area of the ship, streaming into the front cabin. Somebody is belowdecks. If I tilt my head just so, I can see that the door to the cabin is open and I can see the shadow of a person moving quickly back and forth. I look directly down and I can see the form of a person lying on the spacious bed. The light gives it an odd form. It looks like the person is bound, like a small tree is being transported for replanting.

The light goes out and I can hear someone move to the stern of the boat, then a splash. Somebody went in the water after Cephus. I know instantly that it will be a matter of seconds until he finds the big man moored to the props of the boat.

Without thinking, I throw open the hatch. With a very loud clank, it hits the apex of its stays. I punch out the screening underneath it with two quick jabs. The tenacious screen hangs delicately

269

by one corner. I yank it off and toss it through the hole and watch it carom off through the doorway and into the main area of the boat. As I parallel bar the open hatch, head tucked down into quaking shoulders, I think I see the bundle shifting on the bed below. I swing my legs back, then forward, and drop right where I want to, at the foot of the bed. I spin, quickly taking in the cabin.

It's a spacious cabin, and even in the dark I can tell it is not very well cared for. The smell is what strikes me most: a mixture of sweat, salt air, musty cloth, and the sweet acid smell of feces.

I concentrate on the form on the bed. Now that I'm only feet from it, I can make out the shape.

It's Willy.

The world stops.

I feel it in the little forward lean I do to keep from falling over as I stare at the man, studying his contorted body. From above, through the hatch, I was certain the bundle was Chubby and the shock of my discovery paralyzes me with inaction. I can't comprehend the situation. Willy shouldn't be here. And he especially shouldn't be lying on his stomach with his head turned around like an owl, looking up at me with those wide eyes frozen black with terror. I shake my head, trying to shake myself out of my trance. I have to pull myself together quickly and continue the search for Chubby. *Time is running out*, I tell myself.

Clearly it was Tony that went in the water and I have no idea how long he will be. Perhaps he will free Cephus, but it is more likely that he will immediately recognize the situation and come directly to the surface, so it will only be a matter of minutes at the most. Like Cephus, I'm sure Tony isn't a world-record breath holder, so I need to find where they are keeping Chubby and I need to know now.

Unexpectedly, a slight shadow appears on the wall above the bed next to me. I swing my head to see Tony standing in the doorway holding a large butcher knife. Water drips from him and he is breathing deeply. In the other hand he has the screen from the hatch. My eyes keep falling back on the knife. It's as if it's the only thing in the entire world. It's huge. At least ten feet long, in my mind.

Tony is a statue. Clearly, he's as shocked as I am. He looks at me for interminable seconds, also trying to comprehend the situation. He clearly recognizes me but I know he still can't believe I'm standing in front of him. The pieces start to fall together for him, those blocks of knowledge falling into place in his mind. I'm the man from the beach. I'm the man that raced past him just a short time ago. And I'm the man that tied Cephus to the bottom of the boat.

He charges me. Not a word, just a pounce. I instinctively roll onto my back into a ball and fall backward on the bed, sticking my feet up as a shield. I am not a fighter by habit and I don't know all the requisite moves to defend myself. Whenever I find myself in a tussle, and that has happened about twice, my usual posture is much like a turtle. All arms, legs, and other nonvital organs surround my face and stomach until I can find an opening to roll free and defend myself more aggressively. It tends to work. The attacker thinks that I don't want to fight. That lures him into a false sense of security and I can usually catch him unawares.

But I've never fought a guy with a knife.

Fortunately, the feet work. He dives at me and lands squarely chest to soles. He lets out an *oomph* of air that I feel blow past my face and I shove my feet out like I'm leg-pressing weights, sending him flying back where he smashes into the bookcase and small desk to the right of the bed. He slumps there, stunned, knife still in hand. I slide off the bed onto my feet, awaiting the next rush. I try to focus on the man, but my eyes keep moving to the knife, its rusty lifeless blade dull against the brown carpeting of the cabin.

He slowly pushes himself to his feet. He is smiling now. An unexpected challenge, this man in a wetsuit. He moves toward the door, still not saying anything. I don't move at first, wondering why he is backing out. He has the knife. He has the advantage. Why isn't he coming after me?

Gun! The neurons in my brain all fire at once, triggered by some built-in animal instinct that has fallen into disuse. I make a move toward him and he turns and sprints through the doorway. I lose sight of him for a moment before I get to the doorway and when I do see him again, he is at the sink in the galley halfway to the four stairs leading up to the back deck. He has about fifteen feet on me before I can get my fool feet to start moving.

He takes the steps two at a time and is now on the back deck. I'm right behind him. Up the stairs I see his bare feet slide out from underneath him on the wet deck as he tries to make the 180-degree turn to get to the pilothouse. He is hunched over, like a sprinter waiting for the gun, as I too take the stairs two at a time. When I hit the deck, I dive at his knees, knocking his feet out from under him like a bowling ball making the split spare. I roll up and spring on top of him. Lying across him, my chest on the small of his back, I grasp his left wrist, the knife hand, in my right. I snatch up the wrist and slam it down on the deck and, much to my surprise, and much like back on the beach, the move works and the knife pops out and spins on its hilt toward the port gunwale. He flops like a huge fish and bucks me off his back, but I still have a good grip on his left wrist. I yank it violently toward me and I hear the pop of fluid as the shoulder bursts out of its joint. He screams and I give it another yank. I'm sitting on my butt now, digging the rubber heels of my booties into the deck, my left palm flat behind me to steady me. I tug on his arm one last time and far too hard because my hand slips off his wrist and I go tumbling backwards, despite my left-hand brace. He rolls on his right side, pulling his broken wing to his chest. He looks like he's pledging allegiance, but with the wrong hand. He grimaces at me with nothing but hate in his eyes. Those dark, dark pupils wide open.

We move simultaneously, he for the pilothouse and me for him. I win. I catch him by the back of his shorts and with both hands jerk him back. We tumble back onto the deck and he lands on my lower stomach, knocking the wind out of me, and he takes the opportunity to swing his good elbow and smash me on the front part of my right temple. I now know what a boxer sees when his opponent lands a right hook. Stars—constellations of them. And it takes a lot of blinking to clear them.

My grip goes slack and he squirms away from me, heading for the pilothouse again. Woozy, I get to my feet to stop him, not sure I can. He hit me very hard, or in the right place or both, and the cobwebs in my head are pretty thick. I'm having a hard time concentrating as I lean heavily against the door of the pilothouse, looking in. He is nearly to the wheel and the console and then he is there. He reaches around the wheel and spins, pointing a revolver at me. It is a thirty-eight, I think, blue, like a cop gun or an old gun from a western. If the knife looked big, that handgun looks gargantuan. The barrel looks like it is inches from my face when he fires.

The bullet explodes the wood of the doorway jamb directly in front of my right shoulder, the splinters of wood slapping my face and neck. I'm stunned. My God, he's shooting at me—and he missed. It all seems so surreal.

He's stunned, too. He can't believe he missed because he's only fifteen feet away, an easy shot. I'm standing in the doorway, a perfectly framed target.

The recoil of the pistol threw his forearm up, making a ninety-degree angle at the elbow. After coming out of our joint surprise, he quickly lowers the gun and I dive across the doorway and roll up against the portside gunwale as I hear the second shot ring out. I hear it tear into wood, but I don't know where. I feel something underneath my side, but I know I'm not hit. As I roll away, I see it is the machete-like knife. I grab it and scrabble forward on all fours along the side deck.

I feel it before I hear it. He doesn't miss with the third shot. It tears into the hamstring of my left leg with enough impact to knock that leg out from underneath me like someone kicked it out with their foot. I land on my hip, but quickly get back up on all fours and continued my animal-like scramble around to the front deck. Resting with my back against the front corner of the pilothouse, I look down at my leg for the briefest second. I'm pleasantly surprised. Not as much blood as I thought there would be. There is a small exit hole on the front of my leg, but quite a bit off to the side. The bullet went clean through; it's only a grazing wound. It didn't catch anything hard enough to really flatten out the lead so it just spun through, but it sure feels funny. Not pain, really—kind of an irregularly pulsing stinging sensation. It feels like there are little tiny crabs pinching their way around my leg.

I hear Tony slowly moving up the side deck. The creaks are infrequent and long. He is moving slowly and carefully. I'm behind the superstructure of the boat and he can't see me and doesn't want to get ambushed and knocked in the water. Not when he is only a shot away from finishing me off.

# TWENTY-SIX

I SCRAMBLE TO THE open front hatch and tumble through. I land on the bed, my right leg coming down on Willy's back, the spring mattress bouncing me off the bed and onto the floor. In my leg a thousand new crabs come out for dinner.

My dive makes far too much noise. Tony surely heard it and now knows exactly where I am. As if it really matters; a fifty-foot boat doesn't have a lot of places to hide. I think, *right back where I started—in this damn cabin, with Willy's grotesque corpse.*

While deliberately trying not to look at Willy's jostled body, I hobble over to stand in the doorway, half in the cabin, and half in the salon. I want to be able to defend myself if he comes through the doorway, and at the same time I want to be able to duck through the doorway if he starts shooting through the hatch. Either scenario seems plausible to me.

My adrenaline is pumping relentlessly; my chest aches as if my heart is a hammer pounding from the inside. I look down at my leg and it seems like the bleeding has stopped. At least it isn't bleeding very much, that I can see. The crabs are still there, pinching away.

I split my concentration between the doorway and the hatch. I can't hear footsteps or creaking or anything above me, so I reason that he'll try to take me through the doorway. It's probably the best approach. If he tries shooting me through the hatch I can run into the salon. Then Tony is left chasing me around the boat. Here, in the cabin, he has me cornered, and I'm starting to feel it. Just a little panicked, but growing more so with every passing moment.

Chubby.

I look over at the bed where Chubby should be and I'm again reminded that I am not alone in the cabin. My landing bounced Willy half off the bed and like a large puppet with its head twisted backwards, he lies draped across the edge of the bed, upper half on, lower half off. He stares at me with eyes half closed as if he might have stumbled while sleepwalking. I force myself to look away and to refocus on Chubby.

If Chubby isn't in the cabin, then where is he? I retrace my very quick tour of the belowdecks of the *Steel Drum* to no avail. Chasing down Tony, I moved through the salon too quickly to get a good read on how the boat is laid out. But I know for certain that I didn't see Chubby in the galley area because there is no place to put a person without tripping over them in all the clutter. I wonder if there are cabins astern. Probably. Maybe they are keeping him there.

I take a fleeting glance through the doorway but it's too dark as the only light belowdecks is the ambient glow that comes down the rear companionway. I take several deep breaths, attempting to relax, and with each breath, I take in more of the foul odor that drapes the room. It's the smell of death confined. It smells like Willy started rotting right away. My upper lip curls from the stink.

"Hey! Riley, isn't it? I hit you—I can see the blood."

I can't immediately pick up where Tony's voice is coming from. My head swivels like an antenna trying to fix his location. The voice also brings his image back into my mind.

He isn't a large man; slight and wiry with short, blonde hair and skin tanned to the color of wet terra cotta. He is wearing shorts and a T-shirt, both wet from his swim, which reveal sinewy arms and legs. I probably have fifteen to twenty pounds on him, even though we are about the same height.

"We seem to have a stalemate, Riley. You still with me, mate?"

I can fix his voice now. He is above me, on the deck, shouting through the open hatch. I edge a bit more through the doorway trying to put that extra inch between the gun and me.

"You are a pretty quick fellow, Riley. Move like a cat or something. Hey! Why am I doin' all the talking? Hum? You still with me? You haven't bled out on me yet, have you?" He talks in a casual manner. He is the one with the gun; I am the one with the hole in my leg. He can afford to be casual.

I don't respond. Not because it works into my brilliant plan, but because I have no idea what to say to the guy. He is trying to kill me. I am trying not to get killed. What are we supposed to talk about? The weather?

"I know you're down there. There is blood all over the hatch and deck. You also made a big crash when you dove down there. What I say is you come up here and we talk, hum? Sound good to you?" His voice refracts less. He is closer to the hatch, speaking directly through the opening now.

I answer, "Come up there and get shot?" My voice wavers a little too much.

He laughs. A belly laugh that isn't too sincere.

He explains, "I can't kill you, Riley. You've got to untangle Cephus from my props so I can get under way. And Willy yelled at Cephus just one too many times so I can't very well have him do it, as you can see. I figure with that SCUBA gear you got here, you can untangle it quickly—even with a hole in you."

*Shit!* He found my gear. He must have discovered it when he circled the boat looking for me.

"So what do you say? Come on up and talk and maybe we can work something out." There is a short pause. "Or I start shootin' the place up." A hand holding a gun appears through the hatch, pointing in my general direction. Just as quickly, he withdraws it. "You see? You see? You come up."

"OK," I shout. "I come up there, get the boat untangled, then you shoot me and dump me. Might as well do it now and save me the work." The gun appears through the hatch again. Tony screams, "You want to die, my friend?! Huh? You get your fucking ass up here!" He is waving the gun all around the room as he shouts at me.

I fake acquiescence. "OK. OK. I'll come up. I'm coming up. Hold on."

I have no intention of going up. My best chance is to wait it out here and let him come to me. Even if he does start shooting through the hatch, I can scramble into the main area of the boat and be safe. He's exactly right; we are in a stalemate situation here and that is the best I can hope for—for now.

I need to get a look around the boat. Maybe find another weapon more offensive than a knife. And find Chubby. If I can free him, then we will have a numerical advantage. Although, I quickly concede, a gun certainly makes the odds less favorable for us. Nevertheless, it will be a morale boost for me to have someone on my side.

An odd nagging thought sprouts in my mind. Why isn't Tony concerned about me finding Chubby? Is it the gun or has he forgotten about him? That would be great if that were the case because I'll have the surprise element again.

Or, as my brain flashes back to me, Chubby is not aboard.

I can't blink. My eyes are locked on the door handle of the cabin door that gently sways back and forth with the movement of the boat. All my involuntary reactions have shut down and I have to tell myself to breathe while rubbing my chest to coax my heart to stop beating so damn hard. Can I have completely misunderstood? Could it be that Chubby really is not on the *Steel Drum*?

I came out here to get Chubby. I felt responsible for his kidnapping and I couldn't live with myself if he got hurt. I know how much his mother loves him. I couldn't fathom the agony she would have gone through if her son went missing, especially if I could do something about it.

And I know his father is dead.

But the realization—that he might not be aboard—hits me with the force of a truck hitting a little girl on a bicycle.

If Chubby isn't on the boat, I have no reason to be here.

I reach for the wall for support, but my hand finds only air. I stumble against the wall, shoulder hitting it, stopping my fall enough to allow me to shuffle my feet under me. Without thinking that Tony might be on the other side with his gun, I move through the doorway, reach for the wall, and feel up and down for a light. I find it, push in the brass button and the wall sconce casts a meager amount of light through the area, but enough to see that there is not another cabin behind the passageway. The main area—the salon/galley—of the boat is the only living area belowdecks other than the cabin behind me. I look around the large room. No Chubby—of course not. I have jumped to one helluva conclusion and it is going to get me killed. Leaving the light on, I step back into the shadows of the cabin.

I have to find a way out.

I close my eyes and concentrate on pushing down the panic that wells up like spume in my throat. What weapons and tools do I have? I squeeze the handle of the knife and think, *this is about it.*

I consider the hatch. I could try to climb out and make a run for it. Maybe make it into the water and swim far enough away to be out of pistol range. I move under the opening. It's closed. Confused, I wonder when Tony closed it because I didn't hear him close it. Now I'll have to jump up, knock it open, and then try to climb out. I'm not sure I can do that with the bad leg, and I'm certain that I won't be able to do it quietly. I will certainly arouse Tony's curiosity and end up with a bullet in the head for my efforts.

But the swimming idea sounds like a good one to me. I know I can swim to Sandy Hook Key from here—I swam here from there. But I have to quickly get far enough away from the boat so that Tony can't shoot me. He hasn't proven to be an excellent shot, just a decent one, so I'm confident that I can swim underwater for several yards and resurface far enough away that I'll be out of range. Also, he won't be able to pursue me with the props fouled. I realize that I can't wait down in the cabin hoping for a miracle—I need to take action. Swimming may not be the perfect choice but it's my best choice. My body prickles with renewed optimism.

I touch my wound, and my damaged leg is wet and a bit sticky. I've been out of the water for some time now and the rest of me is dry, so I know it is blood. The wound is still bleeding.

I can hear Tony moving around on deck, but I can't quite place where he is. I assume he will place himself so that he can see me coming up the passageway and at the same time not be cornered.

My leg is still throbbing, but not bad enough that I can't walk relatively normal. I favor it slightly as I walk through the salon, but when I climb up the companionway to the back deck, I put on the big act. I drag it behind me like it's a piece of wood, hoping to give Tony a false sense of my weakness. I move immediately, without looking behind me, to the starboard side of the boat. I turn slowly. Tony is standing on the port side, around the corner of the super-structure, shielding himself. He is pointing the gun at my chest.

"Drop the knife," he says, sort of tired, sort of resigned.

*Stupid!* I should have concealed the knife better. I need to get better at this stuff real fast. Clearly, he saw my stiff arm as I walked out to the transom because he was standing at the corner when I came up, the knife in full view. I don't try to be coy. I let the knife slide down my forearm and into my hand.

"Toss it overboard. Eeezy."

Without taking my eye off of him, I give the knife one short false cast and then toss it lightly overboard. It makes a dull *plump* sound when it hits the water.

"Why are you so bloody persistent?" He inspects me, eyes thin. "Why are you on this boat?"

I hesitate a beat and say, "Chubby."

His face wrinkles. "What?"

"Not what, who."

"Who?"

"The young boy that works for me. His name is Christopher, but we call him Chubby."

He laughs to himself, waggling his head. "I don't know who you are talking about. You want who?"

I sense his sincerity. He has no idea who I'm talking about. My aching suspicion is correct, and for the first time I realize that it's a good thing. Wherever Chubby is, he isn't here, and that is a *very* good thing. The thought lightens me.

We look at one another for some time, both weaving and rolling with the boat's movement. He smiles at me, thinking. You can tell when someone is thinking. Their face takes on a certain kind of intensity. Eyes narrow, mouth moves slightly as their tongue probes the inside of their lower lip.

I'm watching him and thinking as well. I'm trying to figure out just what the hell I'm going to do next. The blocks are slowly falling into place in my mind. This guy knows nothing about Chubby. Chubby is not on this boat, and probably never was. That is crystal clear to me now. And what really matters now is that I have a pissed-off Brit with a beat-up old gun pointed at my chest. It doesn't help that I damn near pulled his arm off.

"This isn't any of your business. Why are you fucking with me? Are you some sort of agent or something?" His voice swells an octave. He is enraged. He is spitting his words, accentuating his remarks with short thrusts of the handgun. I instinctively raise my palms, my involuntary gesture to try and calm him. I can almost feel the burn of the bullets plowing through my chest. I'm having a hard time catching by breath, like there is a balloon in my torso and someone is pumping it up way too big.

"Put your fucking hands down." He searches for more words to spew at me, but the thoughts seem to pile up at his mouth before he can get them out. He twists his head back and forth, wetting his lips, starting words then stopping. Finally he simply spits out, "You've made me very mad!"

An unexpected laugh escapes my lips and it startles both of us. Tony freezes, a little disarmed. I try to keep the new spirit going by keeping a foolishly broad smile on my face. It doesn't work.

"You making fun of me now? Huh?" He is around the corner now, slowly approaching me. I can now see his left arm. It's held tight against his waist, his index finger hooked through a loop on his shorts. He stops about fifteen feet from me. "You think this is funny?!" He is screaming. Out of control. He quickly lifts the gun to shoulder level, aims it at my chest, and fires. Click.

I flinched away when he raised the gun, but I'm quicker than him in recognizing the misfire. I take a step and dive at the gun as Tony stands dumbfounded, looking at the weapon like it somehow turned into a banana. I'm just tall enough to reach the gun, and I catch it with both hands and pull it down and out of his grasp. I roll away, juggling it like a hot potato, trying to get it positioned so that I can fire it. I hit the stern transom after three tight rolls and swing the gun up at the looming Brit. I fire. Click. *Keep pulling the trigger, Riley.* Again and again. Click, click, click. *What the hell...* then the proverbial light bulb. *The damn thing is out of bullets!*

It's Tony's turn to comprehend first and thus win the prize of kicking me in the sternum. The kick is not as striking as it should have been; being barefoot took a good deal out of the impact. I'm able to absorb the blow by flexing with it, but not quick enough to grab his foot on the withdrawal, only catching air. He hops back, bouncing on the balls of his feet, left arm tucked tight, right fist up, clenched so tight his knuckles are white. He looks like a Kung Fu fighter from a movie.

This man, Tony, constantly surprises me. Every time he has the opportunity to thrash me, he backs off. I don't know if it's some sense of honor or what, but he always lets me back into the fight pretty much unscathed—except for the little hole in my leg. I push myself upright. Realizing I still have the impotent gun in my hand, I give it a hard, cross-chest, Frisbee toss out into the water. I throw it so hard that I don't hear it hit.

Tony and I crouch opposite one another, boxers in a ring, turning slowly around each other, looking for an opening.

"Maybe we can make a deal, Riley. I can get us money. Plenty of money."

"I don't want money, I want Suzy back."

That makes him stop, and when he does, I do, too.

"What did you say?"

And I dive for his feet in some ill-advised wrestling move. But it works; I have his knees tucked into my left shoulder and I thrust up taking him backwards, his head slamming onto the deck. He is a stunned fish, and I scramble up to his head and wrap my legs around his neck and squeeze, the blood from my leg wound pulsing out and down my thigh, wetting his cheek. He tries to free himself but he is essentially one armed; and from making my living swimming with them, my legs are a vise. He struggles and I squeeze—struggle, squeeze—and I close my eyes to what I'm doing. I don't want to know. It's not me; it's someone else.

The struggling fades but I can't stop squeezing. Then he stops and I open my eyes to what I've done. I release my grip and scoot back from him. He is limp, dislocated shoulder slumping low, tongue tip pointing to the corner of his mouth. I check his pulse. He is dead.

The sound of an approaching boat turns my attention to it and I stand to get a better view but when I swivel my head around, the world is slow to catch up. I blink quickly, trying to help it along. I struggle to focus. I'm dumbfounded. What boat is this?

They are closing fast, maybe a couple hundred yards out, and with the improving light I can clearly tell that it is Isla Tortuga's police boat. My stomach falls into my feet. My mind is swimming. Things are not jibing. Slowly, in snatches, the fog builds, recedes, reforms over in another corner to obscure my mind and keep it from making the computations. Like an engine on fumes, my mind won't fire completely and I feel it fading, slow, slow, slow.

"Riley! Riley! You all right?" So that is the rumbling in my head, Bourgois pulling alongside. I had attributed it to my jelly-thick brain.

One of his men stands on the bow ready to throw me a line so that we can raft off, but I am too preoccupied with my left foot. I look down at it and move my distant foot around in the bootie. Why, my foot is wet. I look at my right foot, move it around, and discover it is dry. Fascinating. I return to my left foot. I can feel the fluid lubricating my toes. Huh. Curious.

I look up to see Bourgois standing aft of the pilothouse, leaning on the port transom, glaring at me with a mixture of contempt, amazement, and concern. I can see his face go through the changes.

My mouth cracks a horizontal grin—the grin of a madman. I'm all right—lightheaded and giddy, my grin widening into full smile, and Bourgois's face locks at the end of its cycle.

"Catch the line, if you can," he coaches.

Behind him, on the horizon, the sun breaks hot orange through filtered clouds. It has baked Africa for twelve hours and now it's our turn. I squint and turn up my chin to the approaching warmth and watch Bourgois, in shimmering silhouette, jump aboard the *Steel Drum.*

Then I fold to the deck.

# TWENTY-SEVEN

My head bounces on the deck one too many times, slowly stirring me. In snatches I see the blue sky overhead—nothing but blue, dark oxygen-rich blue. But my mouth is a desert so I work my tongue around inside to move what little moisture I can find. I try to sit up, but my head is a bowling ball. Then Bourgois's broad face appears above mine, framed in that blue that I can't take my eyes off.

"Hang on, Riley. We'll be back in a moment."

I nod, perceptible only to me. "OK," I answer dryly.

Then he's gone and the blue again fills my eyes. My butt is numb, and I move my legs to shift myself and find the left leg feels stiff. I roll my thick head to see it more clearly. I notice that I'm dressed only in my Speedo; someone took off my wetsuit but I make out that my leg is bandaged thick with a white, gauzy wrap. I shudder slightly—am I cold? Yes, my nipples are firm and the hair on my chest ruffles in the wind. I self-consciously look at myself in the Speedo. Yes, clearly I'm cold. Then Bourgois's big head again.

"Don't try to move. We gave you something. Hang on and we will get you to the hospital right away." He clasps my shoulder.

"Cold," I mutter.

"Yes, yes." He is gone and then I feel the prickly wool blanket on me. It smells comfortably musty. "Better?" I can't see him; I can only hear him. My world is only what is in my line of sight—that blue, blue sky. I struggle to sit up, to see what is going on, but an invisible hand reaches up and pulls me back down. I don't have any coordination at all, and certainly no strength to fight the powerful phantom hand.

It's clear to Bourgois what I'm trying to do because I feel his hand against my shoulder, but this time it's to aid the phantom hand in pressing me down.

"Riley! Damn it, man. Will you relax?" I can feel his breath on my neck, but I can't get my anchor of a head to move.

So I relax. Yes, much better, I confess. Just relax. But I'm anxious, edgy. I have enough awareness to realize that I can't move and that frightens me. But at the same time, I don't care. To complicate the opposing feelings, my senses are not interpreting reality very well. Everything appears as if in a long, well-lighted tunnel. Or my head is fitted in a box with only a small portion of the front cut out—plenty of light and sound, but terribly limited perspective. I'm not claustrophobic, but I do not like this feeling. But then a moment later I'm fine.

A cold, wet something is placed on my forehead. The object goes from my hairline to my eyebrows. It drips water down the bridge of my nose and into the corner of my eye, and I blink until it melds into my own saline. Ah, that feels good. Cool, relaxing, and pleasant smelling. Scented like perfume. No, not the rag, but in the air. Is that a woman's voice? I jerk my two-ton head around awkwardly.

"Shshsh, easy now," she murmurs.

"Allie?"

"No. It's Martha. You are going to be just fine. Rest now. Shshsh." It sure sounds like Allie. The accent is familiar but unfamiliar some-how—I know this person but I'm not sure from where. Hell with it, go to sleep, I tell myself.

So I do, watching Manolin ride on the back of a marlin.

———————

It isn't until later that I learn that my caretaker on the boat was Martha White—Martha, former wife of Tony, mother of little Sophie, and nurse to Phil Riley. Not really sure why she tended to me after she learned I killed her husband, but she did. I won't get a chance to ask her. Bennett took her and little Sophie back to London before I was released from the hospital.

I might have had a chance to learn more, but they, Bourgois and his motley crew, gave me far too much morphine on the boat or I would have been out of the hospital after a day, no worse for the wear except for a couple stitches, some nasty bruises, and every muscle in my body spent. Nothing a little rest and relaxation in the sun wouldn't cure.

But they kept me pretty doped up while I was in the hospital. I guess I was rambling on about fish and lions and little girls on bikes. My incoherence led them to believe that I had a concussion, but the scan said no—just the ramblings of a man in hypovolemic shock, as the doctor described it. Well, he was half right. I might have been in shock from the loss of blood, but the rest is something that I'll keep locked away a little longer.

So I was confined to the hospital for five days, trapped in a cage without bars so everyone I knew on the island could come by and stare at the semi-conscious goof. In my morphine fog, I half expected them to throw bananas to me.

I vaguely remember Alan coming by, head shaking, mouth wide in a smile, to sneak me a relatively cold beer. I barely remember Allie's visit as well. She came by to bring me flowers plucked from her garden on the resort. She also smiled deeply. Chubby, his mother, Bourgois, even Bill in his sling—it was beginning to be a trend. Everyone that visited me smiled that knowing smile. What were they all thinking? Did they think I was crazy? Their smiles and chuckles were similar to ones you would give a senile person that doesn't know what day of the week it is. Maybe they were right.

As the drug load decreased, I started feeling melancholy. I was having a hard time understanding why I did some of the things I did, and how I had it in me to do them, and the massive leaps in judgment. It wasn't like me. Before coming to Isla Tortuga, I would never do something like chase down a boat in the middle of the night on the open water, let alone be the cause of two men's deaths. Maybe I needed to get myself back to St. Paul and see those doctors again.

I relived those insane two days a dozen times as I lay in that bed, in and out of my slumber. Despite my deep unease about my actions, I couldn't help but be interested in learning the whole story behind the *Miss Princess*. I realized that I only had a vague understanding of what really had gone on. I had unwittingly become a central part in the whole mess and didn't *really* know what the whole thing was about. I think that, more than anything, is why I accepted Bourgois's invitation to dinner.

---

At my request, they release me from the hospital without them notifying anyone. I know I don't want any fanfare, I just want one night with the chief to try to piece together as much as I can about what started this ball rolling. I ask the chief to pick me up at the hospital. He obliges and asks quietly, "Where would you like to go for dinner?"

I answer, "The Beachcomber. I need someplace quiet."

Alan is both surprised and delighted to see me, and, again, gives me that stupid smile. Bourgois and I have a very pleasant dinner—grouper for both of us, the garlic especially heavy tonight. We split a couple bottles of red wine, and it's beginning to be all right for me again, the warmth of the wine settling me. As the night progresses, we laugh occasionally, we talk about the ocean and Great Britain and his friendship with Bennett.

And we talk about the *Miss Princess*.

"So, you gonna tell me how all this got started?" I ask.

"I probably should have told you long ago," Bourgois responds.

I nod, gently. I give him room to tell the story at his pace.

"I guess it starts with Cartier. Cephus—the big guy—was Cartier's mate from his childhood."

"Cephus was from Isla Tortuga?"

"No. No, Cartier is from Venezuela originally. He moved here with his father some years ago, when he was a teenager I believe. Cartier knew Cephus from the small town in which they grew up."

"I didn't know that. I didn't know Cartier was from Venezuela."

It's Bourgois's turn to nod subtly. He continues.

"Cartier came to me three days before you found the *Miss Princess*, alleging that two men, Cephus and Willy, approached him about helping them collect some money that a fellow owed them. In exchange for his help, Cartier would receive a cut. Somehow, Cartier also knew there was a family missing, presumed kidnapped a few days ago and that they might be in the area. I, of course, knew of the kidnapping through Don Bennett, but I have to admit I'm impressed that Cartier put it together. Cartier thought that the men might indeed be the kidnappers and that they came to Isla Tortuga because they thought they could conduct business here since they knew the customs official."

"So tell me Don's story."

"Don wanted to bring you in to help search the islands. That's not something he typically does. He likes to do things his own way, by himself. He thought pretty highly of you."

"So Don really is your friend. And is the head of security for Tony's company? Did I hear that right?"

"Yes. Both he and Martha were quite upset by the whole turn of events, as you might imagine."

"Martha. She helped me on the boat. Why did she do that? I killed her husband."

"I don't know, Riley. I really don't know."

I push the remains of my grouper fillet around on my plate. In an effort to excise the image of the dead men on and under the *Steel Drum* that builds in my mind, I ask about my own boat. Bourgois tells me she is fine; that they went back out the next day and drove it in. He also tells me that, because of my condition, they didn't have time to dispose of the *Steel Drum* properly. They had simply left it to drift and when they went back out for my boat, it was obviously gone. He calculated that it would beach on one of the small cays. Someone would report it and his department would retrieve it. I think, *great, let some fool like me find it abandoned like the* Miss Princess *and start the whole thing over again.*

It suddenly dawns on me that I didn't know what happened to Tony. Bourgois doesn't go into much detail. He simply states the body is being prepped for return to Great Britain.

"Things got a little out of hand for me," I confess.

Bourgois shoots me a furtive glance, nods as a response.

"I'm not sure what I was thinking. Things got a little out of hand for me," I repeat, waiting for a response, slowly feeling that my apology is being dismissed. Bourgois stares at me like I haven't said a word, and that he is waiting for me to speak. I'm getting the impression that, in his mind, there is no way for me to apologize for what I've done.

"Hey, I know. It's only words, but I'm sincere. I thought I was doing the right thing," I offer, shrugging my shoulders obviously.

"You killed two men, Riley," he says. The unexpected response brings my eyes up to meet his.

"I've been thinking about my role in this matter as well, Riley. I could have been more forthright in my dealings with you in regard to this matter. I should have listened to Donald's advice and taken you in, so to speak. But I didn't, and gratefully no one got hurt but the bad guys. That doesn't exactly excuse your actions, but I'm not sure, given the outcome, I'm inclined to do anything about it."

Words fail me so my response is a slow nod, and we steal glances at each other, not knowing what to say to each other next.

Bourgois says, "You look exhausted. You should get some sleep. And I could use some sleep, too."

"Yeah. Yeah that's good advice. I am getting a bit tired." But I'm thinking, *I've got to see about a couple friends first.*

---

I munch on one of Mrs. Patois's macaroons as I walk the path that leads to Bill's hilltop home. Chubby and his mother visited me during my hospital stay, but I was pretty out of it then and I wanted to see with clear eyes that the boy was OK. I didn't know what to expect when I walked up to their front door, but I wasn't expecting what I got.

He was more than OK, he was *content*. Not just happy or in a good mood, but content. As long as I've known him, he has always been the restless teenager and now he appeared at ease. Confident, smiling, cracking jokes. Floored by Chubby's reaction, I never got through the front door and I wished him a good night and left feeling a bit foolish for my concern—especially when Mrs. Patois called me back and offered me a cookie. I saluted her with it and scooted back into my pickup.

But as I stride down the path, I imagine it is Bill that I should be worried about. After all, he's the one I left bleeding on Cayo Pardo to go chasing ghosts.

Bill's place is situated similarly to mine, but sits high on the hill behind Chubby's house. It is a cement block house like mine, but Bill painted it a garish yellow and the structure blends into the landscape like an elephant at a cocktail party. The man likes to get noticed—or doesn't care if he gets noticed. I haven't figured out which.

The house is dark, but I push the screen door open and go in anyway. "Bill? You here?"

I stand in the doorway taking in the scene. It would be an understatement to say that Bill likes books. The living room, more like a library than a room to entertain, has books stacked in musty leaning towers against all four walls and any other structure within the room that will support something leaning against it. I've been to his house countless times, but I'm always amazed by the organized chaos that is Bill's house. My house is so different—barren, filled with only the basic necessities. But Bill's house isn't dirty, it's just filled with books. I asked him on my first visit why he kept all these books and his answer was typical Bill: "In time you'll know why."

I walk into the room and with my heel let the door ease closed behind me, my eyes slowly adjusting to the vague light. I reach between two strategically placed stacks feeling for the light switch and when I flip it up, a table lamp throws a muted glow against the light-absorbing books. The light from the lamp glances off a glossy photo that has formed into a droopy *C* from the humidity. Like a moth I go to the light and the photo.

I hold the photo in both hands as if I'm reading a scroll and the image in the photo tilts my befuddled head. I'm not sure I believe what I'm seeing. The photo is black and white but isn't old, perhaps taken five years ago judging by Chubby's boyish appearance. Standing behind Chubby, with his hands on the boy's shoulders, is Bill. They stand on a beach with the surf frozen in time behind them. It all seems like a perfectly natural photograph except for the third man in the photo. Standing next to Bill, with his hat over his heart, is Manolin.

# TWENTY-EIGHT

The Lime 'N Pub is characteristically busy and with the dull thought of the photo of Bill, Chubby, and Manolin still in my head, I stop for a quick beer. I park several cars down alongside The Road because there isn't any room on the crushed coral parking pad of the small establishment and listen to the engine rhythmically click as it cools. The sweet scent of antifreeze rolls back through my open window.

When I finally walk in, I expect the usual reaction—cold indifference. Well, I get that in spades. Like a car that won't stop running but is surely dying, the conversations end in snatches and fits until all I can hear is the creak and scrape of chairs as everyone turns to look at me.

Not quite sure what to say or do, I stand there noticeably embarrassed, until the bartender, whom I remember from the other night, slides up to me and gently places a Hairoun on the bar. He holds up his hands signaling me that the beer is on the house and I nod in response. I lift it and pull hard on it, feeling hundreds of eyes on me.

"Riley! Hey Riley!"

Expectantly I turn to the familiar voice. Next to a corner table, near the rear of the restaurant, I see Allie rise and start to make her way through the tables. And at the table she just left, his limpid grin showing me both fear and anticipation, sits Cartier. In a clearly halfhearted salute, he raises his gin and tonic. Then I'm startled when someone grabs my forearm and I turn to find the ever-ebullient Allie Tennison standing in front of me.

"I didn't know you were getting out of the hospital today. Why didn't you call? I could have given you a ride," she scolds.

"I didn't want people to make a fuss..."

She cuts me off with an upturned hand. "Hush, mate. I don't want to hear that kind of talk. Hey, come on over to the table. I've got someone you need to meet."

And as quickly as that, she is weaving her way through the throng back to her table. My eyes follow her path and as she is about to make her last cut to her chair, my eyes jump to her destination.

My stomach flips. Sitting on the edge of her chair, one slender foot hooked behind one of the legs, is Annick.

It's amazing how quickly one's hands can get sweaty in the presence of a beautiful woman. In mere seconds my hands are so wet I can barely hold on to my beer. I stand there stupidly, until Allie finds her seat, points in my direction, and leans over, speaking inaudible words to Annick. Annick turns, and I watch her smile grow from a pleasant first-hello kind of smile, to an I-know-you smile. But my attention is drawn away from her by Allie's frantic waving.

The crowd slowly loses its interest in me and the conversations begin again in much the same manner as they ended—in fits and starts. I follow the same circuitous path as Allie through the res-

298

taurant and find myself towering over the trio at the table. I squat down on my haunches, bandaged leg extended, and rest my crossed forearms on the table. I'm directly across from Cartier, with Annick to my left and Allie to my right.

"Annick, this is Phil Riley. The guy I was telling you about. The guy that owns the dive shop," Allie explains. Allie turns to me and offers, "Annick would like to learn to SCUBA-dive and I volunteered you, seeing as you're the only dive shop on the island. I hope you don't mind. And have a seat, for pity's sake."

"Of course not. I'd be delighted," I say as I slide a chair up to the table.

"Annick thinks that maybe you've met before," Allie continues.

"Yes. We've met." Annick extends her hand toward me.

"You speak English. I thought you were French," I blurt out as I take her hand in mine.

"Canadian, actually. French Canadian. I'm from Montreal." With a smile, she releases my hand. "Sorry to disappoint you," she coos.

I let her mock apology linger, the weight of her eyes holding me. In the subtle light of the restaurant, her eyes look like shifting pools of silver and tourmaline. I rock back slightly in an effort to break the hold those eyes have on me. I finally continue, "I'm sorry. I've been misjudging a good many things lately. You said we met?" Playing dumb.

"A couple of times in fact, once at a restaurant, and once at your shop. I was with friends both times. Maybe you didn't notice."

"Ah yes. Now I remember. Of course. Of course I remember." I want to say *how could I forget*, but it sounds far too trite. Instead, I ask the obvious. "So where are your friends?"

"Yvette is back at the room—we're staying at the Beach Resort—and the guys sailed on. They're heading south to Grenada to return the boat. I couldn't take another day on that cramped little thing anyway. Plus Yvette and I need to catch a flight in Barbados in two days so we decided not to risk not getting back to Grenada in time."

Wow. A good amount of information there. More than I could absorb quickly, especially because I'm still working on her not being French. Or at least French as I envisioned her. Just one more leap to a conclusion for me. What I want to ask about most is her relationship with the guy on the boat. She speaks casually about him as if they aren't too close, but I'm pretty damn gun-shy about jumping to any more conclusions about anything, and I'm even less willing to come right out and ask her about her and the guy.

"They are my cousins. The great sailors," she says.

My head snaps around as if it were spring-loaded. I catch the slightest twitch in her eyebrows, and her smile broadens steadily to reveal just the tip of her tongue touching her incisor. My God, was I that transparent? This girl is playing me like a bonefish. My throat feels warm from the heat rising out of my shirt collar.

"If you two are finished." Allie to the rescue again.

"I should really be getting back to the room. I told Yvette I wouldn't be late," Annick explains as she and I rise simultaneously. "And I'll see you tomorrow morning? For diving?" She reaches out and grips my forearm, giving it a quick firm squeeze; her French-tipped nails slowly comb the hair on my arm as she withdraws her hand.

"Nine. Bright and early. I may not be the one taking you out, but my divemaster is very good." I point to my leg as explanation.

"I look forward to it and I understand completely."

"As do I—look forward to it, that is." I watch her give quick waves to both Allie and Cartier and glide out the back door of the little pub. She is gone so quickly and quietly, I'm unsure if she was ever really there. I flop down in my chair and realize I don't remember rising, and turn to find both Allie and Cartier staring at me with Cheshire-cat grins. I refuse to give them the satisfaction. "Sam, I came down here to apologize for my actions the other night. I have no excuse for what I did, and I want you to know that I'm sorry."

There is a sizable pause as Cartier's grin grows wide, then draws tight. He snorts quietly, shakes his head, and stands. Looking down on me he says, "Don't apologize to me, apologize to Cephus's daughter."

———————

Exhausted, feeling the weakness in my leg seeping through my whole body, I plod down the path from my truck to my house. The myriad of aches in my body makes me think I've been on a trip around the world by donkey. I can think of nothing better than to lay my tired bones in my own bed and sleep, sleep, sleep.

I stop short when I see it. It's laying upside down, just on the edge of light and shadow, about three feet from the steps to the door. The flip-flop. Cephus's flip-flop. The one that was missing when I dragged him into the house. For some reason, for some very strange reason, I think, *have you seen my shoe?* and the entire episode on the *Steel Drum* streams back into my head. I can see Tony's limp body splayed on the deck, Willy's contorted shape staring back up at me, and I can see Cephus struggling underwater, his huge body bobbing against the tether that holds him mere feet from life-giving air. I imagine that at the farthest scope of the line, if he reaches as far as he can, his fingertips might pierce the surface of the water to feel air one last time—the air that his lungs burn for. Cursing under my breath, I stoop and pick up the flip-flop. I lift it to my nose and it smells like plastic. *What did I expect it to smell like?* I shake my head and step up into the house.

"Hey, bud. How you doin'?" It's Bill. He's sitting on the sofa, back to me, reading my Doc Ford novel.

I nearly have a heart attack. I'm not expecting anyone in my house, and after all that has gone on the last week, this is a surprise I can do without. "Jesus fucking Christ, Bill! You nearly gave me a heart attack. What the hell are you doing here?"

"Reading. And you should watch your language. I wouldn't consider myself a Christian, but those aren't the most respectful words."

With forced calm, I say, "I was looking for you earlier."

"Well you found me. I'm done. Not a bad book." He tosses the paperback on the sofa, and stretches his long arms over his head, yawning wide mouthed. He half pivots on the sofa, throws his good arm over the back, resting his cheek on his shoulder. "Actually, the main characters kind of remind me of you—the hippie guy and the science guy both. They'll do anything for this magnetic lady friend they meet—I'm not ruining the story for you am I?"

I look blankly at him. He takes that as a no.

"Good. So these guys are under this woman's power and one guy gets his head caved in for her, and the other guy goes around the world to track her killer. Sound familiar, huh, huh?"

"I'm no Doc Ford," I mutter.

"In your own way, maybe you are."

"Bill. Stop with this. I'm exhausted. Look, I need to apologize to you for leaving you like I did. I feel terrible. Look, I didn't have a clue what I was doing out there. Not a clue."

"Ah," Bill sings, rising on his knees on the sofa. I sense that somehow, in some subtle way, I have opened the door for him to give me his next great theory on life. "You know what? Maybe your brain didn't, but your heart did. Your heart did." He lets that last comment sit for effect. "You may have acted on those feelings in a weird kind of way, but I think you're kind of new to your atavistic self. You just need to get accustomed to all aspects of yourself." He smiles, letting me know that he wants me to ask more questions.

This is the little game we play. Bill hands me his little nuggets of wisdom, one or two at a time, then waits for me to push the conversation on. Reluctantly, I make the next move in the game.

"Atavistic self, huh?" I question.

"Yeah, yeah. Humans are complex creatures. The world is a complex place. You got to look beyond what you are used to looking at. The world that we perceive with our eyes is only part of what is going on. You can get lured into thinking that reality is the . . ." He waves a finger at the flip-flop in my hand. "What is that?"

"The shoe of the guy I drowned."

"Ah! See!" He is animated now, almost bouncing on the cushions of the sofa. "Like I was saying, you get lured into thinking that reality is the shoe you're holding in your hand, and it is, to a certain extent. But there is more. Why is that shoe here? Why did that guy happened to lose his shoe at your house?"

"Because I whacked him in the head and dragged him in here."

"Ah man, you're not trying here. The dude lost his shoe for some reason that we will never know. Some force in the world put that guy on a collision path with you, and him leaving that flip-flop is like him leaving a part of himself for you to remember him. To make you think of him and his impact on your life."

"Bill. I killed the guy. It's not something that I particularly want to remember."

"You got to try and be open about this kind of thing. It was the guy's time, if you want to look at it that way. Don't get hung up on that kind of thing. Besides, they shot your best bud in the back, right? I ain't losing too much sleep over it.

"Anyway, we are all put on this Earth for a reason, and none of us really know why. We have a guess or two, but we never truly, for certain sure, know why. You can't get caught up in the hard, tactile reality stuff—the flip-flop again. That is hard reality, but it means something more. Kind of a symbol."

"I'm sorry Bill, but that's bullshit. The guy lost his shoe, that's it."

"Well, you're still learning. Maybe I'm overloading you. You're still fishing for your atavistic self. It'll come around—I can see it awakening already. It's in you—you just don't want to admit it. You are like that young pelican that dives for every flash in the water until he finally learns that you see only what you are prepared to see. Not every flash is a fish and like that young pelican, you need to learn that life lesson. You need to learn to fill in the voids—and you need to learn where the voids are so you *can* fill them in." He gently pats his chest.

"You can't get caught up with what you're used to seeing and expect it to be your forever reality without understanding that there is more. Stand back, baby, it's there for you to see—but not necessarily out there." He throws his good hand toward the door.

"I learned that this last trip. I was looking for my usual kind of vision, you know, and I saw this odd funky kind of boat, which of course turned out to be the *Steel Drum*, and I thought that the boat was my vision. I was kind of pissed, you know, 'cause I usually get these glorious visions, not some beat-up old boat. But then, about two minutes later, I see an angel or a vision or whatever you want to call it. Don't smile, I saw a little twelve-year-old blonde-haired angel who led me to you. Swear to God. And that's not swearing. So you see, you got to be open to new stuff, 'cause new stuff is gonna happen, and you gotta let all your senses be free to take in that new stuff or you'll miss it." Again the smile.

"Give it some thought. Be open to new ways of looking at your reality. It makes getting up in the morning a whole lot more interesting." Sermon complete, he unfolds from my sofa, glides past me, gives me a slap on the side of the shoulder, and skips down the stairs to the lawn.

"All right then, so I can fill in some voids—tell me about how you know Manolin," I call after him.

He spins with a flourish, face aglow. "See, you're not as exhausted as you think. Your neurons are still firing away, putting those pieces together."

"So? You gonna tell me?"

"Ah, what's the fun in telling you? The real fun is in the finding out. Kinda like fishing. Your dad ever take you fishing, Phil? Sit on the edge of a dock and dip your line in the water?" He's walking back to me now, head bobbing, big smile.

"You go hunting for sunnies and you end up with big ol' largemouth bass on the end of the line. But you don't throw that bass back even though you weren't fishing for him, do you? You take what you catch and you enjoy the surprise—that's life, my little fisherman."

"Bill, stop with the mumbo jumbo BS, will ya? Tell me who took the picture of you three. And why didn't you tell me you knew Manolin?"

"Ah, yes, you said you were looking for me earlier. You were at my house. You saw the photograph." He stands on the ground the two steps below me, looking up at me.

"Because I like you, man. I think you have great potential and I don't want to ruin it for you by putting that largemouth bass on the hook pretending as if you really caught it. That's your problem: you want everything right now—right now. Life comes to you, be patient. All you need to do is be open to it—remember what I said before—wait for it, set the hook when it strikes and reel that bad boy in."

"It sure feels like you're hiding something from me, Bill."

"Ah, Philly my boy, I'm not hiding anything—I'm giving you something!"

"And the fishing metaphor is getting kinda old."

"The world is emblematic. You should read Emerson, man. Every step downward is a step upward. The man who renounces himself comes to himself."

"Emerson again?"

"Yeah, Emerson." He's quiet now, almost like he's spent.

I look down at my friend, not wanting to push him, but wanting some sort of reasonable answer to my question. "I just want to know about the picture. It's clear you and Chubby know this Manolin guy. I just want to know the story."

Bill looks up at me and says, "He's just an old man from the sea."

I watch him lope through the milky moonlight to the path that leads down the hill to The Road. He stops at the trailhead and half turns. "Hey, Paddy. A man can be destroyed but not defeated. Never forget it."

"Emerson again?" I call after him but I'm not sure I understand his response. I heard the word "No" but not what came after. I watch him disappear in pieces as he walks down the hill.

The screen door slams behind me and I make my way to Manolin's wooden fish scattered on the table in my living room. Picking up a couple, I massage the small sculptures, rolling them and kneading them. They feel electrified in my hands—charged with some sort of energy. I don't like the way they feel in my wet palms so I force myself to put them down even though I feel compelled to keep playing with them.

———

The night has grown impatient as squalls flash silently off on the horizon. The wind keens in the palms and by three o'clock I find myself in the state of consciousness that is both asleep and awake. I lay in my bed not quite fighting my deeply aching leg as the pain is almost meditative, the constant, throbbing rhythm of it. Slowly, in rhythm to my leg, I slip into a restless slumber.

I dream it is dusk and I am at Pelican Bay. Suzy stands in front of me and I notice she has one shoe on her foot, the other in her hand. The girl stares blankly, her eyes murky, wet. Without a sound, she turns and in that thick dreamlike way, runs toward the water. In the void behind her stands Manolin. Without a sound, he points after the girl.

I understand his meaning and at a slow lope I follow her into the water and dive as she dives, cutting deeper into the sea, giving chase, endless air filling my lungs. I am one with the water.

The girl swims deeper, unaware of my presence so I give chase, swimming easy and strong. As she rounds a mound of coral she joins up with Tony, Cephus, and Willy. They are waiting for her. Suzy stops and sculls around to face me. My four victims sway, suspended effortlessly. They study me with eyes that are blank and unemotional—like fish eyes. And that is when I realize that I too am a fish. That I am a marlin hunting the deep blue sea.

# Dear Reader...

The first book club I was a member of was pretty small. In fact, it was just my older brother, my dad, and I. And I didn't contribute all that much to the discussion—I was only four, after all. But I sure loved being in that group!

I remember Dad reading us novels like *Treasure Island* and *The Adventures of Tom Sawyer*—adventure stories; stories of exotic places with guys doing cool and exciting things. That's when I got hooked on books. Hooked on the ideas that they conveyed. And the dreams, the places, the deep, dark, and romantic secrets that the characters carried into Injun Joe's Cave—or buried in the sand under that "X" on the treasure map.

Sure, it was about the action, but it was about the characters, too. Who were they? Why did they do the things they did? After Dad (and sometimes Mom as a more than capable stand-in) clapped the book shut for the night and said, "good night, sweet dreams," I'd lie under the covers and think about Tom or Jim Hawkins as if they were chums from the playground. They were real to me—with real lives.

That's what books do—they transport you into another place and time—and into the characters' lives. I still do it now—and I'm a fair shake past four years old. But as Jimmy Buffett advises, you should grow older, but not up, and I've taken that advice to heart. So I hope your book group hasn't grown up so much that you can't pull those covers up over your head and ponder what Phil is thinking. I hope you too can make these characters real in your life. If so, I've done my job.

Good night, sweet dreams.
MS COMBES


*The author would like to talk with your group about your thoughts about* Running Wrecked. *In fact, if details can be worked out, he might even be able to personally meet with your group for an evening of discussion. If your group is interested in speaking to the author personally, whether it be in person or via phone, please contact him at mark@ markcombes.com.*

## READING GROUP QUESTIONS

1. Discuss the animal/fishing symbolism found throughout the book.

2. Discuss the concept of starting over/rebirth that is found in the book:
   a. For Riley
   b. For Tony

3. How is Riley different from other "heroes" in the male adventure/suspense genre?

4. Is Riley a hero?

5. Discuss the relationship Riley has with Bill Tomey and how it differs from his relationship with Allie.

6. Discuss the relationship between Riley and Donald Bennett.

7. Why does Riley not trust the government of Isla Tortuga?

8. Why does the government of Isla Tortuga not trust Riley?

9. Who is Manolin—both "literarily" and symbolically within the book?

   Hint: Manolin is a major character in a very famous novel.

10. Discuss the relationship between Chubby and Manolin.

11. What do you think *really* happened to Chubby's father?

12. Why does Martha comfort Phil on the boat?

13. Who do you think took the photograph that Phil finds in Bill Tomey's house near the end of the story?

14. At the conclusion of the story Riley has a lucid dream. What does it mean?

Read on for an excerpt from the next
Phil Riley Novel by Mark Combes

# Clowns and Chameleons

COMING SOON FROM MIDNIGHT INK

# ONE

"What would you do if your kid was born without a skull?"

"Ah man, don't lay that shit on me. It isn't going to change one damn thing. I have to do this because it's the way it works and you know that."

"Why? Why does it have to be this way?"

"Because you fuck with Nowak and you pay the price. Simple as that. Judge, jury, and executioner. That's it." Bart swallows hard, the words like chicken bones in his throat. "And a word of advice. I'm leaving the gag out for a reason. Take a lungful of water and end it fast."

"No! What is your name? Wait!"

Bart lets the lid of the freezer drop under its own weight. When the heavy lid seals, the *woof* of escaped air makes him flinch. He snorts and shakes his head. Bart feels the vibrations of the man struggling in the freezer, his bare hands on the cold metal of the lid. He flips the hasp down and moves toward the stairs that lead from the stern deck up to the top deck of the thirty-seven-foot Nordic tug. He leans out, looks down portside, and finds Finn standing half out of the pilothouse, looking back at him, eyes soft with resignation.

"This is the last one, old man. Just fire this bitch up, will ya, and let's get this thing over with."

Finn nods. His eyes sweep away from the big freezer on his stern deck, the freezer now visibly rocking.

Bart half looks over his shoulder and kicks back, his big boot heel slamming into the metal of the freezer, denting it. "Give me a break, will ya!"

Bart looks up just in time to see the back of Finn's head as he spins and disappears from view. Bart slumps against the rails of the stairs, hands gripping tight, head slung between them, looking at his blood-splattered boots. He rolls his ankle, scraping his right boot against the textured fiberglass, but the guy's blood has dried into the leather into some incomprehensible cranberry-colored Rorschach blob.

The now-subdued pounding from the freezer makes him half look back. "This is the last one, Nowak. This is the last one," he breathes to himself.

The engine comes to life and the pounding from behind him is lost under the grumble of the tug's big diesel.

Bart climbs the stairs to the top deck and begins to ready the crane davit, but he realizes he has a solid hour before the boat will be in position to drop the freezer, so he slumps down on the deck and hugs his knees against the early April cold. He could go below with Finn, but the old Scandinavian has always made him nervous—the man is so damn quiet. Never talks, never makes eye contact of any duration, just runs the boat in silence. Bart doesn't know what Nowak has on Finn, but it must be something pretty good because ol' Finn sure as hell doesn't look like the kinda guy that would choose to be a part of "dumping trash," as Nowak liked to call it.

But Nowak sure had *Bart* by the short and curlies. If he hadn't gotten involved with those crazy fucking bikers and wound up running meth all over southern Wisconsin, he wouldn't have needed the big Pole, and he wouldn't have to be Nowak's "refuse specialist"—again Nowak's clever term.

He should have done the jolt in Boscobel. He should have never let Nowak get his hooks into him. At least if he were in prison, he'd be his own man. Even if it meant fifteen to life, he'd be making his own decisions. He wouldn't have to do this fucking Polack's dirty work.

*Fuck man, what are you talking about? Doin' time ain't being your own man. Having some fat guard that washed out of cop school telling you when to eat, when to sleep, when to shit . . .*

"I don't like the decisions I've made," he whispers to his left knee, a confession breathed in fog into the cold of the early spring evening. It's a confession he's made before—and increasingly more often these past few months. But he never seems to do anything about it. He looks down at the freezer on the back deck and realizes he could let the blubbering man with the fucked-up kid out of the freezer. That would be a different decision. That could be his first step to being his own man. But he wets his lips and looks away, knowing he won't make that decision. He won't take that chance. Sometimes it's just easier doing what you know than taking that chance.

Fat boy in the freezer took a chance, and see what it got him. Nowak didn't tell Bart what the guy did—just told Bart that the man lied to him and that he need to go away. Bart found the man right where Nowak said he'd be—at the Children's Hospital, in the pediatric ICU unit, looking at some kid whose head was wrapped in gauze like some miniature mummy. The guy went down easy with one punch to the kidney. But he's a big boy, and it took a bit of work to muscle him down the stairs to his van. Once in the van, the guy didn't put up much of a fight. Bart went with it and played it like he was just taking fat boy back to see Nowak. That he had some explaining to do. The guy just nodded and massaged his lower back, but when they got to the marina, fat boy wised up and knew he wasn't off to see Nowak. He was off to see the fishes. That's when it got ugly. But he couldn't outrun ol' Bart in those wingtips, and after a couple kicks to some tender areas, he was once again accommodating. Bart bound his hands behind him and led him to the boat, but when the big boy saw the freezer, the fight was back on. Blood needed to be let then and Bart felt the rush of violence that got him in hock to Nowak to begin with. But beating this boy was a whole lot easier than the storekeeper over in Waukesha. That old Hmong put up a pretty good fight, even against a guy crazed by meth. Bart hadn't seen anything like it—this little five-foot-four dude kicking and clawing—but the old man simply gave up too much weight, and Bart was able to wrestle him onto the floor of the storeroom and crush his face into the floor drain, like pressing bony garlic through a press.

But he didn't feel that way this time. This dude cowered when hit and it took the fun out of it. It was like the guy didn't want to fight for his life. Like his life wasn't worth fighting for. But he never begged, and Bart admired that. He may not have wanted to fight, but he never begged or cried. He had to give fat boy a certain amount of respect for that.

When he got him bound up and into the freezer, then fat boy started talking. Like that was going to help. Bart wasn't the guy he needed to convince to let him live. Bart was just the guy that followed the orders—he never made the orders. Not by a long shot. But that didn't stop him from rambling on about needing the money for his kid. His kid with the weird disease causing him to be born without a skull or some crazy shit. No way a kid lives without a skull, so the guy was clearly blowing smoke, but Bart let him ramble on. It seemed to calm the big guy and Bart was tired and wished for something to pick him up. He'd flown straight all afternoon and he was getting a bit edgy, but he needed to finish the job first. He remembered the Hmong and knew that straight he could control himself. High—it was anybody's guess what might happen.

Bart looks up and sees that Finn has taken them out of the marina and is heading north, following the Milwaukee River toward its mouth at Lake Michigan. They are abeam of Kaszubes Park when he sees the police boat idle out of the canal just north of Greenfield Avenue. Even at that distance, he can tell the cops had seen them—and he and Finn must have looked awfully suspicious out on the water this early in the season—and at dusk. Bart's suspicions are confirmed when the cop boat explodes up on plane and hits its lights, the wail of the siren catching up seconds later.

"Fuck."

Finn clearly saw them, too, because he slows the boat.

Bart pounds on the cabin roof, "Don't you stop this fucking boat, old man!"

Bart scrambles to his feet and half skips, half slides down the ladder to the rear deck. The police boat is upon them already, the siren winding down but the lights twirling in some crazy blue dance, looking garish against the smudgy sunset behind them. The cop behind the wheel is clearly showing off as he whips the boat alongside the tug, tossing a wake that nudges the big boat enough to make Bart take a correcting step to keep his balance.

"Good evening, officers."

"Tell your skipper to put the boat in neutral. And have him come out back with you. Are you two the only ones on the boat?" It is the other cop, the one with the silly-looking bomber's cap on, earflaps cocked at the four and eight o'clock positions.

"Finn. Neutral. And come out here. These boys want to talk to us."

"Don't be cute, mister." It is the cocky cop, the one driving. He doesn't wear a cap. He may not have thought he needed one, but judging by his red ears and face, he could use one.

"You fellas are out kinda early in the season, aren't ya? Kinda cold yet."

*Ah, good cop, bad cop*, Bart gathers. Probably wasn't planned that way, but that's how it is playing out.

"Where the hell is your skipper? You in the pilothouse—come out to the stern of the boat, please." Bad cop is getting impatient.

"Jim, easy." Good cop puts his hand on bad cop's arm. "Why *are* you out early in the season? There are only a handful of boats in the water this early."

"Just an early shakedown cruise, officer. Such a mild winter— hardly any ice and all—we thought we might be able to get in an early charter. Make the most of the season, you know?"

The cops don't buy it and they both let their eyes fall on the huge freezer, which had been surprisingly quiet during this exchange. The only sounds are the mechanical whirling of the cop lights and the grumble of engines at idle.

"What's with the freezer, buddy?" asks good cop with a thrust of his chin.

All three men look at the freezer as if some Las Vegas magician had just made it appear. And then it starts to rock and fat boy screams for his life. Bart can't make out what he's saying in the freezer, but it's pretty clear he wants the hell out of there.

Good cop reaches over to grab the gunwale of the tug to pull their boat closer, and bad cop goes for his gun. But he's not as quick as Finn.

The blast from the old man's 12-gauge explodes bad cop's life vest into a cloud of red blood, white stuffing, and blue uniform. The man is dead before he hits the deck, dropping like a sack of wet laundry.

Good cop, hand still on the gunwale of the tug, looks up at Finn in shock. Bart reaches out and grabs the man's forearm and yanks him off his feet, and the man lands half over the rail, half in the water, feet pedaling to get traction on the side of the tug. With a second pull, Bart hauls the man into the boat like some trophy fish. The cop slams into the side of the freezer, and Finn is there to smash his face with the butt of his shotgun. Again. Again. And again. The man stops flopping and Bart flashes back to the Hmong in the grocery store, and he wonders what the hell he is doing on this fucking boat with this fucking crazy-ass old man.

"Goddamn, old man! You could have hit me with that blast!"

Finn looks up at him and his eyes say, *Yeah, so?* "Put this one in the freezer."

"This dude won't fit in the freezer. Not with the fat boy in it."

Finn rests his shotgun in the crotch of the gunwale and transom and reaches for the boat hook. With practiced agility, he hooks the rear quarter cleat of the police boat and slowly pulls it closer. He rafts off the tug to the police boat with a flash of dock lines. He looks back at Bart and cocks his head in surprise that the man hasn't done what he said. He reaches for the shotgun and gives it a one-hand pump. "Put him in the freezer, son. Do it now."

"Jesus." Bart flips the hasp on the freezer and hefts the lid. Fat boy stares back up at him, eyes wide with fear, mouth round with shock. "You got company, fella." Bart grabs the cop by his boots and pulls him over the end of the freezer, the lower half going better than the torso. The cop's service belt catches on the rim of the freezer, and Bart curses to himself as he folds the rest of the cop on top of fat boy in the freezer. And fat boy doesn't complain once. Not a whimper, not a shout. Bart looks back into the freezer, and he can see fat boy's face looking past the profiled face of the cop. Bart is thankful that the smashed part of the cop's head is down, but he bets fat boy isn't happy about it. Bart tosses the cop's silly bomber hat onto fat boy's face, flips the lid down, and turns to find Finn standing profile to him, shotgun in the crook of his left arm, pointing at Bart's gut.

"What? You gonna shoot me, too? Ain't any more room in the freezer, old man."

Finn barks a sharp laugh, and Bart is startled.

"Climb over and drop their anchor. Let's move it along. I don't want to be bobbing out here for much longer."

With an obvious waggle of the head, Bart carefully crawls over to the cop boat and gingerly steps over the slumping cop. "Why the hell do I have to do this? Huh, old man?" He's at the anchor locker in the bow of the boat and looks over his shoulder to find Finn back in the pilothouse staring back at him. Bart thinks, *man, he moves quietly.*

"Pull the anchor, son. Let the rode run all the way out."

"I don't know what the hell you mean by a 'rode,' old man. Remember? You're the boat guy. I'm just the muscle."

"Just throw the anchor over and let all the line pay out."

"You know what? Who made you boss? You ain't Nowak, dude."

"Right now I'm worse."

Bart stares back at the old man, contemplating his comment. It's hard to argue with. "Fuck me," he mutters to himself as he hefts the Danforth over the side and watches as the line uncoils from the locker. It's a hypnotizing sight: that perfectly coiled line unrolling in perfect circles. He can't help but smile, but he instantly wonders why.

"Turn their lights off. We are drawing *enough* attention."

Bart deliberately takes the side of the boat opposite the dead cop and studies the toggle switches on the console. He finds the switch marked *pursuit lights* and flips it down.

"Might as well kill their engines, too."

Bart wonders if Finn chose the word "kill" on purpose and turns the key. Quasi-silence only broken by the deep rumble of the tug. Bart relaxes just a bit.

"Come on back over, or do you want to stay with your new friend?"

Bart looks down at the dead cop. In the failing light, the blood has turned black, and the man looks like he's taking a nap. But the almost perfect circle of blood under him tells the truth.

Bart makes the jump from the cop boat and unties the lines connecting the two, tossing his end into the police boat. Finn immediately throws the tug into forward and they creep away like ghosts. Bart feels the slightest pang of remorse as he watches the police boat settle back on its anchor, rolling slightly but enough to make the cop slouch sideways and then finally fall on his side, now out of sight below the gunwale.

Finn punches the throttles and the engine responds without complaint, but Bart can't take his eyes off the police boat. He feels like he's abandoning a defenseless child on the side of the road, and he's surprised by this newfound emotion. He leans his rear against the corner of the freezer, and he can feel fat boy squirming, his movement being transmitted through the cold metal.

A loud finger whistle turns Bart's head toward the pilothouse. Finn is waving him closer. Bart reluctantly plods to the rear of the pilothouse and slumps against the doorjamb, the front of his shoulder keeping him from toppling in.

"Get the crane ready. We're dumping them just outside the breakwater. We've got to get back before the entire Milwaukee police department is swarming the river." Finn spins back into the pilothouse without waiting for a response. Bart stares at the empty space where Finn was standing just seconds ago. He snarls and gives the finger before moving astern and climbing the ladder to the crane.

He unhooks the cable and spools it over the side of the top deck. He slides the control box over the side and scurries back down. On the rear deck he hooks the U-bolt through the prefabricated cables bolted into the freezer. He looks to his side and does a double take as he realizes they are through the breakwater and heading straight out into the lake. It's a calm evening, and it's otherworldly out on the lake. The sun hides behind a smear of gray clouds, adding to the effect.

The engines step down, and that's his cue to get the freezer overboard. He looks toward shore and realizes they aren't very far out, maybe only a half-mile or so, but he doesn't care. He wants the job to be over.

He reaches behind him and presses the up button on the control box, and the cable from the crane takes up the slack. The crane lifts the freezer easily, and when it is above the plane of the gunwale, he walks it over to the port side, the crane spinning in its base, taking all the weight. Once over the side, he lowers the freezer until it's just in the water, floating ever so much. But it's enough to take the tension off the pin in the U-bolt.

He jerks the pin out, and the freezer hesitates only a second before it slides below the surface, water roiling up in its wake as it rides to the bottom, followed by a huge burp of air.

"Let's go home, old man."

Finn throws the tug into gear and turns sharply back toward the entrance to the river.

But they should have waited a few more seconds, because if they had, they would have realized that the huge burp of air that Bart witnessed was trapped air—trapped air from the freezer. And quickly rising after that escaped air is fat boy riding up with the dead cop and his life jacket. The man bobs wide-eyed and gasping as the tug motors back toward shore, directly into the setting sun.

## ABOUT THE AUTHOR

Mark Combes is an avid sailor and SCUBA diver and travels extensively in the Caribbean pursuing his passions. He works in book publishing. This is his first novel.